MORE *than* HIM

MORE THAN SERIES
- BOOK THREE -

MORE THAN HIM

More Than Series #3

JAY MCLEAN

*"Every morning you have two choices.
Continue to sleep with dreams, or
wake up and chase them." - Carmelo Anthony*

NOTE TO READERS

Please note than More Than Him (More Than #3) is part #3 in the More Than Series and should not be read prior to reading More Than This (More Than #1) and More Than Her (More Than #2) More Than This

PROLOGUE

Five Weeks Post-Logan

IT HAD BEEN five weeks since I'd seen him. I hadn't heard from him once. Not a thing. And I think it's for the best. I think that maybe I needed a clean break, a way to completely erase him from my life. I'd told Micky and Lucy, and they understood. They knew that being around them might mean being around him or even hearing about him. And I couldn't do that to myself. Not yet. I was back to where I was when I'd first got here, trying to do everything I could to avoid him.

"I have something to tell you." Ethan turned the TV off, and I faced him. He was home more often now, and I knew why. He was worried about me. He thought I'd turned into the girl from that summer. But I wasn't. Not really. I was nowhere near as broken as I was then. Maybe it was because I was immune to the fucked-up ways of Logan Matthews. Maybe it was because I'd come to accept the fact that maybe—just maybe it was my fault. That I never should have taken him back the first time. Or the second time. Or the third. Whatever it was, I didn't care. I was over it.

"Dimmy." He tried to get my attention again.

"What? What do you have to tell me? If it's about his room—not yet, okay? Just wait … another week. I've got to go in there and clear out my stuff."

Okay, so maybe I wasn't over it yet. But I was close.

"No." He shook his head. "That's not it. But, uh, it's about him."

I looked away. "Then I don't want to know."

"Dimmy, I think you *need* to know."

"I don't think I need to know shit about him anymore, E. I'm done with him."

"He's gone."

My head whipped to face his. "What do you mean he's *gone?*"

"Like, gone. Away. Out of the country. He's traveling the world or some shit. I don't know." He shrugged.

"What? How? What about college? What about med school? Traveling where?"

"Dim, I don't know. I bumped into James today, and he asked how you felt about Logan experiencing the world indefinitely or something."

"Indefinitely?"

"Seriously, I don't know. I know as much as I just told you. Look, I'm just telling you so that you know it's okay. You don't have to worry about bumping into him on campus or anything. You can hang out with your friends again. He won't be there. I just wanted you to know. And honestly, Dim, you fucking deserve to know. He should have at least told you that much."

He was right. I at least deserved that.

"Don't cry," he said, standing up. I didn't know I was. "He doesn't deserve any more of your tears. I won't let it happen."

I couldn't speak, and even if I could, I don't think I'd have the words.

He left the room just before there was a knock on the door.

"Hey." It was Jake. He removed his cap and ran his hands through his messy, dark hair. "Uh, how... how are you? Is that a stupid question? Stupid, right? Of course you're not doing well. I mean, with the whole beating and... shit... I'm sorry ... Um, can I do any—"

"Jake," I cut in. "What's up? What are you doing here?" I told Micky and Lucy I just needed some time to get over what had happened, and I wanted to cut off all ties I had with Logan. This included Jake—so I had no idea what the hell he was doing standing at my front door. I raised my eyebrows.

"Oh." His eyes widened in surprise. Clearing his throat, he said, "Look, I know that you don't want to see me or anyone who has—" A car pulled into the driveway interrupting his speech. Cameron stepped out, throwing the keys in the air and catching them.

What the hell?

"Hey," Jake said to Cam.

"'Sup?" Cam replied, walking toward us.

"You made good time," Jake spoke, looking at his watch.

"No traffic," Cam responded.

"That it?" Jake asked, jerking his head behind Cam.

"GUYS!" I snapped. "What are you doing here?"

They both turned to me.

Jake cleared his throat again and then sighed. Cam spoke for him. "Logan gave us a task. Actually two tasks, well three if you include—"

"What are you talking about?" My arms crossed and my eyes thinned to slits. I was irritated, close to shutting the door in their damn faces.

Jake stepped forward. "Logan wanted us to take care of some stuff for him."

I waited.

"Shit," he mumbled.

Then Cam spoke. "He got us to trade in his car, and he got you this." He handed me the keys.

I threw them back at him like they were a ball of fire in my hands. "I don't want anything from him."

"It's kind of our mission you accept them," he stated, shrugging.

"His dad wrote out a check with the leftover money from the trade and paid some of your tuition," Jake said.

"What?" I didn't know if I was angry or pissed or hurt or grateful. I wiped my face and squared my shoulders. "I can't accept this."

"You kind of—" Jake started, but Cam cut him off.

"Leave it, man," he told Jake, then asked him, "Could you give us a minute?"

Jake nodded and headed for his car. Then, it was just Cam and me.

Face-to-face.

Awkward.

"Logan's an asshole," he said, breaking the tension.

"No shit."

"He really wanted to give you this." He jerked his head in the direction of the car behind him. It was a green hatchback of some kind.

"I'm not taking it." I was firm, probably harsher than I should be.

"Fine," he sighed. "Look, I know we didn't really get to know each other that well, and we didn't really run in the same circles or whatever, but um, Lucy—she kind of misses the shit out of you. So, I don't know. Maybe you could call her or something?"

I nodded.

"Don't cry," he said.

"Shit," I spat. "I keep doing that."

"Doing what?"

"Nothing."

Silence.

Awkward.

"I might see you around, Amanda."

"Okay," I said.

He lifted his arm, threw the keys into the house behind me, and bolted for Jake's truck.

My head spun to find where the keys had landed, and by the time I'd turned around, he was gone, and so was Jake, and so was Jake's truck.

"Assholes," I said to myself. I closed the door and picked up the keys.

"What was that about?" Ethan asked. His hair was wet, his clothes fresh out of the laundry; he must've just gotten out of the shower.

"Logan traded in his car and got me one and used the leftover money to pay my tuition," I said flatly.

"Good." He made himself comfortable on the sofa, picked up the remote and turned the TV back on. "At least he's done one thing right by you."

1

AMANDA

"Are you actually going to drive it today or just stare at it again?"

"Shut up," I told Ethan as he stepped out of the house and started making his way over to his own car.

"All I'm saying is you may as well drive it. It's been sitting there for two weeks. Who fucking cares where it came from? It's yours, and you deserve it."

I looked down at the keys in my hand. "Okay," I said under my breath. I wrapped my fingers around the metal and nodded my head once. "Okay," I repeated, reassuringly.

I opened the car door and sat in the driver's seat.

And that's all I did.

Then the passenger's door swung open, and Ethan slumped into the seat. "Drive," he said, facing forward.

"Huh?"

"Drive. Let's go home. It's Tristan's birthday. Let's hang out there, forget this space for a while." He waved his hand in a circular motion. He didn't have to say the words; I knew what he was getting at. I hated this house and all the memories that came with it. He faced me. "Okay?" he asked.

"I have to work."

He took the keys from my hand, stuck one in the ignition, and turned it over. "I'll call them, tell them you've got lady cramps or whatever. They

won't question it. Come on, Amanda. Let's just... I don't know..." He
shrugged. "Let's just find a way to bring you back, even for a little bit."

I DROVE THE two and a half hours home in my new car. I couldn't deny it.
I liked having a car; it felt like I was gaining some freedom.

I pulled up to the curb and parked. Ethan and I got out at the same
time. He wanted to go to the liquor store and get some beers for him and
Tristan, and I wanted to stretch my legs. We were both underage, for the
next few months at least. Ethan had a fake ID, and we were in a different
town. I knew this area only by the few times I'd come here with *him*.

I must have been daydreaming while I was walking, because I didn't
see the store door swing open or the body that walked out of it.

Obviously.

Because I slammed right into it.

"Shit," I muttered, trying to regain my footing.

"Fuck." A deep rumble voice came from above my head.

Somehow, my hands had flattened against—what I assumed—was the
person's chest. I couldn't be sure, because it felt like steel. People aren't
made of steel. I shut my eyes tight. The person's hands grasped my
elbows, trying to hold me up.

I finally settled, but my head was still down and my eyes were still
closed. "You all good?" Man of Steel asked.

I nodded.

He cleared his throat. "Amanda?"

My head whipped up. My eyes snapped open. "Hey, Dylan."

He let out all the air in his lungs and took a step back. And then he
smiled—this huge, megawatt smile I'd never seen on him before. "How
are you?"

I smiled back—genuinely—for the first time since *he'd* left. "I'm doing
okay."

"Good."

Then it was quiet. I shuffled my feet. He crossed his arms over his
wide chest.

"Are you doing anything right now?" he asked. His words were rushed,
like it took all his energy to speak.

I shook my head. "Not really."

"Do you want to maybe go somewhere and talk? Look, I know that we didn't really—or don't really—know each other that well, but I think maybe I need to talk to someone I don't know—about something that—"

"Sure," I cut in. If I didn't, he'd never stop rambling.

"Yeah?" He raised his eyebrows. His hands went into the pockets of his jeans.

I looked away. The mannerism was too similar to someone else I know. Or knew. Whatever. "Uh-huh," I murmured, pulling out my phone to text Ethan.

WE ENDED UP sitting on the grass in the park on the other side of the road. I didn't know what he wanted to talk about, so I stayed quiet, until finally, minutes later, he spoke. "You didn't see where I was coming from when you ran into me like a linebacker, huh?"

My eyes narrowed at his question, then trailed to where we collided. "Oh," I said as understanding dawned. *Marine Corps Career Center.*

"Yeah," he replied.

"You're joining the Marines?"

He cleared his throat and leaned back on his outstretched arms. His legs kicked out in front of him, crossed at the ankles. "I think so."

"Huh."

He sat up and faced me, with one eye squinted to block out the sun. "Actually, I don't *think*. I'm almost positive I'm going to enlist."

"Wow."

"Yeah."

"No one knows?"

"No. I haven't told anyone."

"Why?"

"Why haven't I told anyone, or why am I doing it?"

"Both."

"I don't know." He sighed. "Truthfully, I always planned on it after high school, you know? But then I met Heidi—" He paused, waiting for an emotion to settle before continuing. "I met Heidi, and I didn't want to be without her. She wanted the college life—I wanted her. It wasn't a hard decision. I'd have followed her anywhere."

"And now?"

He shrugged. "Now, she still wants the college life, and it's not for me."

"I'm sorry," I told him. I didn't know either of them well enough to give more support or advice. Maybe that's why he'd thought it was okay to talk to me about it. Maybe he'd needed someone who wasn't going to talk him out of it.

"Me too," he deadpanned.

"So, are you and Heidi done?"

He shook his head. "I don't think that matters."

"How can it not? I'm sure she—"

"Amanda," he cut in. His tone was flat, serious. He turned his entire body to face me. "I'm sorry."

I reared back a little, surprised by his words. "You're sorry?" I laughed once. "What? Why?"

He shrugged. "For Logan."

"I don't want to talk—"

"I know," he said. "Micky and Lucy warned us... but I *am* sorry."

I swallowed my emotions. "You don't need to be sorry."

It was quiet for a moment. The birds chirped above us. Their sounds seemed to be magnified by our silence. "I get why he did it—why he left."

I opened my mouth to speak, but he stopped me. "You were his girl, Amanda. He loved the shit out of you. And somehow, his life, merged with yours, caused a horrible outcome. Ask any decent guy; they'd tell you the same thing. It's our job to protect our girls, to keep them safe, to make them happy. He thought he failed. If it were me, I'd do the same thing. I'd run. Hell, I'm probably doing it now—joining the Marines. But it doesn't even compare to what happened with you. And Logan, he's a great guy, the best, but he doesn't know how to handle that kind of hurt, you know?"

I blinked and let the tears fall.

He kept talking, "I just—I know you hate him, or at least you want to. But don't blame him for what he did. Maybe running away was the only way he thought to make it right."

I nodded. It was all I could do. Maybe he was right, or maybe I just wanted him to be. He stood up and offered me his hand. I took it. Then we stood in front of each other, my face to his chest—the guy was huge. I tilted my head so I could see his eyes. "Whatever Heidi is making you feel, she's wrong. She has no idea what she's about to lose."

Suddenly, his arms were around me. "Thank you for listening," he said, his voice rough.

"No, Dylan, thank you for speaking. It's rare."

He laughed.

So did I.

I missed it—the laughing.

"HAPPY BIRTHDAY, HOMO," Ethan sang. We were in Tristan's yard, sitting at our usual spot of the dock on his private stretch of the lake. His parents were loaded, but the type of loaded that meant they were absent more than they were home. We'd spent way too many quiet nights here drinking.

"Thanks, baby," Tristan blew him a kiss.

Ethan belched.

I nudged Alexis next to me. "You think that's hot?"

Her eyes were half-shut, her face a shadow of red from the firepit in front of us. "Dude, your brother is hot. You can't deny it."

"I can totally deny it."

"Shut up," she huffed. We both watched the guys, about ten feet away, with their beers in their hands, play-fighting. "Ethan's always been hot."

It was my turn to tell her to shut up.

She snorted.

"Have you ever told him?"

"What?" She sat up. "That I want to hump him?"

I threw my head back and laughed. "Ethan!" I called out.

"Shut up," she warned.

I didn't care. I was having fun tonight. I wasn't drinking, but I wasn't brooding, either. "Lexie said she wants to hump you."

They stopped play-fighting and immediately faced us.

"Oh my God," Lexie moaned into her hands that were covering her face.

I laughed at her and then looked up at the guys. They were standing close to each other, having a heated discussion. Tristan chuckled, pushing Ethan toward us. They walked the few steps until they were around the pit with us. Tristan took a seat while Ethan stood in front of Lexie. I watched him, confused. *What the hell was going on?* He must have noticed, because he gave me that shut-the-fuck-up look I'd gotten used to in our almost twenty-one years together.

Lexie's face was still buried in her hands. He cleared his throat. She didn't move.

"Lex," he said quietly.

"Go away."

"Lex," he said again, firmer.

She still didn't move.

He sighed and then moved her hands away from her face. Finally, she looked up at him, her face red—from embarrassment this time.

He tugged on her hand to get her to stand up. She did, but her eyes were huge with shock. He sat on her chair, then brought her back down on his lap, whispering something in her ear.

She nodded.

Good for them, I thought.

———

THAT WAS AS far as they went. She sat on his lap, with his arms loosely around her. They didn't make out; they didn't even kiss. At one point, I saw her flip his cap backwards so their faces could be closer when they whispered quietly to each other.

I had to turn away then; it was too much.

Too familiar.

HE SAT BACK in the car after walking her to her door. It was nearing four a.m., and we were heading home to Mom's house. "I've always like her," he mumbled. His head fell back against the headrest.

I watched him for any sign of amusement or mocking—there was none. "Yeah? What took so long?"

"She's your best friend."

"So?"

He sat up and faced me, motioning his head for me to start driving. I did.

"I heard her once—telling you she wouldn't date a guy she couldn't be around whenever she wanted. She said she had trust issues and didn't know how you did it with Tyson."

Tyson. My heart hurt. I wonder where we'd be...

"Sorry." He pulled me from my thoughts. "I shouldn't have mentioned it."

I glanced at him and smiled. "It's fine." It really was. Tyson wasn't a sore subject. "What makes you think she won't make the exception with you?" I asked.

"Because." He took off his cap. "I just asked her. She said she's happy to fool around, but she doesn't want to be anything more—not when I'm there and she's here. She doesn't want an emotional attachment or whatever. She says she doesn't trust me."

"So that's that?"

"That's that," he confirmed.

2

AMANDA

It had been a month since we went home for Tristan's birthday. A month since I ran into Dylan, and a month since I'd decided that I was no longer going to live my life in a state of post-Logan depression, *again*.

I was going to live my life for me, and only me.

Ethan was the only one who was stopping me from doing that. He never left the house anymore. He was in class or home, and that was it. I was never home alone. He never dated, he never partied, and he never went out. If I wanted to go somewhere, he was with me. Like my bodyguard. Only he wasn't. He was my brother, and he shouldn't be living his life like this.

So, that's what I told him.

He just stared at me, unblinking.

I raised my eyebrows.

He sat up on the recliner and rested his elbows on his knees. He opened his mouth to say something, but the words got caught in his throat, and then he let out a long sigh. "No," he said, his voice firm.

"Ethan." His name came out like a whine. "I'll be fine."

"No," he repeated, coming to a stand. He pointed two fingers at me as he walked past. "And we're done talking about this."

He walked into the hallway, and seconds later, the sound of his door slamming echoed through the house.

I let out a frustrated breath, got up and walked to his room. He was sitting on the edge of his bed, staring down at the floor. "E." I tried to get his attention.

"Quit it, Dim. I mean it," he warned.

"You have to stop doing this. It's not your job to protect me."

He stood up. "Get out," he spat, pointing at his door.

"What?" I reared back in surprise.

"Don't talk to me about what my role is—or whatever." He was pissed. "I know what I should be doing. I know that I should be protecting you." He was shouting now. "You don't think I fucking know that? I've failed you how many times now? First with Greg and now this shit. Don't fucking talk to me about—"

"Holy shit," I cut in. "Ethan, none of this is your fault." I took a step closer to him. "You can't blame yourself."

"Shut up, Dimmy. You don't fucking get it. Dad's not around anymore. It *is* my job." He sucked in a huge breath, sniffed back his emotions and ran his hand through his hair. I watched his chest rise and fall, trying to regain control of his breathing. He walked to his desk and leaned back on it. "I'm sorry," he finally said. "I'm just... I don't know what I am, but I shouldn't be yelling at you."

I stayed quiet. I didn't know what to say. Ethan had always been protective, but not like this. I'd never considered Ethan's feelings. I'd never even thought of him, or how he'd felt when Dad left, or when that shit had happened with Tyson and Logan and Greg, and now this. "It's not your place to be Dad, E. We have a dad; he's just an asshole. But you're not it. You're not him, and you never will be. You couldn't have done anything—"

"Amanda." My real name leaving his mouth made me pay attention. "I should've been there to protect you. I'm your brother."

"I love you, Ethan, but you're right. You're my brother, and that's *all* you are. It's not on you to be more for me. Don't do that to yourself. Promise me."

He crossed his arms over his chest and looked away. "Okay." He nodded. "But I need you to do something."

"What?"

He opened his desk drawer and pulled out a brochure, then walked over to me. "Self-defense classes." He handed the papers to me and then waited.

I looked up at his anxious face. He looked so much like Dad; he always did. "Sure," I agreed.

So that's where I found myself two days later. Ethan was with me. He'd wanted to check out the place before I'd agreed to lessons. It was at the same gym I went to for yoga, so I was familiar with the building. Ethan didn't even try to hide his protective stance in front of me as the instructor introduced himself. "Jordan," the instructor said, shaking hands with Ethan.

"This is Amanda." Ethan pointed at me. I raised my hand in a wave.

Jordan smiled warmly. "Amanda," he repeated. He was only a few years older than us and well built. Good-looking guy, if I cared—which I didn't.

Ethan cleared his throat. I rolled my eyes.

Jordan continued to discuss my future lessons with Ethan. Sitting back, I let him have control. I think he needed to know that he was doing something to help fix me. Honestly, I really didn't think I was that broken.

"I don't like him," Ethan stated from the driver's seat of his car. We were on our way back home.

"Who?" I asked.

"That Jordan guy."

"What? Why?"

"He looked at you like *that*.."

I laughed.

"Not funny, Dimmy. Last time I was pissed at a guy who looked at you funny it was Logan. Look how that turned out."

My mood switched. "Okay," I told him. I wasn't going to argue; he was right.

"Just don't get involved with him—"

"I don't even know him."

"Just say you won't start dating or whatever, not yet, okay?"

"Okay," I said again.

Dating was the last thing on my mind.

I was home half an hour before I started getting bored. Thanks to

Logan's leftover rent money and the money he'd put into my tuition, I
was able to cut back a day or two on my shifts. This made Ethan happy. It
made me insane, especially with being alone most of the time. Ethan was
in the house, but it wasn't like we hung out or anything.

The urge to listen to my music set in, but my iPod was in *his* room. It'd
been there since that night. I hadn't been inside since the day I'd gotten
home from hospital and found he was *gone*.

"Come on, idiot," I said, whispering to myself. My hand was on the
doorknob. "Just do it. It's just a room." I took in a deep breath and
mustered up all the courage I had.

I turned the knob, blindly stepped forward, and let out all the air in
my lungs.

Then I felt him.

Wherever he was in this world, he was only there physically. Everything else was in this room, with me.

My hand brushed against something soft, causing me to open my eyes.
My breath hitched, and all the memories came back. I focused on the
bed, not wanting to take in too much at once. It would overwhelm me. *It
would break me.* My iPod sat in the middle with my headphones wrapped
around it, right next to my e-reader.

I had been reading and listening to music when he'd come in from a
run. He'd said he wanted to tell me something. He'd wanted to tell me
that it was his birthday, but I'd already known. Of course I'd known—I
loved him.

I loved him too much.

I ignored the ache in my chest and looked around the room. Everything was so Logan. Not a single thing out of place. He was meticulous
and kept his room so clean. I'd always wondered why he did. Even his
pool house was like this, but I'd figured his housekeeper kept it that way.
I'd never asked. I should have. I should have done a lot of things. I guess
it had never occurred to me that our time was limited.

I did this sometimes—thought or talked about him like he'd passed
away. Dead. Never coming back. I think it was my way of dealing
with it.

Without knowing, my feet had me walking around the room toward
his desk. He kept a framed picture of us right in the middle. Micky had
snapped it when we were at their house once. We didn't know she'd taken
it until she showed us weeks later. I was sitting on his lap, with his arms
tight around my waist. My head was thrown back, laughing at something

he'd said. His face was so close to mine, we could've been kissing, but we weren't; he was just watching me.

He'd made Micky e-mail him the picture right away. We'd stopped by a store on the way home, and he'd asked me to pick out a frame for it. He'd said that the picture resembled us, who we were, and how he wanted to remember me for the rest of his life. He wanted to put it somewhere he'd see every day, to remind him that not all memories are distinct moments. Some are moments just worth remembering. My laugh—he'd said—is a memory that should be treasured—not just remembered.

That was one of the moments that led to me falling so deeply in love with him.

I felt the sob creep up my throat, and I held it back. Gripping the frame to my chest, I quietly shut the bedroom door and walked into his closet and shut that door, too. My crying was the last thing Ethan needed to hear. I sat on the floor, turned on the flashlight app on my phone and looked at the picture in my hand.

Then I let it out.

The hurt, anger, sadness and the loneliness of it all.

I missed him.

I missed him so damn much, and I couldn't even cry openly about it. My tears landed on the glass of the frame, and I wiped them with my thumb. "You asshole," I whispered, figuring if I could feel his presence in the room, then maybe he could hear me, wherever he was. "I hate you." *Lie.*

Then I saw the box I'd put his birthday present in. It was the last thing I'd given him.

Stupid present.

Stupid stethoscope.

I laughed bitterly and studied my wrists.

Stupid.

I cried so hard that I ended up in a ball on the floor. I don't know how long I was there , until finally, the sobs wore me out and I fell asleep.

———

THE VIBRATING OF my phone woke me right before music filled throughout the small space of the closet. I was in a daze of half-sleep before I realized what was happening. My head pounded and my eyes hurt. I felt drunk, but I wasn't.

I was just stupid.

I picked up the phone and sat up—and only then did I work out that "Hey There Delilah" was playing.

For some reason, I smiled. "Tyson." I spoke quietly into the phone.

"Dimmy," he sighed out. He was less enthusiastic than I was. Something was wrong.

"Tyson? What's wrong?"

"Nothing." Looked like I wasn't the only one in the mood for lying.

I stayed quiet and waited. Tyson was like that; he just needed time.

I heard him sniff. "I just walked in on Ally and some guy in our bed."

"Oh my God."

"It's our fucking apartment, Dimmy. She was fucking some guy in a space we shared."

My blood boiled. "Fuck her."

He chuckled, but it was sad. "So lady-like."

"Seriously, Ty. If that's how she treats you, fuck her."

"I think some asshole already did."

"I'm sorry."

"Yeah. Me, too."

"So what are you going to do?"

"No idea."

"Are you kicking her out?"

"The lease is in her name. I just packed some shit, and now I'm sitting on a park bench with two bags and my guitar like an upper-class, street-performing bum."

I snorted.

"Not funny, Dim."

"Sorry."

He exhaled loudly.

"What about classes?"

"I'm done. I don't even have to be here to graduate."

The words were out before I could stop them. "Move in here. We have a spare room."

3

AMANDA

I PICKED HIM up from the airport and brought him home. Ethan was fine with him living with us. He and Tyson had always gotten along, so it was never really a question.

Then the awkward moment of which room he was going to have took place. The three of us stood in the hallway, eying each other. It was almost like Logan's room was haunted. Tainted. *Ruined.*

"Rock, paper, scissors?" Ty asked. He smiled sadly at me.

"You take it," Ethan said to me. It was an order.

"What?" I panicked.

"You have to get over it at some point. This is step one." He walked away.

"Is he okay?" Tyson's eyes moved from Ethan to me.

I shrugged. "What do you mean?"

"I don't know. He just seems ..." He laughed once. "Older?"

I rolled my eyes. "He thinks he's my dad now."

"Oh," is all he said. He walked into my room—or my old room now, and I walked into mine. It should have been *ours*.

"WHEN DID YOU get a car?" Tyson flopped down on the sofa next to me. It only took him an hour or so to unpack his bags and move my things to my new room. Logan had emptied out most of his stuff; he didn't have much.

"A couple of weeks ago."

"It's nice."

"Thanks," I replied, not wanting to go into detail. I feigned interest in whatever was on TV. Baseball. Great.

Ty cleared his throat. "Did he pick it out himself?"

My eyes snapped to his.

"Ethan told me," he stated.

"Geez, gossip much?"

He shrugged.

"I don't know. His friends dropped it off..." I trailed off, watching his face for any emotion. I couldn't see any, but he looked tired, more mature. He wasn't the lively Tyson I'd known when we dated. The Tyson I knew was a boy; the one sitting in front of me was all man. He'd gotten bigger, more masculine. He'd been a jock most of high school, but in his junior year, he'd decided to focus on his music. He'd always been good at both, but he was amazing with his guitar.

"What?" he asked.

I must have been staring at him. His deep brown eyes bore into mine. "Nothing."

He laughed quietly. "Were you just checking me out?"

"No!" I yelled and then laughed. It felt *so* good to laugh.

"I miss that sound," he said.

My lips thinned to a line.

He blew out a breath and rested his head on the back of the sofa. "What the hell happened to us?"

I mimicked his position. "I know, right?"

"Dimmy... I'm not saying this to make you feel like shit or anything... but do you ever wonder? I mean, do you ever think about where we'd be if we'd stayed together?" He rolled his head to the side and faced me.

I did the same. "Sometimes," I told him honestly.

He smiled, then eyed the ceiling again. "I already miss her."

"Ally?" I sat up, wanting to pay more attention to him.

"Yeah. I shouldn't, right? She's a whore." He grimaced at his own words. "I shouldn't say that."

"It's okay," I told him. "She is. You don't deserve to be treated like that."

"Yeah," he agreed. "Not twice."

I sucked in a breath. His words hurt, especially in that moment. When it was all for nothing.

"Sorry." He nudged my side. "That was a dick thing to say."

"You're right, though. You don't deserve that. Not at all, Ty. I hope you know that. You're a good guy, one of the best, really."

He laughed once. "Maybe that's the problem. Maybe I should've been an asshole—worked for Logan. He got the girl."

His words stung. "Did he? Because I'm here, and he's not. So I don't really see how he got the girl."

He didn't say a thing.

Neither did I.

We just sat there, looking at each other.

I heard Ethan walk in and sit on the recliner. My eyes didn't move from their spot.

"Well." Ethan broke the silence. "Aren't you two a party?"

"Party," I said.

"What?" they both asked.

A smile pulled at my lips. "Let's have a party."

A FEW HOURS later, the house was filled with the familiar odor of beer, perfume, and sweat. I sat outside by the fire with a soda in my hand. Ethan was next to me, of course.

"You should go have fun. That girl's been eying you the entire night." I jerked my head toward a blonde a few feet away.

He lifted his head and looked at her, but only for a second before facing me. "Did you invite Alexis?" he spoke over the music.

I nodded.

"And?" he asked.

I hesitated, before telling him the truth. "She had a date."

"Fair enough." He sat up a little in his chair and eyed the girl again. Tyson came and took a seat next to me. "Stay with her," Ethan ordered, then got up and made his way over to the blonde.

Tyson hit my leg with the back of his hand, getting my attention. "I just saw a drunk girl dry-humping some guy's leg in the hallway... he was barking at her."

I laughed so hard I spat out my soda, causing it to drip down my chin.

"That's so sexy," he teased.

I tried to swallow the remaining amount in my mouth. My eyes stung from the acid building behind my nose.

He moved his hands up and down as if comparing the weight of two things. "Spit... swallow ..."

I spat.

His laugh was a slow build-up, a chuckle turned guffaw.

I wiped my face with the back of my hand. His laugh had quieted by the time he leaned closer and wiped my chin with the sleeve of his sweater. "You're such a kid," he murmured, shaking his head from side to side.

He was so close, I could smell the beer on his breath. My own breath hitched when I noticed his eyes go from mine to my mouth. He licked his lips.

Shit.

I held his hand that was on my face and tried pushing it away, but he gripped my wrist and turned it to face him.

"What's this?" There was confusion clear in his tone.

I pulled my hand out of his grip and sat on it so he couldn't see.

"What is it?" he asked again.

"Nothing, Tyson. Leave it alone."

"When did you—"

"I said leave it alone."

He didn't mention it again.

THE SUN HAD started to come up by the time everyone left. I'd wanted to go to bed earlier, but I knew Ethan would shut the party down if I did, so I dealt with it.

I couldn't sleep, even if I wanted to. I lay in his bed, staring at the ceiling, trying to drown out the silence with music, but it made me feel worse.

Tyson knocked on my door before coming in. He didn't say anything, just lay on the bed, on top of the covers.

"I'd gotten so used to having someone else in the bed. It feels strange now," he explained.

"Yeah." I knew exactly what he meant. "Have you heard from her?"

"Yeah, I just got off the phone."

"And?"

"Nothing. She said she was sorry."

"Do you think you can forgive her?"

"No. I think my mind's pretty set on the whole cheating thing. If I was able to forgive, I'd have forgiven you, you know?"

I didn't know what came over me, but I reached over, felt for his hand and held it. "Yeah," I whispered.

"I'm sad, Dim." His voice broke. "Are you sad?"

"Yeah," I repeated quietly.

"You don't seem sad."

I thought about my next words. "I have to numb myself emotionally, you know? I mean, it's not just me who's in this. It's Ethan, too. If I show him how bad I'm hurting, he'll want to fix it, and he can't."

He squeezed my hand once.

I continued, "We're going to be okay, Tyson."

"Yeah," he agreed. "And if not, we'll be broken together."

A FEW MINUTES of silence passed before he started to chuckle.

"What?" I asked.

He laughed harder.

"What?" I asked again.

"You should've seen this kid barking at that girl," he managed to say.

I started to giggle. "What do you mean bark? Like, howl?"

"No, Dim." His words came out in a rush of excitement. "I mean... ruff, ruff ... ruff, ruff ..."

I laughed into my pillow. "Why was he doing that?"

"I don't know." He turned to face me, leaning on his elbow and resting his head in his hand. "This is your school. You tell me."

"Ooh, sorry," I mocked sarcastically. "We can't all go to musical genius school. That was just your run-of-the-mill college party."

"You can say that again." His smile came through in his tone. "No musical geniuses bark where I come from."

I giggled. "Well, that's a shame. You're missing out."

A loud, girly shriek echoed through the house.

I rolled my eyes.

"Ethan got a girl in there?" Ty asked.

"I assume so."

Then a rhythmic banging sound filled my ears. "Oh God," I moaned. It wasn't the first time I'd had to hear it, but it never got easier.

Tyson chuckled. "How awkward for you—having to listen to your own brother banging—"

"Shut up!" I pulled the pillow from under my head and used it to cover my eyes and ears.

Then we heard her speak again. "Say it!"

"No." Ethan's voice was firm.

The banging stopped.

I pulled the pillow away from my face and looked at Tyson.

His eyes were huge, waiting. "I feel like we're kids eavesdropping."

"We kind of are," I whispered.

She was louder this time. "SAY IT!"

"Oww. Fine!" Ethan bellowed. "Ruff, ruff... ruff, ruff!"

Instantly, Tyson and I were kicking our legs, laughing into the pillows. "No way!" Ty laughed.

I couldn't speak. My body wouldn't stop shaking from laughter. Tears had pooled in my eyes.

"Ruff, ruff... ruff, ruff!" We heard once more.

Then the rhythmic banging started again.

TYSON AND I moved into the living room to watch TV so we didn't have to listen to them... um... bark?

"What are you planning on doing tomorrow—actually, today?" I handed him a coffee and sat next to him.

"I don't know. Sleep a little, find a job, I guess."

"So you plan on staying for a while?" I couldn't help the excitement from showing. It felt good to have him here. It felt familiar.

"If it's okay with you. I kind of just want to hide out for a bit. I haven't even told my parents I'm back."

I nodded. "I get that. It's fine."

A door opened. Tyson and I quickly looked at each other and then pretended to pay attention to the TV.

"You guys still up?" Ethan asked, walking toward the sofa. A brunette walked behind him, adjusting her dress. Tyson chuckled under his breath.

"Yup," I answered for both of us. I watched Tyson pretend to be engrossed with what was on the TV.

"Dimmy, Tyson," Ethan started. Tyson looked up. Ethan pointed at the girl behind him. "This is Kat."

Tyson fell into a fit of laughter. I held it together. "Nice to meet you, Kat. Sorry—" I pointed my thumb at Tyson. "—he's drunk."

She smiled right before Ethan led her out of the house with his hand on her back. When I heard the door click shut, I turned to Tyson. His face was red from his attempt at containing his laughter. I slapped his shoulder.

"Holy shit, Dim." He held his stomach. "Her name is *Kat*, and she makes guys bark like a *dog*. What the fuck?"

My head flew back with my laugh. I snorted. Multiple times.

Ethan interrupted us. "What's so funny?" he asked seriously.

"Kat?" I asked, at the same time Tyson started barking.

"Fuck you," Ethan said, but he was laughing, too. He exited the room and left us in our state of idiotic bliss.

And for a moment, I forgot who the hell Logan Matthews was.

And soon enough, I determined, I'd make it permanent.

4

AMANDA

It didn't take long for Tyson to make himself at home. A few weeks had passed, and he'd landed a job at a record store. He didn't really need a job. He lived off a trust fund left to him by his grandparents, and he was getting paid monthly royalty payments for a few songs he'd recorded on compilation albums. Things were just starting to take off for him in New York when that stuff happened with Ally. He said he'd go back to it eventually but was happy just to sit back for a few months and wait it out. Music would always be there, he'd said, but being young with no major responsibility is limited. He just wanted to live a little. Good for him.

Summer break went by quickly—way too quickly. We spent the time working and lazing around. Ethan's shifts were sporadic, but he made sure someone was always home with me. He and Tyson had come up with a schedule.

I'd thought it was stupid, until I was left alone in the house, and it no longer seemed that way. I felt like a child afraid of monsters. Maybe I was.

I tried calling Tyson first, but he didn't answer. Ethan picked up on the first ring.

"I'm sorry," I told him.

"Where are you?"

"Home."

"Where's Tyson?"

"Don't know."

"Are you okay?"

"I think... maybe... I'm not sure." I paused and pushed aside my damn pride. "Can you just come home, please?"

"I'll be there soon."

"Ethan..."

"Yeah?"

"I'm hiding in the closet."

He cursed before hanging up.

I was weak.

Pathetic.

Scared.

Stupid.

"DIMMY," HE CALLED out. I heard his footsteps get closer just before the closet door swung open. His expression went from panic, to relief, to sympathy. "You're okay," he soothed, taking a seat on the floor next to me. "You're okay," he said again, but this time to himself.

"I'm sorry. I don't mean to worry you." I looked up at him.

"Don't ever apologize for that." He ran his hand through his hair and wiggled a little on the floor until he was comfortable. "You want to talk about it... what you're feeling... or whatever?" He seemed uneasy.

"I don't know. I thought I was okay, E. I really did. But then I was here alone and I just... started to remember..."

"And you got scared?"

I nodded.

"Do you remember it?"

I nodded again, biting my lip to stop the sob. "I just wanted them to stop. They wouldn't stop. They just kept hitting him—"

"That's it?" he cut in. "*That's* what you think about? That they hurt *him?*" His tone was sharp. "What about you, Dimmy? How about the fact that they hurt *you?* How about the fact that Logan just fucking left and hurt *you?* Or the fact that he's *still* hurting you? Every day he's gone, and you're hurting. That's all you can think about—that asshole?"

I stayed quiet, waiting for him to calm down.

"How are those self-defense classes going?" He changed the subject.

"Good," I said truthfully. "I'm getting more confident."

He squeezed my hand. "Good." Then he lifted it and studied my wrist. "He doesn't deserve *this,*" he stated, motioning his head toward it. He stood and offered me his hand. "I called Tyson. He's coming home; we're going minigolfing."

"Minigolf?" I asked, incredulous.

"Yeah." He pushed me out of the closet, through my bedroom, down the hallway and into the living room. "It'll be good times, promise."

Tyson came home five minutes later, apologizing for leaving. He hadn't realized I was home. He kept apologizing, even though I kept telling him it was fine. I wasn't his responsibility. I wasn't Ethan's, either.

An hour later, we were minigolfing. Ethan and Ty shared a flask. I drove, opting not to share in the extracurricular.

It was the first night since he'd left that I felt like myself again, even for a little while.

We laughed. Hard. It really was good times.

Tyson knocked on my door and popped his head in. "You decent?"

I was already in bed, ready to call it a night. "Yup."

"Dammit," he joked. He made a show of jumping on the bed before lying next to me. He turned his head to face me, blinking hard a few times.

"Are you wasted?" I asked, giggling when he scrunched his nose. They hadn't stopped drinking whatever was in the flask until a few minutes ago. I eyed him, waiting for his answer. He'd gotten so handsome over the past few years. His features were more defined, manlier.

"I think so. I don't know what Ethan had in that flask, but it's worked its magic into my system."

I laughed. "Magic?"

He nodded, turning his entire body to face me. I did the same. His scruffy, dark hair was all over the place.

"Quit checking me out," he teased.

I laughed into my pillow. I wasn't going to deny it; I kind of was.

I felt him move forward until his body was flush against mine. The heat of his arms as they wrapped around me engulfed me. He pulled me in so my face was on his chest.

I muffled into his chest. "What are you—"

He cut in before I could finish. "Sshh, Dim. Just let me do it." I let my body relax. He must've felt it, because he brought me even closer. "I've wanted to hold you like this since I moved in," he said, pulling back and looking at my face. "Are you okay?"

The concern in his face broke my heart. "Yeah, Tyson. I am." I put my arms around him. "I promise."

"I'm not talking about *him*. I mean ..." He cleared his throat. "You were almost raped."

My breath hitched. No one had ever said those words aloud. Not to me, anyway. "I don't think about it. *Almost* doesn't count."

"That's bullshit. It has to count for something."

"It could've been a lot worse."

"Yeah, or it could have been prevented completely."

I reared back, a little pissed off at his words. "What's that supposed to mean?"

He exhaled loudly. "Nothing. I don't know what I'm saying. I'm buzzed. Sorry." He brought my head back closer to him, but we were face-to-face, his nose against mine, our lips almost touching. He closed his eyes slowly. "Good night, Dim," he said, right before he kissed me.

I let him.

It wasn't passionate. It wasn't intimate. There was no tongue. No movement. It just *was*. When he pulled back, he sighed. "I know you're still in love with him."

I didn't speak.

I didn't agree.

I didn't deny.

I didn't know how I felt.

I WOKE UP the next morning and he was gone. I must have fallen asleep in his arms. Some nights, I'd had nightmares. Last night, I didn't.

I don't truly understand why, but the fact that I was almost raped didn't really ring true. Maybe I'd blocked it out, or maybe I was just so scared for Logan at the time that I didn't really understand what was happening until afterwards.

I remembered most of it so distinctly. I remembered him being held up, me saying his name, him finding the strength to break free, but then he fell to the floor. I'd wanted to reach him. I kept thinking that he'd find the strength again, but he couldn't get up; he just kept crawling toward me. It had all happened so fast, but his movements—they were so slow.

I'd heard him say my name, right before he got kicked in the head. I'd screamed. It was so loud, it had echoed through the house. I'd screamed some more, and I'd thought for sure that if he could just hear me screaming, he would wake up. Surely, he would wake up. He had to.

I think my body shut down then, because I don't remember anything that happened after.

When I woke up in the hospital, the first thing I remember thinking was maybe Logan and I were connected somehow, more than just a boy and a girl in love. Maybe our souls were entwined—if he hurt, I hurt. If he stopped breathing, I did, too. If he died, maybe I would die with him.

I was alive. I was awake. Which meant that he was, too. But I didn't see him; he never came for me.

He just left.

WE DECIDED TO go home for the weekend to visit Mom. She'd started to date some guy, and she wanted us to meet him. I'd invited Tyson to come along; he assumed he already was.

My mom loved Tyson—always had. We took Ethan's car, as mine was too small, and Tyson didn't have one. Tyson wanted to drop by the store and get a bottle of wine and some flowers for Mom. Ethan left his phone charger back home, so he went to the electronics store to buy a new one. I waited in the car for both of them.

A knock on the window caused me to jump out of my skin. I held my hand to my heart and turned to see a familiar face.

He knocked again.

I should've expected to see him; we were parked out front of his practice. I wound down the window.

"Hey, Amanda," he said, then rubbed the scruff of his beard with the back of his fingers. "You got a minute? I'd like to have a quick word, if that's okay?"

It could only be about one thing, and for a second, I hesitated. But I wouldn't let this ruin what I'd spent months trying to build. "Sure." I smiled at him and got out of the car.

He motioned for me to sit on a bench a few feet away. The cool metal chilled the back of my thighs when I sat. "How have you been, Dr. Matthews?"

"You know to call me Alan, Amanda."

I giggled. "How have you been, Alan?"

He blew out a breath, his smile completely gone. "I've been better." He cleared his throat. "That's actually why I wanted to speak to you."

My eyebrows drew in. "What do you mean?"

He took my hand in both of his. I let him. I swallowed down my emotions and blinked back the tears. I don't know how he'd suddenly made me feel like this.

"I owe you an apology—"

I opened my mouth to interrupt, but he lifted his hand to stop me. "Please, sweetheart," he said. "I need to apologize to you. Logan—"

My breath caught. My insides turned to cement. His name alone still had the power to ruin me.

"He was in a bad way after what happened to you. And even though it happened to him, too, he never saw it like that. All he ever saw was you. He blamed himself. He thought it was his fault it happened. And he thought that if you hadn't met him... well..." He let out all the air in his lungs. Then he looked at me, right into my eyes.

Blinking, I let a tear drop.

"I thought I was helping him. It was my idea for him to leave and travel. I thought that maybe it would help him if he saw things differently... but hell, I never even thought about you."

I let the dam break, let it shatter into a pool of uncontained emotions.

"And I'm sorry," he continued. "I'm sorry that he's gone."

"Please," I managed to say, trying to stop him from continuing. I wiped my face. "I appreciate what you're saying, I really do, but you're not the one who should be apologizing."

He nodded. "Do you want to know about him?"

"No," I said quickly. "I can't."

"Okay."

He removed his hands from mine and leaned back on the bench, and I mimicked his position. We stared straight ahead.

"You know," he said, his tone a little lighter. "When he left for college, it started to get real lonely in that big, old house, but he would come by and visit on weekends. Now, though—I miss him."

I swallowed the knot in my throat. "Yeah." I did, too. But I wasn't going to admit that to anyone.

He laughed once. "I looked up taco casserole recipes on the internet."

I smiled. "Yeah?"

"Yeah," he replied. "Mine came out black, though."

I laughed, that awkward crying-type laugh.

"Just saying—if you ever feel the need to make it and want to visit a lonely old man in a big, empty house, the invitation is there."

I turned to him. "Maybe."

"There you are!" Tyson's voice came from behind me, interrupting us.

I stood up, and so did Alan. I waited until he was next to me before I made the introductions. "Um, this is Tyson." I pointed my thumb at him. "Tyson, this is Dr. Matthews." I felt Tyson tense.

They shook hands.

Alan smiled and then faced me. "The invitation will always stand, *pretty girl*."

5

AMANDA

"I swear Mom loves Tyson more than her own kids." Ethan stood next to me while Mom gushed all over Ty.

"Oh, my," she swooned. "You've gotten so damn handsome."

I smiled. It was true; he had. I didn't miss the look she gave me over his shoulder while she was hugging him.

"Well," Tyson started. "You haven't changed a bit. I swear you and Dimmy could be sisters."

I snorted at the same time Ethan scoffed, "Lame." Mom smiled warmly at me.

While Ethan looked every bit like Dad, I was a fine mix between the two. Dad was Mexican, and Ethan got all his dark features: his dark skin, hair and eyes. Mom was almost the opposite. She had fair skin and natural blonde hair; and her eyes were the color of the ocean. She did look younger than her years, and even after everything she'd been through, it hadn't affected her looks.

"So, when do we get to meet this asshole?" Ethan joked.

Mom laughed at him. "Soon."

Scott, his name was.

Dinner went smoothly. He even managed to keep up with Ethan's fifty questions. Ethan played the overprotective son perfectly. I think Scott found it more amusing than anything else, but he hid it and treated Ethan with the respect he seemed to think he deserved.

Tyson sat next to me and occasionally nudged my leg. It was this stupid game we'd played when we'd dated. Back then, it started with nudges on the leg, and eventually it had turned to him trying to sneak his hand up my thigh.

He didn't do that tonight.

AFTER SCOTT AND Mom retired to the living room to watch TV, we went up to my room. Ethan had a date; he wouldn't say with whom. Alexis also had a date that night. Funny how that happens.

"Am I sleeping in here?" Tyson asked, walking around my room. He was taking everything in, like it had changed since the last time he'd seen it.

"I don't know; I didn't really think about it. I mean, I'm fine sharing a bed if you are."

He looked at the bed and then at me. A slow smirk pulled on his lips. "Hey, remember that time..." He walked over to the bed and sat on it. "We snuck here after school once. The first time we fooled around was right here—on this bed."

I nodded, biting my lip. I remembered.

He leaned in closer. "Shit, it was good times. You were so responsive, too."

"Tyson," I warned. We were about to go somewhere I didn't want to be.

He just nodded and cleared his throat. "I'm glad I was your first," he said, removing his socks and jeans. "That way you'll always remember me." He took off his shirt and stood in nothing but his boxer shorts.

I looked away.

I waited for him to get into bed before switching off the light on the nightstand. "So does that mean you can easily forget me?" I asked him. I knew I wasn't Tyson's first. He was two years older and had been open about the fact that he'd dated and slept with other girls before me. We never got into the specifics of it. I didn't want to know. Some girls may have wanted a list of names and locations, but I was happy being naïve.

He laughed quietly. "No, Dim." He rested his hand on my stomach. "I'd never be able to forget you. I don't think any guy would be able to forget you."

I wondered for a second if Logan had forgotten about me. It'd been months.

"Trust me," he said, pulling me from my thoughts. "He hasn't either."

I turned to my side to face him, causing his hand to wrap around my waist. "Why are you so nice to me? I mean—you don't need to be. I was horrible to you. I treated you so badly, and you still talk to me. You still care about me. Why?"

He pulled me closer to him. "I don't know. I'm not going to lie; it really hurt—what you did to me, but I guess I learned to accept it. Truth is, I'm always going to care about you. You're my best friend, Dim. Shitty things happened to you, and you just keep getting up and fighting. You could've easily turned the other way. You could've shut everyone out and let that consume you, but you haven't. And I admire that. I admire you. In fact, I'm pretty sure I love you."

I gasped.

"Shut up, idiot. Not like that." He laughed.

"Oh." Relief washed through me.

"Plus, I keep you around because you're easy on the eye."

I shook with laughter and pushed him away.

He brought me closer. "I'm serious, Dim. In high school, you were cute, you know? Now... you've gotten so fucking hot—"

"Shut up!" I tried to pull away from him, but his hand on my waist kept me there.

"Fine," he sighed. "You want to just fool around for a bit then?"

"Okay," I joked.

"Yessss!" he mocked.

We didn't fool around. We fell asleep.

He kept his hold on me.

And I let him.

I WENT TO the store the next day, got all the ingredients I needed, put on my big girl panties and drove to his house. A part of me hoped he wouldn't be home. The other part of me wanted to see him.

I knocked on the door. He answered almost immediately. His eyes went from my face to the bags in my hand. "Amanda, you have no idea how happy I am to see you."

"Dr. Matth—"

He raised his eyebrows, the gesture alone interrupting me.

I smiled. "Alan." I jerked my head in greeting.

He sat on the counter, like he had the first time I'd cooked for him.

He didn't speak much, just watched me. He offered me a beer; I declined, opting for a soda instead.

"Is he safe?" I asked him.

He swallowed his mouthful of taco casserole. "Yes. He's safe."

"Is he happy?" The words were out of my mouth before I could stop them.

Alan sighed and rested his elbows on either side of his plate. "I wouldn't say he's happy... but he's... coping."

I placed my fork on the table. "Do you speak to him often?" My voice broke.

"He calls when he can."

I nodded and looked down at my plate.

He perked up. "You want to see pictures of him when he was a kid?"

My lips lifted at the corners. "Yes," I said sheepishly.

"He'd kill me if he found out."

I shrugged. "He's not really here to do that, is he?"

WE BROUGHT OUR dinner into the living room and finished up eating in there. Alan found six photo albums and placed them on the coffee table. "I know everything is digital now," he said. "But I like to have something physical to hold, you know?"

I smiled, remembering Logan's words. "Yeah, Logan said the same thing about CDs."

"Really?" He smiled back at me. "He told me you said the same thing about books."

I nodded shyly. "Did he talk about me a lot?"

"Are you kidding?" he said. "You were all he talked about." He took his glasses off and pressed the bridge of his nose with his thumb and finger. "I know it doesn't mean much anymore, but he really loved you, Amanda."

Ignoring the conversation, I picked up the first album on the pile and started flipping through it. The first picture was of him as a kid in his Little League outfit. You could tell right away that it was Logan. Even through his forced smile, his dimples still came through.

"That's one of my favorites," Alan said. "Look at him. He was so little for his age, so skinny, not like now." He laughed once. "His clothes are hanging off him." I watched an emotion take over his face. Pride. "His hat's so big, it's almost falling over his eyes." He took the album out of my hands so he could get a better look. An envelope fell out and landed on the floor. I picked it up. "Oh no." He sounded panicked. He held out his hand and said, "You don't want to see those, darlin'."

My eyebrows pinched in confusion.

"They're not... *happy* pictures of him."

"What do you mean?" I squeaked.

He sighed and placed the album back on the table. "They're... uh... evidence."

"Evidence?" I whispered.

He nodded and cleared his throat. Then he lifted his eyes to meet mine, and I knew instantly what he meant.

"Can I?" I asked.

"Sweetheart, they're not—" He blew out a breath, a look of acceptance on his face. "Okay."

I opened the envelope slowly and shook out the pictures. They landed face down in my hands. Taking a huge breath, I carefully flipped them over.

I stopped breathing at the same time Alan gasped.

This is what monsters are capable of.

I pushed down my emotions and looked up at Alan. "This is what he was like when he was brought in?"

Alan just shook his head, his eyes unfocused, his mind elsewhere. "He was a lot worse. That picture was taken a few hours later, after we cleaned up all the blood."

I slowly flipped through the pictures, one by one. Each one told a different story. With each angle, each body part, I could see Logan as a kid, fading slowly with each hit. Then I got to the last one. It was different than the others; it didn't belong. He was smiling. I heard Alan laugh softly and take the picture from my hand. "He's smiling at me because I wouldn't stop laughing. You know those laughs that build up inside your belly? When you're just so damn happy you can't contain it? It was the first time he spoke to me." He wiped his eyes and replaced his glasses.

"What did he say?"

"What's that, love?"

I smiled and covered his hand with mine. "His first words to you, what did he say?"

He sniffed once, his lips curling into a smile. "He'd just fallen off his bike. I was putting a Band-Aid on his knee and he said, 'You're a nice doctor man. I want to be you when I grow up.'"

My eyes went wide with surprise. "And look at him now. He's all grown up and on his way there." I tried to comfort him with my words.

"Yeah."

It was silent for a moment as I flipped through the horrible pictures again. "How long did it take him to speak?"

"He didn't. Not until you showed up."

My eyes snapped to his. "What do you mean?"

His eyebrows drew in as he watched me. "Oh. You mean the first time? Sorry. My mind was—"

"Wait. There was a second time?" My voice rose. I couldn't control it.

He let out a slow breath. "Sweetheart," he hesitated a second. "After that night, with everything that happened to you, and to him, he shut down. He blocked out the world, and he turned in on himself. He didn't leave the pool house; he didn't speak to anyone. He barely ate. He barely existed. He turned back into that little boy who I'd first met."

"I'm sorry."

"You have no need to be. That's how he copes with things. He doesn't know how to verbalize things properly. His child psychiatrist warned me about it—that it might never solve itself. She said maybe someday, something might happen, and he could turn right back around. I guess that night, when his father came back—that was someday."

I tried to picture it in my mind—Logan, alone in that pool house, barely existing. And then I imagined me—alone in our house, barely existing. We could have barely existed together.

"Anyway," Alan's tone brightened, "I have pictures here of when he was around thirteen. I'm pretty sure that was the age he started to believe he was God's gift to women."

I couldn't help but laugh. "That's so Logan."

"Yes. Yes, it is." He started to flip through the albums. "There are a few where he's flexing his scrawny, little muscles. He thought he was jacked."

I threw my head back in laughter.

"Here it is," he said handing me the album. Sure enough, there he was, flexing his nonexistent, prepubescent muscles. He had that same cocky smirk I was so familiar with.

I shook my head and ran my thumb over the picture. "This is so Logan."

My Logan.

So THAT'S WHAT we did—talked about past-Logan for the rest of the night.

And then, somehow, I found myself cooking taco casserole in his kitchen every other Sunday.

6

AMANDA

I DIDN'T DO much else apart from school, work and the occasional gym session. The self-defense classes Ethan made me do were actually a blessing. I'd learned more about male genitalia than any girl needed to know—unless, of course, you're using that knowledge to battle monsters.

I'd started running, too—on a treadmill. I never really understood running as an activity. It always kind of confused me why so many girls in books ran. Then I read a book where the hero explained to the heroine the benefits of running—about how it releases endorphins and can make you *feel*. I needed to feel, so I jumped on the treadmill, and forty-five minutes later, when I finally hopped off, I felt different. Maybe it was just in my head, or maybe it really did help.

"WILL YOU RUN with me?" I turned to face Tyson on the sofa next to me. His eyes moved from the TV and slowly made their way to mine. He had a mouthful of popcorn. "What?" he said, popcorn falling out of his mouth.

"You're such a kid. Don't talk with your mouth full."

He swallowed. "You want me to run with you?"

I nodded.

He shrugged.

The front door creaked open and banged close, and I felt Ethan behind me. He tapped me on my shoulder. When I turned to face him, he had a solemn look in his face. Then he showed me the envelope in his hand. I was confused for a second, but then I saw the international stamp and my name on the front.

Logan.

I closed my bedroom door and sat on the edge of the bed. My knee bounced like crazy. My hands shook. My heart pounded against my chest. Sweat built on my forehead. I inhaled deeply and then let it out slowly. "Okay," I encouraged myself. I slowly opened the envelope and pulled out the letter.

Pretty girl,

I don't even know where to start. You've probably heard that I've been traveling around. Dad contacted a few people, and I'm working with Doctors Without Borders. I don't know if you've heard of them, but they do a bunch of relief work all over the world. I was helping this one kid, and his mom went into labor, right in front of me. One of the doctors delivered the baby, and I was there. I witnessed it all. I was the second person to hold the baby. And you're right—what you say about them. That they're miracles. They really are. I wanted so badly to call you after it happened, to tell you all about it. And to tell you that you should do it, become a midwife, or at least try, because it's such an amazing feeling, and you would be so perfect for it.

But I didn't call, because I knew it wouldn't be fair to you. Neither is writing this letter, I guess. But I don't know. I just kind of felt like I needed to. I just needed you to know I was thinking of you.

Anyway, I'm sure you don't care about what some asshole thousands of miles away is doing. I just wanted to tell you I'm okay ... not that I expected you to worry about me or anything.

I guess the real reason I'm writing is because I wanted to tell you that I hope you're doing well. And I guess I wanted you to know that I understand. I understand that you hate me. And as much as it hurts, I know that I deserve it. But I just didn't want to go another day without telling you, just in case you had any doubts, that there's not a single part of me that feels that way about you. All that we had, every moment we shared, it meant everything to me. Everything you felt, I felt it, too. It was the hardest thing to do, to walk away from you, from us, but I had to do it, because you deserve so much more. And I hope you see that. I hope you've moved on and found some guy who treats you like the amazingly beautiful girl you are. And that he knows how lucky he is to have you. I hope he appreciates every single thing about you. And I hope he loves you and gives you the world, Amanda.

Because I would have.

If shit didn't get in the way with us, I would have.

I would've given you the entire universe, because that's what you deserve.
And I want you to know that I wasn't lying. Those last words I said to you, they
are yours. And so am I. Forever.
Because I do love you, Amanda.
And that's the truth.
Logan.

TY LAZILY WALKED into the room and sat on my desk chair. I was still staring at the letter in my hand.

"You okay?" he asked, jerking his head towards the letter.

I cleared my throat. "Yeah." I put the piece of paper back in the envelope and placed it in my handbag on the desk. I started to walk away, but he held on to my hand, stopping me. I turned to face him, confused. "What's up?"

He pulled on my hand and spread his legs so I could stand between them. A part of me started to panic. Another part of me was curious.

He shook his head slowly, his eyes never leaving mine. "Was it from him?" he said.

I nodded once. He put one hand on my hip and brought me closer to him. "Come here," he said quietly, pulling me down until I was sitting on his lap.

"Tyson, I don't think—"

"Don't think," he cut in, resting his hand on the side of my face. My eyes drifted shut. My breath hitched. Then his lips were on mine. Slowly and softly, he kissed me, and I kissed back. He made a sound and brought my face closer to his; his tongue darted out and licked my lips. I opened my mouth for him. The instant our tongues touched, we both pulled back.

He had a disgusted look on his face; I don't know what I looked like.

"That was gross," he announced.

I chuckled. "Way to make a girl feel special."

He lifted me until I was standing and then stood up himself. "I mean..." He eyed me up and down. "You're hot and all, don't get me wrong, but dude, that was like kissing my sister."

I laughed. "You're an ass."

He sat on the bed, and his features turned serious. "So, I have some news," he announced.

"Yeah?"

"I, uh, got offered a job today."

"You already have a job." I sat on the bed next to him.

"No, I mean a proper job. One where my Juilliard education is actually going to come into play."

"Yeah?"

Nodding, he said, "I've been asked to go on a worldwide tour with a band. It's actually a pretty big deal."

I couldn't hide my smile. "That's amazing, Tyson. Who is it?"

His small smile turned into a massive shit-eating grin. "John Mayer."

"No fucking way!" I pushed him. I was so excited for him.

He nodded, his smile huge.

"No. Fucking. Way!" I repeated.

"Yes way," he spoke through his laughter.

"Congratulations!" I jumped on him and hugged him tight.

He started to pull me off him. "Okay, crazy, calm down."

We sat on the bed opposite each other, our legs crossed. He took both my hands in his. "I have to leave in two days," he said, his voice softer.

"Oh." I couldn't help the disappointment coming through. "That's... soon."

"Yeah." He blew out a breath. "Look, Dim. If you need me here, I'll stay—"

"What? No. Just... no."

"But if you're not going to be okay—"

"Shut up, Ty. You're going. I'll be fine. I promise."

"I don't want to leave you if—"

"Tyson, I love you. I love that you care about me. I love that you'd give up this opportunity for me. I love that you somehow think I'm your responsibility. But I'm not. I'm no one's but myself. It's been months, I'm okay."

He leaned forward and kissed my forehead. "I love you, Dim."

I jumped off the bed and pulled him up with me. "Let's get you packed."

He smiled and then pulled me in for hug. "I'm gonna miss you," he said, his voice low.

I held him tighter. "I'll miss you, too."

A FEW HOURS later, most of his stuff was packed. He didn't have much with him, just the couple of bags he brought from New York.

"Why did you kiss me?" I asked.

He shrugged. "To prove a point."

"What point?" I looked around his mostly-empty room. My old room.

"That you still belong to him, whether you know it or not. A piece of you left when he did, and I don't see it coming back until he does."

My heart dropped. He was right—I didn't want him to be—but he was.

"Besides..." He stood up. "I've been here for months, and you've resisted me... and all of this..." He made a show of pointing up and down his body. "If I can't tempt you, then no one can."

I laughed and threw a pillow at him. He blocked it, took two steps forward, and looked me right in the eyes. "You wanna fool around, for old time's sake?" His tone was serious, but his eyes danced with amusement.

"Fiiiine." I feigned annoyance.

We didn't.

WE TOLD ETHAN that Tyson was leaving. He was happy for him, but I knew that he'd worry about me. Turned out, he didn't have to worry long, because Tristan called that night. When Ethan told him Tyson was leaving, Tristan jumped at the chance to move in.

That's the story Ethan's pushing. Personally, I think E asked him to be our housemate slash babysitter. Either way, I was excited to have Tris here.

"Minigolf," Ethan announced. He lifted the flask in his hand and pointed at me. "You're driving, Demander."

I turned to Tyson, who was already getting ready to leave. "Done." He walked over and put his arm around me. "Let's make minigolf our bitch."

"I'M REALLY GOING to miss you, Dimmy. I mean it." Tyson and I were lying in my bed, my head resting on his chest. He lifted my chin and made me face him. I could smell the booze in his breath. "I hate that sometimes I get to see you, you know? Like, a glimpse of who you used to be. The sixteen-year-old Amanda I fell in love with. The one who lived life and wanted *more*. I really hope you find her again. And when you do, I hope the guy who gets that part of you treasures it, even if that guy is Logan. I just want you to be happy."

"Tyson." My voice broke.

"You know..." He kept talking. "You really broke my heart, Amanda. Fuck." His eyes started to drift shut. "I loved you so damn much. I dreamed about it last night—you and me—what our future would have been like if you'd never met him. I pictured us in an apartment in New York, like I wanted us to be... you know... before you broke my heart. I always told myself it was for the best, but I don't know anymore. I planned on marrying you. I told Logan that... when I told him about what happened to you that summer... I told him I wanted to. Maybe it's not right for us to be together; maybe it's timing." He was rambling. I let him. "I hope he was worth it. I don't think your story is over yet. But I really, truly hope he's worth it, Dim. After everything you've been through, everything we've been through, he better be it for you."

7

AMANDA

IT'D BEEN ALMOST six months since Tyson left. He would call, text, or contact me on Facebook almost every day. I told him he didn't need to, especially since he was traveling around the world. He told me it kept him grounded, reminded him of home. I wasn't going to complain. Tyson—he was my constant. I needed that. He never brought up what he'd told me that night. Sometimes I wondered if he remembered it at all or if it was just a drunken rambling. Either way, I remembered his words. I would always remember them.

"So?" Tony pulled me from my thoughts. He was drying some wine glasses behind the bar.

I scrunched my nose. "Definitely not a date?"

He sighed and rolled his eyes. "Yes, Amanda. Not a date. You've made it very clear the last thirty times I've asked you out that you're not interested in dating or in me."

"It's not personal," I tried to soothe. "I'm just not ready to—"

He raised his hands in surrender. "I know, I know. I get it. So tonight? It's just a bunch of Twiggy's friends, not the usual college crowd. Come on, it'll be fun. A bunch of hipster stoners? What's not to like?"

I chuckled under my breath. "Fine." I caved in. "But I'm driving, and I'll meet you there." I pointed my finger at him. "Not a date."

"Not a date," he repeated.

A FEW HOURS later, I pulled up at the front of Twiggy's house. He worked most shifts with me and Tony, and even though he was nearing thirty, you couldn't tell from the way he behaved. Tony and I never knew when he was high or when he was straight; maybe he was just high on life.

THE SMELL OF weed was overpowering the moment I opened the door. Bob Marley played through the speakers. I had to laugh at how stereotypical it all seemed.

Tony's voice boomed from somewhere in the house. "Amanda!" he yelled. I spun in a small circle until I saw him jumping and waving his hand in the air. I carefully maneuvered through the people in the living room until I got to him. "You want a drink?" he yelled into my ear. I lifted the bottle of water in my hand. "Okay," he said, then motioned for me to sit on the chair he'd just occupied. I dropped my ass on the plastic, fold-up seat. He left but came back seconds later with another chair and positioned it next to me. He placed his arm on the back of mine and leaned in close to my ear. "This is exactly what I pictured Twiggy's parties to be like."

I laughed. "I know, right? Bob Marley and everything."

He leaned in even closer. I felt his warm breath on my neck, right before his lips brushed my earlobe. "I know we're not on a date," he said, his voice low. "But you look amazing tonight."

It's nice to be complimented, even if he were nothing more than a friend. I turned to face him to say thank you, but something, or *someone*, caught my eye.

My heart thumped against my chest.

Once.

Twice.

Thump.

And then nothing.

It stopped beating. My eyes drifted shut. I had to be seeing things.

Tony—he must've taken it the wrong way, because the next thing I knew—his warm lips met mine and he was kissing me. I don't know how long his lips were there, until finally, my heart started up again.

Thump, thump.

I audibly sucked in a lungful of air and held it.

He pulled back. "I'm sorry," he said.

I let out the air in a rush. "Not your fault."

He turned and eyed the floor. "Not a date," he mumbled.

My breath came in short spurts.

My eyes lifted and locked with *his*.

LOGAN

HEART—STOMACH. STOMACH—FLOOR.
Our eyes locked.
There was no one else in the room.
She raised her hand in a small wave.
I raised my beer toward her.
Then she smiled.
Smiled.

"GET YOUR SHIT together," I told my reflection in the bathroom mirror. I dropped my head between my shoulders and splashed water on my face and then faced the mirror again. "You knew you'd see her at some point. Quit being a fucking pussy." I rolled my eyes at myself. "Great. I'm fucking talking to myself." I jerked my head toward the mirror. "Dick."

SHE'S HERE WITH Tony—they're dating. It's been a year; of course she's moved on. He seemed like a nice enough guy.

"Not your problem," I said aloud.

They kissed. That's *fine*.

I closed my eyes and tried to erase the memory of her kissing some other asshole.

My hand shook as I turned the knob on the bathroom door. She still had the power to make me nervous.

I tried to muster up the courage to go over and speak to her, hoping that her boyfriend would let me. I didn't know what I'd say. Maybe I should just leave her alone. Maybe she didn't even care that I was here.

I cursed under my breath, opened the door, and stepped out. But before I had a chance to make up my mind, fate had decided for me.

Her eyes went wide when she saw me. "Logan," she breathed out.

My stomach flipped. "Hey..." My voice cracked. Fuck, I was nervous. I cleared my throat. "Hey," I tried again.

She stood with her back against the hallway wall, waiting to use the bathroom. I kept my eyes focused on her face; I didn't want to see the rest of her. I didn't think I could handle it.

A bunch of girls tried to get past. I moved forward so they could get through, causing my body to push against hers. "Sorry," I told her.

"It's fine." She said it so quietly I almost didn't hear her. Then she cleared her throat and stood straighter. She pointed her water bottle toward the bathroom door. "My turn," she informed.

"Oh. Yeah, of course." I stepped back and let her out. This was it. This was our goodbye. She pushed off the wall and walked around me. My eyes focused on where she'd just been.

"Logan?" I felt her hand on my arm. My eyes shut tight, not wanting to remember what her touch did to me. "Logan?" she repeated.

"Mm."

She gripped my arm tighter and turned me to face her. She bit her lip, her eyes unsure. "Will you wait for me?"

I nodded, my tongue too heavy, my mouth too dry to speak. She walked into the bathroom and closed the door behind her.

I let out the breath I didn't know I was holding. Only then did I let my body relax, my muscles aching from the tension.

AMANDA

"GET IT TOGETHER," I told myself in the mirror. I splashed water on my face and neck and filled my bottle of water. *Why did I ask him to wait for me?* Oh God, this is going to be so awkward. He's going to be outside, thinking I'm going to say or do something phenomenal, and I don't even know what the hell I'm doing.

When I stepped out of the bathroom, he was there, leaning his shoulder against the wall with his ankles crossed. His hands were in his pockets, causing his arm and shoulder muscles to flex. I didn't take him in; I didn't want to remember how his body made me feel.

I cleared my throat.

His green eyes lifted to mine.

He stood to full height.

I froze.

Thump. Thump.

I opened my mouth to apologize and to let him get on with the rest of his night, but he spoke first, "You want to get out of here?" he asked. His eyes on mine were so intense, so full of promise. Then he shook his head, as if clearing his thoughts. "I'm sorry. Fuck, I'm a dick. You're here with your boyfriend." He kept shaking his head from side to side. He took a step backward, his hands going up.

I watched him, confused, but then it hit me. "Oh!" I rushed out. "He's not—I mean—Tony—he's not my boyfriend."

"It's okay," he talked over me. "You don't need to explain."

He took another step back and bumped into someone, who pushed him forward and into me. I tried to help steady him. "Sorry," he said. I noticed his hands clenched at his sides.

Once he was on his feet again, he blew out a breath. "You don't need to tell me anything, just—"

"I'll just tell him that I'm leaving, okay?"

He shook his head again. "It's fine... you don't need—"

"Just wait out front for me?"

He nodded, then turned and headed for the front door.

I watched him. And finally, I let my body relax.

I WALKED OUT the front door and looked around for him. He was leaning against a car, one knee bent with his foot on the wheel. His head was down, looking at his hand. He shook it a couple of times and then went back to examining it.

Weird.

I strolled over to him; he must not have heard me coming, because his eyes never lifted. I kicked his shoe with mine, and his gaze moved from his hand, to my shoe, up my legs, higher, over my body and finally, after what felt like a lifetime, my face. His eyes shut tight as he looked away from me.

"Are you okay?" He was acting strange, or maybe this had become normal for him. *Who knows? It's been a year.* He pulled a can of beer from both pockets of his sweater and silently offered one to me. I shook my head, declining.

"Walk?" he asked, kicking off the car and replacing one can back in his pocket. He pulled the tab off the beer, placed it to his mouth, tilted his head back and chugged. After his Adam's apple bobbed for the fourth time, his eyes shifted to mine. Pulling the can away, he straightened up, but his gaze remained on me. He licked his lips. I unconsciously did the same. He cursed under his breath and took a step toward me. Panic kicked in, but he just walked past me and started leading me away from the house. I followed, crossing my arms over my chest and hiding my hands under my armpits. I needed to hide my wrists. He couldn't see them.

LOGAN

SHE'D GOTTEN EVEN hotter, if at all possible. Her heels just helped show off her legs. Her goddamn legs. She didn't wear heels that often when we were together, but when she did, it drove me crazy. I wonder if I'd ever told her that. I should have told her a lot of things, and more often.

Like the fact that I loved her.

Or the fact that I still love her.

I stopped walking, turned to face her, and waited for her to catch up. "Sorry," I told her. "I shouldn't have turned my back on you." I watched as her steps faltered.

Fuck. Nice choice of words, asshole.

WE WALKED HALF a block until we were at a baseball field. She led the way to a swing set, and sat down. I did the same, sitting opposite, so we were face-to-face. She smiled at me, but it was off—it didn't reach her eyes. Her legs pushed off the ground only enough so that they straightened. Her eyes focused on the dirt underneath us.

Her arms were still crossed with her hands tucked under them. She must've been cold. I pulled the full can of beer from my sweater pocket and shrugged out of it, stood up, and then placed it around her shoulders.

"Oh," she said, surprised. "You don't have to do that."

I sat back on the swing. "It's fine."

She put her arms through the holes and zipped it up. "Thank you."

"You're welcome."

8

AMANDA

BEING IN HIS sweater was a bad idea. I could smell him all around me. I let it control me for a second, but only a second, before I got my bearings back.

I looked at our surroundings. It was so dark, the only light coming from the moon and the one street lamp lighting part of the field.

Of course we'd end up at a baseball field. I laughed under my breath. "Do you miss it?" I asked him, jerking my head toward the field.

"Of course I do, Amanda. Every day." His words were rushed. It surprised me. It must've shown in my expression because his eyes went huge and then looked toward the field. "Oh," he said. "You mean baseball? Um. Yes, I guess. Not really, no. I mean... I don't know," he rambled under his breath and then shook his hand out a couple of times before he examined it again.

Something was wrong.

"Logan, are you okay?" I stopped swinging and faced him.

"Yes." His voice was hoarse.

"You keep looking at your hand."

He focused on it again. I followed his gaze. "It won't stop shaking," he said.

I watched as his fingers trembled. He flexed them a few times. "Why?"

He laughed once. "You make me nervous," he stated. "You've always made me nervous." He looked up, his gaze intense. "I guess nothing's changed."

I looked away. I felt myself coming undone, and I couldn't have that. "Everything's changed," I told him.

It was the truth.

Then we just sat there, in the deafening silence of our own thoughts.

AFTER A WHILE, I stood up. I didn't know why, but sitting there with him was too much. It was too hard. But it was also too easy—it shouldn't be easy.

He stood, too. "I wrote you."

I sucked in a breath. "I know. I got it."

He just nodded and looked away. I didn't think it was necessary to tell him I kept it in my handbag and carried it everywhere.

"Look..." he said, his hands going in his pockets. "Can we just talk for a bit? I know that I'm the last person on earth you wanna be seeing, but I don't want this to be awkward, and I know that I have no right to ask anything from you, at all, but I don't know..." he said and shrugged, "it would just mean a lot, if you could talk to me... for a bit..."

He took my hand in his and placed it flat against his heart. I could feel it pounding against my palm. He ducked his head so he could look clearly into my eyes. "Please, Amanda," he pleaded.

He covered my hand with his and placed the other on the side of my face.

I stopped breathing. All I could hear was the blood pumping in my ears.

Thump, thump, I felt against his chest.

His mouth parted, but he didn't move. His eyes stayed focused on mine. He rubbed his thumb against my cheek. "Please," he said again.

"Okay." I nodded.

"Yeah?" His features brightened.

I couldn't help the smile that formed. "Sure."

He led me onto the field and stopped in the middle, never once releasing my hand. Lying down, flat on his back, he tugged my hand until I was down on the ground. I sat next to him and waited, but he just looked up at the stars and stayed silent. Then, finally, "You hate me, don't you?"

I tried to silence my gasp, but I don't know if it worked. "I want to," I told him truthfully. "I mean—how could I not, right?"

His eyes finally left the stars and focused on me.

He waited for me to continue, so I did. "There are so many reasons why I should hate you, but I can't, Logan." I swallowed the knot in my throat. "I can't hate you," I repeated. "But I can't feel anything else for you."

Lie.

He sniffed once and nodded, looking back at the stars. "So I take it you're still at UNC?"

My body relaxed. I could do this. We could talk. "Yup."

"Still childcare?"

My eyebrows pinched. "No, um, I changed majors."

He sat up, a smile taking over his face. "Really? To what? Nursing?"

"You don't know?" He had to know.

He shook his head. "No," he laughed out. "Why would I know?"

"Your dad didn't tell you?"

"What? Why would my dad tell me?" He sat up straighter and turned his entire body to face me.

I got more confused. "Wait. Your dad knows you're home, right?"

He laughed again. "Yes, of course he knows I'm home. What are you talking about?"

"Huh."

"Huh?" he asked. "What does 'huh' mean?" He bit his lip, but his smile still came through, causing his beautiful damn dimples to appear.

I sucked in a breath. "I don't know..." I started to mock, playing along with his amused tone. "If he didn't tell you..."

He threw his head back and made a frustrated sound. "Wait." All of a sudden he turned serious. "You haven't started dating my dad, have you?"

"Ew!" I squealed, pushing on his chest. He fell back on the ground, laughing. "That's just wrong."

"I know." He actually sounded relieved. "You don't need to tell me that."

I couldn't help but laugh. "You're such an idiot."

"I know. You don't need to tell me that, either."

Then it was quiet for a beat.

"So?" He raised his eyebrows. "What's your major, and what does Dad have to do with it?"

I tried to pick my words carefully. It wasn't just about my major or his dad. It was about him, too, but he didn't need to know that. "Your dad helped me decide, I guess. I've switched to psychology."

His lips turned up at the corners. His expression was one I knew well:

pride. It made my heart hurt. I swallowed, wary of his reaction. "I want to focus on children's services. I want to work with neglected and um..." I paused to take a breath. "...abused kids."

He sat up, resting his weight on his arms behind him. "Huh." His eyes were unfocused, staring into the distance. He pulled his knees up and settled his elbows on them. "That's great, Amanda." He tilted his head to face me. "You're going to be amazing."

Yeah, I thought. We could've been amazing together.

"So." He nudged my side, trying to lighten the mood. "How did my dad help you decide?"

"I think I may have said too much already. Maybe you need to ask him that one."

He chuckled. "Okay then..."

We both started to speak at the same time, but he held his hand out toward me. "Ladies first," he said.

"How long have you been back?"

"A couple weeks."

"So everyone knows you're here?"

"Nope, just Dad, and now you."

"Why?"

"I don't know." He shrugged. "You know Micky, she'd throw a party."

I laughed. She would.

"I just want to lay low for a bit, have time to get my shit together." He lay back down on the grass and linked his fingers behind his head.

And that's when I saw it—words tattooed on the inside of his bicep. My fingers moved on their own, lifting his sleeve so I could read it.

His entire body stiffened when my skin made contact with his. "Sorry," I whispered but didn't remove my hand. Tilting my head to read the script easier, I said the words out loud, "Transit umbra, lux permanet..." I looked at him, confused.

He raised his hand to move my hair behind my ear.

Thump. Thump.

LOGAN

HER PHONE SOUNDED, interrupting us. "Hey There Delilah" played.

Tyson.

I watched her face light up. She excused herself and reached for her phone. "Tyson," she greeted. "Do you have any idea what time it is?"

She waited for a response and then a slow laugh built up. "I was just at a party, you know Twiggy...uh-huh...Yeah."

She paused, eyeing me with a seriousness I hadn't expected. "No, nothing exciting, I'm actually just heading home now." She got to her feet. "Skype me tomorrow, okay?"

I came to a stand. She fidgeted with the hem of my hoodie; it was longer than the dress she wore. "Yeah," she said quietly, looking away from me. "I love you, too."

For the second time that night, my stomach hit the floor.

She loved Tyson.

She placed the phone in her bag, then looked up at me and smiled. "You'll never guess what Tyson's doing now."

Like I fucking gave a shit. "Oh yeah?" I faked. "What's he doing?" Apart from banging the girl I'm in love with.

"He's on a world tour." She sounded so proud; it kind of made me sick. "Guess who with?"

"Who?"

She started walking back to the party. "John Mayer."

I choked on air. "No way!"

She nodded enthusiastically.

"So, that must be hard, you guys dating and him all over the place."

"What?" she huffed. "We're not dating."

"But you told him you loved him?"

"I do love him." She shrugged and started walking faster.

AMANDA

I DON'T KNOW why I openly announced that I loved Tyson. Maybe it was because I wanted to see his reaction. Maybe deep down I wanted him to hurt.

The second the words were out of my mouth, it seemed like a light switched off inside him. His eyes dimmed, his features flattened.

I walked faster away from him. I couldn't stand to see it. His pain would still cause my heart to break, and I didn't need that.

I didn't deserve that.

THE WALK BACK to my car seemed to take forever. I made the mistake of moving closer to him when a bunch of guys started walking toward us. The self-defense classes had helped, not just my confidence in unknown situations, but also the immediate panic I would get when faced with the slightest of threats. I felt his body stiffen next to me, and then slowly and carefully, he placed his arm around my shoulders, bringing me even closer to him. As soon as I felt *safe*, I shrugged out of his hold. I didn't want to mess with his head. I didn't want him to think it was okay to do stuff like that, to feel the need to protect me or whatever.

"So, this is me." I unlocked the car, opened the door, and threw my handbag in.

He stood in front of me, nodding slowly. "Is this—I mean—this is the one they picked?"

"Ha! You mean the one you bought me?" The words came out harsher than intended.

He must've noticed because he didn't respond, just moved around me, stuck his head in the car and looked around. "So, it's good?" he asked. "I mean, it doesn't break down and shit? It's safe, right?"

He pulled back and waited for my response.

At the word *safe*, something in me shifted. "Yeah, Logan." I started to unzip his hoodie. "It's *safe*."

He raised his hands as if to stop me. "Keep it," he said. His single-dimple half-smile appeared. "Give it back the next time I see you." It came out as a question.

I continued to shrug out of it and handed it to him.

His expression changed immediately, and sadness washed over him. He took it from my hands, cleared his throat and nodded, as if understanding an unspoken word that lingered between us.

"It was really good seeing you, Logan. I'm glad we did this. I'm glad you're... *safe.*"

His lips thinned to a line. He didn't speak, just nodded.

I turned to get in my car, but his hand on my arm stopped me. He spun me to face him, and before I knew it, his arms were around me and our bodies were locked.

His hard chest was against mine, one hand on my back, the other in my hair. I could feel the heat of his breath against my shoulder.

"Amanda," he whispered, and then he slowly sucked in a breath.

Without realizing, my hands came up to rest flat on his back. I felt his fingers curl into me, holding me tighter. I shut my eyes and let myself have this moment, this last moment with me in his arms. I wanted to remember this, savor it, drown in it. I swallowed the lump in my throat and pushed back the tears.

And that's how we stayed.

It could've been hours, it could've been seconds—it didn't matter. Time didn't exist.

We pulled back simultaneously. He sniffed once and wiped his eyes quickly. Then his red-stained eyes met mine with an intensity that knocked me back a step. He leaned forward, wet his lips and placed them on my forehead. It was warm, and soft, and everything I remembered from the past. He cupped my cheek and pulled back slightly but not enough that I could see him. Then I heard him speak, his voice low, but clear. "Goodbye, pretty girl."

He stepped back, turned around and walked away.

And I watched him.

I got in my car, put it into gear, pulled away from the curb, turned a corner, parked on the side of the road, and let it out.

All of it.

I love him.

I still fucking love him.

I couldn't control the sobs that shook my body. I'd cried for Logan in the past, but I didn't cry for Logan in the present or in the future. And he was here.

I would not let him break me.

After a few minutes, I tried to regain control of myself. I pulled out my phone to message Ethan and let him know I was fine. He was okay with me having more freedom, as long as he knew where I was. I think it helped that he'd started officially dating Alexis a few months earlier and wanted to spend some alone time with her. I also think she'd helped persuade him to give me a little space. She was over most weekends, or he was there with her. It worked, and I couldn't be happier for them. I'm glad they finally found each other. She was exactly what he needed to stop whoring around. I laughed to myself, wondering if Logan's friends had ever thought that about me.

Fucking Logan.

I started crying again. My head hit the steering wheel, and the horn sounded. I jerked up in surprise. Then a knocking on my window made me squeal. I reached in my bag for the mace before turning around to find the person responsible.

Logan.

He was wearing his sweater again with the hood over his head. I wound down my window, a little suspicious of why he was here. "Are you following me?"

His eyes narrowed. "I could ask you the same thing."

"What?"

He jerked his head to the building behind him, but his eyes never left mine. "I live here."

"You all good, man?" a guy behind him asked. He had a girl under his arm. The girl had bleached blonde hair, dreadlocks and piercings. They were the type of people you'd expect to see at Twiggy's party. I guess that's how Logan ended up at a place like that. "I'm good," he told them. "You guys head in." He turned to me and spoke, concern dripping from his words. "Are you okay? I mean—have you been crying?"

I sighed. "Yeah. I mean no. I'm not okay, and yes, I have been crying." I didn't see the point in lying.

He straightened to full height. "Because of me?"

"Yes."

He rubbed the back of his neck with his hand, his eyes cast downwards. "Do you—I mean—do you want to talk about it? About what happened to us?"

I shook my head out of habit, but then I calmed down enough to think about it. Maybe I needed to speak to him. Maybe I needed some form of closure. "Okay," I whispered.

"What?" he asked. His head jerked up in surprise.

"I think that might be a good idea, you know...closure and all."

"Closure." He repeated my words as if tossing the idea around in his head. "Okay."

I grabbed a sweater from the back seat and put it on, making sure to cover my wrists. He opened my door and helped me step out.

"Closure," I heard him whisper.

9

AMANDA

"THE ELEVATOR'S BROKEN; we're gonna have to hoof it five floors." He smirked at me. "Are you going to be okay, or do you want me to carry you?"

"Ha ha," I said, pulling the sleeves of my sweater past my fingers. "I'll have you know I've started working out." I raised my eyebrows at him.

"Aaah." He had a knowing look on his face.

"What?"

"Nothing." He shook his head slightly and motioned for me to go ahead of him on the stairs.

I took five steps up before I turned to him. "What do—" My words cut off when I noticed his gaze lift to mine. His eyes were wide, as if he'd been caught doing something he shouldn't be. Then it hit me. I glared at him. "Were you just looking at my ass?"

He chuckled, low at first, and then it turned into an all-out laugh. "I'm sorry," he managed to get out. "I'm still a guy, and you—you're still smokin' hot." I don't know what emotion showed on my face, but his smile disappeared. "I'm sorry," he repeated. "I won't say stuff like that again." He swallowed and took two steps forward, until we were on the same step. "See, I won't perv. Promise."

We made the rest of the way to the fifth floor in silence. The building was old, not what I'd expect Logan to live in, not with the money I knew he had. We stopped in the middle of the hallway when we saw the same couple from outside making out in front of a door, the guy trying to get his key in the hole while pressing the girl into it. Logan laughed under his breath and walked over to the couple. I stayed close behind him. "Yo, Eli." Logan tried to get his attention. They didn't break apart; they didn't even notice he was there. He put his hands on the guy's shoulders and moved him across the hall. "Wrong door, guys," he told them, before moving back to where the couple had just been. He pulled keys out of his pocket, unlocked and pushed the door open, and then motioned for me to enter.

I did.

THE APARTMENT WAS simple, to say the least. A kitchen on the left, living/bedroom and that was basically it. He had a sofa bed, and his bags and boxes were still unpacked. "This is...nice," I told him.

He laughed. "This will do," he replied.

I turned in a circle, taking it in. "So, it's like a studio apartment?" I motioned toward his sofa bed.

His eyes narrowed, as if confused. "Oh, no. There are two bedrooms down the hall." He pointed to a hallway I hadn't seen yet.

I shifted on my feet. "So, you have housemates?" It was my turn to be confused.

"No." He opened the fridge and stared at the contents.

"So, you sleep on the sofa-bed of the living room because...?" I waited for him to finish my sentence.

He closed the fridge door, turned, and leaned against it and then exhaled loudly. "Because I have this thing with needing to be able to see and hear the front door," he confessed.

Our eyes locked, focused on each other, as if doing so for long enough would help me understand what he meant. Or maybe it might make it easier to explain why we were both here together, but not *together*.

Finally, I looked away, not being able to handle the intensity in his gaze. My eyes roamed around the little space he'd created for himself. Even with the boxes and bags everywhere, it was still neat. Everything had its place. There were piles of clothes in the corner of the room, but they too were folded and stacked perfectly. Apart from those items, the apartment was empty. There were no personal touches, no decorations, no lamps, no pictures. Nothing.

"I like what you've done with the place," I teased.

He reached up into a cupboard and pulled out a packet of something. Gummy bears.

He placed a bowl on the counter and started taking all the red ones out. "Funny," he retorted, not looking up from his task. "Actually, my ex-girlfriend was into all that interior design stuff, she had an eye—" he cut himself off, but then raised his head and stared off into the distance. His eyes narrowed. "Huh," he said to himself. "I've never called you that before—an ex-girlfriend, I mean. It just seems wrong. You're just so much more than that, you know?" He turned to face me. "We were more than that, right? Or was that just me?"

My breath hitched. The walls closed in. I couldn't be here with him. Not when he said stuff like that. Not when he didn't know how badly it affected me. "I think I should leave," I told him. I panicked. I didn't know what else to say.

"No," he said quickly, stepping in front of me and blocking my way. "No, please. Stay. I'm sorry. I won't say stupid shit anymore, please. Just... just stay. We don't even have to talk about us. We can talk about anything, or nothing. We don't even have to talk at all." He looked at his hand and shook it again, then blew out a heavy breath.

I've seen a lot of sides to Logan before, but I've never seen this. I've never seen this type of vulnerability in him. This need for approval or just...*need*.

"Please," he said again, his voice breaking.

And I knew it then—how much trouble I was in. Because Logan—he *still* had that power over me. "Okay," I told him. "I just need some air."

His smile was instant. "I've got the perfect place." He grabbed his keys and took my hand, leading me out the door and up a different staircase.

LOGAN

I TOOK HER out to the rooftop of the building. When I'd first moved in, the landlady told me this wasn't the type of building that allowed drug use and loud parties. I laughed and told her that wasn't me at all. I told her about how much I planned on doing nothing but studying to try to catch up on as much as possible. She'd smiled then and made me follow her up here. She'd told me that it was the only place in the building that had enough quiet so that my ever-progressive brain would work properly. Only she and I had a key, and no one else knew it existed. I bought some outdoor furniture the next day, and this place became my safe haven.

I tell all this to Amanda. She just smiles warmly at me and says, "It's real nice, Logan." Like I'm a fucking kid she needs to talk down to. I knew what she was doing. I saw it in her eyes when I practically begged her to stay. I knew she pitied me, and it was probably the only reason why she was here with me. But I didn't care. I'd take anything she gave me. I walked us over to the outdoor sofa set I bought and motioned for her to sit down.

"So," I started.

"So," she replied.

"How's Ethan?"

Her shoulders visibly relaxed. Maybe she'd be happy to talk, as long as it wasn't about us. "He's good. He and Lexie have been dating for a few months now."

I sat back and tried to feign comfort. Inside, I was a wreck. I tried to hide my shaking hands in my pockets as much as possible, but I couldn't do it from a seated position. "That's good, right?" I asked. "I mean—are you okay with that?"

She shrugged. "Yeah, I'm happy for them." She brought her legs up and under her. "And Tristan lives with us now, so it's kind of like old times —like high school."

"So Tristan—he's in my old room?"

"Um." She leaned back so her head rested on the top of the sofa and she was looking up at the sky. "No. Actually, I'm in your old room."

I tried not to picture her in our bed, probably with other guys. I didn't know if she was dating anyone or if she had in the past. Fuck, surely she would've had sex with—

"So, Logan Matthews—gallivanting aimlessly around the world for an entire year. That must have been fun—I bet you drove the ladies wild." Her tone was part-mocking, part-teasing and part-anger, and I felt every single one.

"No gallivanting. Not unless you count sleeping on dirt in third-world countries and watching sick kids get sicker gallivanting. And no. No girls."

Her head whipped to face me, her eyes narrowed. "No girls?" she asked incredulously. "Why do I not believe you?"

I shrugged. "What about you?" I asked.

It was her turn to shrug. "Don't really think it's important. Do you?" She slowly turned to face me and then let out a breath, picking at the sleeve of her sweater. "Tyson moved in after you left."

I tried for the same reaction she gave me but failed. "Huh."

"Yeah," she said, dreaminess in her voice. Fucking Tyson. "He asked if

I ever wondered what would've happened between us if I'd never met you."

My chest tightened. I wondered the same thing all the time. "What did you tell him?"

"I don't know. Different time. Different place. I guess anything could have happened."

I didn't know what she meant, but I didn't press further.

It was quiet for the longest time, neither of us knowing what to say or how to move on from the awkward conversation.

She shifted until her long legs stretched out in front of her, with her feet resting on the table. My eyes trailed from her feet, up her legs, over the rest of her body.

"How are you so neat?" she asked out of nowhere. "Your room, and now your apartment, it's so clean. Why?"

I had to laugh. "I'm gone for a year, and that's the question you ask?"

She squared her shoulders. "Fine then—why did you leave me?"

I opened my mouth to speak, but she stopped me. "Actually. You know what? I don't want to know."

She started to stand, but I pulled her back down and turned my body to face her. She kept looking straight ahead, refusing to meet my eyes. "When I was adopted, I thought that if I wasn't good enough, my dad would send me back, so I kept my room clean and hoped it was enough, you know? That he might keep me if I was a good kid. That was my way of showing him I was. I guess it kind of stuck."

I felt her warm hand cover mine. "I'm sorry," she said, turning to face me. She looked down where our bodies joined. "I didn't know that it had to do with that."

I flipped my hand over. She brushed her palm softly across mine and then started tracing my fingers with hers. I watched as she focused on what she was doing. "Amanda?" I croaked out. "You don't ever have to apologize, for anything, ever."

"Why did you come back?" she whispered. Her eyes lifted, and I could see it—her pain. "I thought I was getting over it, over you...why did you have to come back and ruin everything?"

She stood up quickly and started to walk away. I followed, pulling on her arm to stop her. "Baby." The word slipped out, like verbal vomit.

"Baby?" she rushed out. "Baby," she repeated, louder this time. Then a rage switched on inside her. She'd gone from upset to pissed, in two-seconds flat. "You don't get to call me baby."

I let go of her arm. "I know, I'm sorry."

"Are you, though?" she hissed. Her words were harsh, punishing. "Because you're acting as if nothing's changed. But it has. Everything's changed."

I reached for her again, but she'd stepped back, tripping over herself. Her hands came up, as if protecting herself from me. She had no reason to be afraid. "Stop," she breathed out. "Just stop."

She turned and headed for the door again. Blood rushed to my ears. I blinked, trying to focus. I couldn't let her go. I couldn't lose her. Not again. "Wait!"

Her body stiffened.

"Wait. Please," I said. I was begging, and I didn't give a shit.

She turned quickly, her eyes glazed with tears. "Wait?" she spat out. "Fuck you, Logan. I did wait. I waited for you at the fucking hospital. I waited for you when I got home, and you weren't fucking there. I waited a week before showing up at your house and begging—fucking *begging*—for you to take me back." She pushed against my chest. I fell back a step. "And then I waited for you to come back to me. But you never did, Logan. You never came back." She wiped her tears and sniffed once, straightening her body. Then she looked me square in the eyes and through gritted teeth said, "You just fucking left me."

Her words left me shattered.

10

AMANDA

MY BODY SHOOK from the anger that overcame me. He had no right.

I watched the emotion on his face. He looked dejected, broken. *Good.* Maybe he understood just a small amount of how he'd made me feel.

His shoulders lifted with each breath, as if struggling to find the air. It felt like an eternity. "Baby," he said again.

And something in me snapped. I lost control. I didn't mean to do what I did next.

My palm stung the instant it made contact with his face. I don't know what was louder, the sound of the slap or my gasp that followed.

"Shit." I stepped forward. "Logan, I'm so sorry." My hand reached up to cup his face, but his sturdy grip on my forearm stopped me. He pushed my arm away forcefully. I wanted to cry. I'd never want to hurt him, especially not like that.

"It's fine, Amanda," he croaked.

I'd broken him.

I shut my eyes tight and let the tears fall. "Logan." My voice was strained.

He licked his lip and then wiped it with the back of his hand. That's when I saw it—blood. It didn't affect me the way it used to. We'd studied something similar in my psych class, and I'd learned to control it. I'd taught myself how to mentally separate the site of blood from Ethan's accident.

I cursed under my breath and stepped forward, but he took a step back, afraid of me. I let out a sob. "Logan," I said again. I didn't know what else to say.

He looked away from me. "I think maybe you should leave. I'll walk you to your car."

I just nodded and followed behind him. We walked to my car in dead silence. He opened the door for me when I unlocked it. He even made sure I was seated properly before he closed it. But he didn't say a word. I wound down my window and opened my mouth to speak.

"It's fine," he said, interrupting me. He placed his hands in his pockets and took a step back. "Take care, okay?"

I HELD IT together long enough to nod and pull away from the curb. It wasn't until I got home and under my sheets that I let it out. Tristan came in after a few minutes and wordlessly joined me. He wrapped his arms around me and assured me that whatever was happening—it was going to be okay.

I looked into his green eyes, so similar to Logan's. "I don't think it will be this time."

"I'm sorry," he said.

So was I.

LOGAN

FIVE FLIGHTS OF stairs later, I was back in my apartment. I triple-checked the four deadbolts on the door before finally throwing myself onto the bed. "Fuck." I rubbed my tender cheek and tried to ignore the metallic taste of blood on my lip. Reaching into the small box next to my bed, I felt around until my fingers skimmed the worn leather of the book. I pulled it out and fanned the pages, looking for the first blank one. The picture fell out. It was beyond faded, but it didn't matter. It could've been completely erased, and the image would still be etched in my memory. I had the same one on my desk back home. *Home.* There was no such place for me. Not unless you counted Amanda as *home.*

I flipped to the beginning and read the first sentence I ever wrote.

Five weeks post-Amanda.
There are no dates here. Only time passing with each moment.
Dear Diary—says the twelve-year-old girl in me.

Manny, one of the guys in the field with me, told me I was depressed. I don't think I am, but whatever. He said 'Loma, go write down your shitty feelings in a journal and you'll feel better.' Loma—that's me. Apparently it stands for LO-gan MA-tthews. It's a thing here. I asked him what his name stood for; he looked at me like I was crazy. "It doesn't stand for anything, asshole. My name's Manny."

So that's Manny.

I don't know if he was kidding or not, but here I am, writing my shitty feelings in a journal.

I miss her.

That's the only feeling I have.

I miss the absolute shit out of her.

If I sit around and question the reason I'm here, I get even more depressed. Fuck. Manny was right.

Location: Africa

Am I doing this wrong? Should I be writing where I am at the beginning? Fuck it.

Nightmare count: 16

On the upside, every day I'm here, I feel like I'm doing something good for the world. If I were to die today, people would say, "Hey, that Loma asshole was saving the world one cholera vaccine at a time. Also, he missed the shit out of his girl."

Amanda.

Fuck.

Whose stupid idea was it to write a journal? This shit doesn't help. Stupid Manny.

Seven weeks post-Amanda.

Today, this kid called me Sir. And then he kicked me in the shin. The kid next to him laughed. Their laughs were so contagious, I found myself smiling. It kind of hurt. I imagine it's what old leather feels like when it has to form to a different shape.

A new guy started today. Jason Malone. We call him Jamal. Doesn't suit him at all but now it's stuck, and he has to deal with it.

We're still going strong with the vaccines.

I'm still missing the shit out of her.

Last night I dreamt about her. It felt so real that when I woke up, I actually walked around our camp looking for her. I even whispered her name a few times, thinking she might really be here.

Maybe I've gone crazy.

Legit, certifiable-type crazy.

Jamal asked if I had a girl back home.

I told him I didn't want to talk about it.

He said, "Pic or I call bullshit."

It made me think of the picture back home on my desk. I closed my eyes and tried to imagine it. There was no problem seeing it in my mind.

Then Jamal called me out, asked me if I was about to cry.

Fucking Jamal.

Nightmare count: 20

Ten weeks post-Amanda.

I'm crying.

A woman just brought her baby in. She was crying hysterically. I took one quick look at her child and knew whatever it was she needed us to do, it was too damn late.

I turned away and puked.

Manny told me to go back to our tent.

So that's where I am.

In the tent, crying my ass off, and questioning how the fuck I'm going to be a doctor one day.

Diary, if I ever complain about my life, tell me to buck the fuck up and get over it. Shit could be a hell of a lot worse.

Ten and a half weeks post-Amanda.

A little girl came in today. She was holding her brother's hand. They could've been twins. She told me her name Amuhda. Definitely the highlight of my day.

Nightmare count: 21

Fourteen weeks post-Amanda.

I laughed today. You'd think I'd be happy about it, but I feel like shit. I wonder how she's doing. I wonder if she ever laughs. I fucking hope so. Otherwise, all of this would have been for nothing.

We were moved from the field to more admin-type roles for the time being. They do that. Change things up. I'm not complaining. Even though it's still kind of a campsite, this one has actual roofs, walls, and showers.

Last night, Jamal's girlfriend called him. He wasn't around to answer, so Manny did it for him. Manny—being Manny—told his girlfriend that he'd been sick the last three days with the worst case of diarrhea he'd ever seen. Which is pretty bad, considering one of our main goals here is to treat the disease. Apparently, it was so bad he had to wear adult diapers and was in quarantine. He even referred to him as Jamal. I don't know what his girlfriend was thinking.

So, of course, Jamal gets up in my shit to help him find a way to pay him back.

We waited until he was in the shower—one of those open shower stalls, like they have at public pools. Anyway, Manny faced the back of the stall where the shower head was, washing his face, shaking his ass and singing "Wrecking Ball" by Miley Cyrus. I had Jamal's cell phone in hand, filming. Jamal was standing behind him with a full bottle of shampoo…We waited for him to start washing his hair, then when he was under the spray washing it out, Jamal squirted more shampoo in there. After a couple of minutes, Manny started getting pissed because he couldn't fucking get rid of the suds. In fact, it was getting worse. His eyes were closed the entire time while Jamal and I tried to contain our laughter. Fuck, we're assholes. Manny was cussing and spinning around in circles, blind as shit because the excessive shampoo was getting in his eyes. After a good five minutes of me filming and Manny losing his shit, Jamal finally spoke up, only he yelled, scaring the shit out of the still-blind Manny. Jamal went right up to Manny's ear, who was of course, clueless, and at the top of his lungs yelled, "I CAME IN LIKE A WRECKING BAAAALLLLLL!!!"

So fucking funny.

Manny's eyes snapped open, and he started chasing Jamal around the campsite, barefoot, bare-ass naked. Dick swinging from side to side. He didn't even hear me laughing or see me filming it all. Once they were out of filming view, I uploaded the video to YouTube and Jamal's Facebook and tagged Manny in it.

Manny had no idea until his mom called him.

Good fucking times.

I wish I could call Amanda and tell her the story. She would've loved it. I could imagine her face as I told her. That slow smile build-up. The low laugh that turns to something so much bigger. I can imagine her head thrown back, her hand on her stomach. She used to do that when I made her laugh too much. Then, when it was over, she'd sigh, almost like she was thankful for that moment.

Fuck, I miss her. So damn bad.

September 24th.

Today has a date. Today deserves a date.

Amanda turns twenty-one today.

I'd planned to take her and Ethan to Vegas. I wonder what they're doing.

She's probably moved on. Has a boyfriend or whatever. He probably thinks he loves her more than anyone's ever loved her. He's fucking wrong. No one could love her as much as I do.

I was so out of it today, Manny told me to take the day off.

Valid.

Now I'm sitting alone on this stupid bed feeling sorry for myself, as if I don't deserve to feel like this.

I picked up my phone a thousand times to call her. I have her number saved. I changed my cell at the airport before I got here. I thought that maybe she'd call and ask me to come back, and I wouldn't be able to say no.

I gave in and actually called her. She answered. I heard her voice. She just kept saying hello. I didn't speak. I hoped maybe she'd know it was me without me having to say anything. Maybe she'd know I was calling to wish her a happy birthday. After a few seconds, I heard a guy's voice. She told him to wait and said hello a few more times. I still didn't say shit. I swear to God she whispered my name.

I hung up and called Jake.

He asked if I was okay. I told him I wasn't. He knew it was her birthday. He said that Micky was Facebook friends with her and that it alerted her, but they weren't speaking yet. Amanda's wishes. From what he knew, she was okay. That was as much as he could tell me. I asked him to get Micky to email me that picture of her —the one from my desk. I hung up, and a minute later I got the email.

I stared at it for five hours.

Then I figured I should do something else to stop myself from going crazy. I picked up one of Jamal's self-help books.

That's where I found this: Transit umbra, lux permanet.

How fitting.

Diary, no one else will understand this, so I'm gonna let you in on a little secret. When I started planning the Vegas trip, a part of me hoped that she'd think I wanted to take her there to get married. I would have. Married her, I mean. People might not have understood. People might have hated the choice we made or be upset we didn't do it properly. But she was my person. Nothing else mattered. Not back then. Now everything matters.

Because I was the match that started the inferno.

Seventeen weeks post-Amanda.

Nightmare count: too fucking many.

Manny seems to think I'm getting better. I don't know. Maybe I am. Or maybe I've just gotten better at faking it.

Eighteen weeks post-Amanda.

The worst day of my life was my twenty-first birthday.

The second worst day is today.

Today, a woman came in carrying a little girl in her arms. There was blood all over them. Especially in between their legs. A boy walked in behind them. They were all beaten and bruised, barely recognizable. But I knew who the girl was right away. Amuhda. She and her mom had been beaten and raped. Raped. What the fuck is wrong with this world?

The little boy, barely able to stand upright, held Amuhda's hand while we tried to stop the bleeding. The entire time we worked on her, he stood by her head, whispering things in her ear.

I wanted to puke. I wanted to cry. I wanted to scream. I wanted to kill someone. I wanted to go back home and fall asleep with Amanda in my arms and tell her how much I love her. I wanted to hear her laugh, snort, cry, yell, anything. I just wanted her.

Last night I dreamt of her. No shitty nightmares. Just her. She told me she loved me. It felt so real, I think my heart actually broke when I realized it wasn't. All damn day I'd heard her voice in my head. **I love you so much, Logan.** *That's what she kept saying—in my head—over and over again.*

Maybe it was my punishment. Like karma. Here—have this moment with the girl you love and the words you've always wanted to hear—and then watch as a mother and her kids almost die on a table battling monsters.

Fucking monsters.

I can't sleep.

The ache in my chest prevents it.

Twenty weeks post-Amanda.

I still can't sleep. Lie. I can sleep. I just don't want to. Every time I close my eyes, there are monsters. Only this time, they're not just mine; they're Amuhda's, too.

I know I look like shit. Manny's starting to worry. He says he's calling my dad. I told him to fuck off, then apologized, blaming it all on the lack of sleep.

Two days ago, I realized I hadn't showered for five days. I still had blood under my fingernails. Good times.

Diary, you're a fucking asshole; you don't do shit to help me. No one does shit to help me. What's wrong with me?

My real name is Logan Declan Strauss. Did you know that, Diary? Did you?

Twenty-one weeks post-Amanda.

The last three nights I've had the nightmares. I wake up, screaming in a pool of sweat. Last night I pissed the bed. Jamal's worried, threatens to tell Manny. I'm not dealing with that shit. It was just a nightmare.

I got locked in a cupboard for my sixth birthday. I think it was for three days. I remember my parents high-fiving each other; apparently it was a new record. I stopped crying after the first day. After I worked out that me crying made it worse. Funny, how six-year-olds work that shit out.

I shared a birthday with this kid in my class. I can't for the fucking life of me remember his name. But I remember him coming to school with a new Gameboy and flashy clothes. I came to school with an eye patch and a bruised back. My mom told the teachers I was going through a pirate phase. My mom was a smartass.

Still twenty-one weeks post-Amanda.

Location: I don't know.

Nightmares: Even when I'm not sleeping.

Dear Diary,

Manny called my dad and told him I needed help. We played two truths for fifteen for three hours. I miss him. Almost as much as Amanda. I told him that. He said he knew. He missed me, too. I needed to hear it. Dad told me to come home. What the hell good would I be there? But then again, what the hell good am I here? Manny talked to him afterwards and offered a solution, a deal of sorts.

Xanax.

Six weeks.

Then I'd come home.

Or—I could go home now.

I chose Xanax.

Whatever.

Nothing was waiting for me there.

Twenty-two weeks post-Amanda.

Xanax.

Treatment for anxiety.

I admit, I needed it.

Dad calls almost every day. He says he can already hear the change in me. It's only been a week, but it doesn't surprise me; he knows me better than I fake it.

The nightmares are still there, but I don't panic when I have them. It's almost like they're dulled down. I've only dreamt about Amuhda once. She's healing well, just FYI.

I've been on very light duties here, but Manny thinks I should maybe go into town and start pushing paper, go back to the admin side, just until I get my shit together. There's still a medic site there, but it's closer to facilities so it makes it easier. He says he won't strip me completely of the medical side; I'm here to learn, after all.

Manny—he's an asshole, but he cares. He cares more than he probably should.

Twenty-four weeks post-Amanda.

The Xanax helps. A lot.

I moved to the admin camp.

The dreams are less frequent, but there are other side effects I'm hoping will pass. I've been told Amuhda is recovering well, so at least there's that. Things are a lot less hectic here. I feel like I'm not doing enough, but I know that it's probably all I'm capable of at the moment.

A new girl started today. She has an accent, from what I've heard of her speak. She hasn't introduced herself yet, but I've caught her looking over at me a few times. She seems nice enough.

Twenty-five weeks post-Amanda.

I helped deliver a miracle today.

I swear to God, this place ... I don't know. There are so many emotions that come with being here. So much sadness and heartache, and then this happens. I get to hold a brand new life. Rebekah, the girl I wrote about earlier, she was there, too. I think our smiles matched each other's. What an experience.

She came into my room afterwards, her smile still huge. We talked about it for a bit. She's from France. She sat on the bed next to me. I freaked out, jumped up, and moved as far away from her as possible. Is that weird? I think it's weird. I just didn't want her to get the wrong idea. Plus, I kind of just wanted that time afterwards to think about Amanda. I wanted to call her. I wanted to tell her all about it. I wanted to encourage her to follow that path, but then I thought about it some more...And really? Who the fuck was I to encourage her to do anything?

Nightmare count: too many.

Flashback count: too many.

Dreams about Amanda: not enough.

I look at her picture too long, too often.

I wonder if she's forgotten about me completely.

Twenty-eight weeks post-Amanda.

I got a paid position here. I applied for anything and everything, and I got one. I wasn't ready to leave. Or maybe it was that I wasn't ready to go home. They're two completely different things.

I'm a coward. But I'm also realistic. I just wasn't ready. Dad was not happy.

A psychologist came to camp today, hired by Doctors Without Borders, to make sure we're all mentally stable. I was with him for two hours. I'd gotten used to the whole talking and listening and back and forth that comes with those meetings from when I was a kid. I'm not a kid anymore, but it's all the same.

He said I had PTSD.

I couldn't argue with him.

I knew it was something similar.

I begged Dad to let me go home after what happened the night of my birthday. I didn't want to stay in the hospital. Not with her there and me not being able to do anything about her state. I was bad, but nothing that bed rest and decent painkillers couldn't fix. The beating I could take—it was what happened to Amanda that I couldn't deal with.

That first night I came home, I had the first of many nightmares. This one wasn't really a nightmare though; it was just a replay of what had happened that night. The vision was so raw, so real, it hurt just as much as it did the first time.

Then something happened. I'm not entirely sure what, but it was like I reverted back to the seven-year-old me. I think it was my way of dealing with it. I didn't want anyone asking questions, and I didn't want to offer anything.

Truth is, I know it was my fault. First, the shit that happened that summer with her. And then that. How could it not be my fault? How can anyone ever say that if she hadn't have met me, if she wasn't part of my life, that that shit still would have happened? No fucking chance.

I switched my phone off and refused to answer the door. I know Jake was there a few times, and even Cameron and Lucy, but they knocked a couple times and left. That was it.

Dad came in and told me that she'd been released a few days later, and everything was fine. Of course, I didn't say anything. I laugh about it now, because it seems so pathetic, but I hid out in the darkness of my closet. I had no idea why until I told the psychologist today. He thought it was my way of punishing myself, like they used to when I was a kid.

It makes sense.

After the fifth day, Dad told me about how he went to 'find himself' after Tina, his high school sweetheart, died. He said he gave himself six months to sort his shit out, and then he'd come home. He said it helped him. It even motivated him to make the most of his life with or without her. I wanted that. I wanted that reassurance that I'd still be able to live a normal life without her. He offered me the same thing. Six months. No more.

I agreed.

He made the plans.

All without me saying a word.

Then Amanda showed up.

Diary, I'm going to skip the part where my heart breaks, because there are no words.

I almost stayed. I almost took the few steps it would have taken to have her in my arms and fake that everything was okay.

Then I remembered what I'd caused. I remembered the first thought I had when I decided to leave her there in that hospital. What if I leave and her life is better? Like my asshole parents left me, and my dad came along. He gave me this life, gave me a home, and somehow, made me feel worthy of it.

What if someone else offered her that? Some other guy she meets a week from now, a month from now, a year from now? What if he could give her the world, and all I could give her was a broken heart and a broken arm? Then what?

I told her I loved her. She needed to know.

And then I left.

Thirty-two weeks post-Amanda.

I've been MIA, and for that, I'm sorry, Diary. Truth is, I've been doing better. The meds help.

I wrote to her. It took all the courage in me to actually send it. I wonder if she burned it. I probably would have.

Thirty-five weeks post-Amanda.

Rebekah, that girl from France that I wrote about before, she tried to kiss me. I pulled back so fast I think I scared her. She said she didn't know I was with someone. I told her I wasn't. Not really. But then again, really. Does that make sense?

She said even if they didn't know it, or I didn't know it, my heart belonged to her.

"Tell me about her," she said.

So I did.

Not all of it. Just the good stuff. It felt nice to talk about her. To remember her the way I wanted.

When Rebekah left, my thoughts were still on Amanda. I always thought about her.

Thirty-eight weeks post-Amanda.

Jamal and Manny organized for me to come back to medic camp, just for a few days. I was excited to see them again. But what was even more exciting is why they asked me to come back.

A fully-recovered Amuhda waited for me.

Call me a pussy, but she was a sight for sore eyes. I admit, I cried.

"Hello, Mr. Loma," she'd said, with the quietest, softest voice I'd ever heard.

I smiled huge. First time I'd smiled like that since leaving Amanda. She had to have a translator, but we talked for a bit. She said I was handsome and that I was her prince. I was no one's prince, but I'd let her call me whatever she wanted. Then she asked me if I would marry her. Poor girl. I told her I couldn't. I said my heart belonged to another girl. Her name was Amanda. She found that hysterical. Amanda and Amuhda. I loved her laugh. She held her stomach just like Amanda does.

Diary, I know you're sick of hearing this. But I miss her.

Nightmares: getting better.

Dreams about Amanda: Too many. And they're all so, so good, that it hurts so, so bad.

Forty-three weeks post-Amanda.

Dear Diary,

It took forty-three weeks, but guess what? I think I'm healing. Being here has opened my eyes to so many things, and even though I didn't travel so much, I saw the world. I saw what I needed to, and that was enough. I've learned to control my anxiety when necessary, but honestly, it's gotten a lot better—to the point where I can go a day or so without flashbacks. The heart palpitations are few and far between, the shakes...they're there, but it's better than screaming and pissing my bed at night.

When I was kid, I used to always find it odd when bullies made fun of other kids and asked them to go cry to their mommy. I remember wondering if they knew that some kids' moms were the cause of their cries, not the other way around.

Huh. I wonder who I cried out for.

Forty-five weeks post-Amanda.

I have nothing to write. Just that I'm here, and I'm okay.

Fifty Weeks post-Amanda.

It's time.

I'm ready.

Dad and I have been talking about what I'm going to do when I get home. He'd organized that I defer, so UNC still awaits. I don't know if Amanda is still there. I still haven't spoken to anyone yet. Apart from that one phone call to Jake, no one else knows anything. That's the way I wanted it. Dad said housing was full on campus dorm-wise, and he'd prefer that I live off-campus anyway, just in case...

Just in case.

I don't know what he meant, but I sure as shit would prefer it, too.

Because I was getting back a month or so before summer break started, we'd have enough time to get things sorted: a place to stay, a car, all that shit. I made sure he knew that he wasn't to spend a single cent on me. Not until I got there. Sixteen-year-old Loma—fuck—I'm calling myself Loma now! Anyway, sixteen-year-old me loved that Mercedes. Twenty-one-year-old me? Not so much. I'd be happy with something that gets me from A to B.

To be honest, a part of me hoped that Dad would transfer me to a different college, somewhere farther away. But I knew he wouldn't. He wanted me to face things head-on, deal with the consequences of my actions, all that shit.

I'm prepared. I think. Actually, I have no fucking clue. All I know is that I'm ready to face it. I'm ready to take whatever the world has to give.

"You're staying in the main house when you get home," Dad said. It was my punishment for being gone the extra six months. Whatever. The pool house just reminded me of Amanda, anyway.

First date. Final goodbye.

Sill missing her, Diary.

Next entry. I'll be home.

Home.

It's been three days.

I'm still hiding out.

Bought a car, though, so that's something. It's a shitty old truck. It'll do. Anything will do. Dad said he wants to sell the house, find something smaller. The largeness of it makes him lonely. Truth—it's kind of upsetting. I grew up in this house, learned to ride my bike in the driveway. This house holds a lot of good moments for me.

When I told him, he just smiled, said maybe it was worth keeping.

He'd also done some upgrading to the house, high cement fencing and a security gate. He even got security lights and cameras in certain spots. He told me that there had been a string of burglaries in the area. I knew it wasn't true, but I didn't call him out on it. Honestly, having that extra security helped me to actually sleep easier at night.

I'm better, but I'm not, not really. If I were to use psychology terms, I'd tell you I was quiet, withdrawn, introverted. Not my usual asshole-self. Dad said he missed his asshole. That made me laugh.

I did something stupid today. I drove my car two hours away. Guess where? Not hard. I don't know why I did it. I just wanted to see her, maybe just to assure myself that she was okay. Ethan's jeep was in the driveway, along with a green hatchback. It could be hers.

Three hours I sat in front of the house like a creeper, then the front door burst open. Ethan first, then Alexis, her best friend. And then Tristan. The outside security light turned on, she walked out, locked the door, and checked it at least five times. My hands shook. I sat on them, moved further down my seat and pulled my cap down past eyebrows. Fucking creeper.

Then I heard it. Her laugh. 'Oh my God,' she squealed, holding her stomach.

I drove away.

It was too much.

I shouldn't have been there.

What the hell was I thinking?

At least she was happy.

That's something, right?

A few hours later, I had the words that seemed so fitting tattooed on my arm. One day, I swear, I'll look at it, and maybe it won't hurt so much.

Three weeks of being home.

I saw her.

I don't think I fully understood how broken I was until my eyes caught hers and she smiled up at me.

Suddenly, it felt like all of the broken pieces of me locked into place, one by one. I felt it physically as much as mentally.

We talked. I can't for the life of me even remember what was said. It's like my heart and my mind were constantly battling, and I didn't know which one to voice. At one point, my heart won out, and I let a familiar comfort settle over my actions, or it could have been the panic that kicked in.

Baby, I called her.

And something in her snapped.

I deserved the slap.

Just like I'll deserve any and all future punishment I get from her.

AMANDA

I WOKE UP the next morning feeling worse than I did the night before. It had never been my intention to hurt Logan, not even emotionally. What I did was horrible. The guilt of it consumed me.

What hurt the most was his reaction. It was as if he saw me for the first time—who I really was. I thought he'd known me better than that, but I guess a year can change a person's perspectives.

It sure as hell changed mine.

At first, of course I hated him. I hated that he could just leave, without a single warning, not even a goodbye. But slowly, with every day that passed and every visit with his dad, things started getting easier. With each piece of the puzzle that was his life, his decisions and actions began to make sense—to me, anyway. It wasn't as if I forgave, and I definitely wouldn't be able to forget what he did, but I'd slowly begun to accept it.

Each conversation I had with his dad was like peeling away a layer. Logan—he built these high walls around him. He put on a persona so that no one got close enough to care for him. With me, those walls came down. I couldn't tell you why he let me in, or what it was about me, or about us, that led him to believe that it was okay for us to fall in love the way we did. The kind of insanely deep, destructive love.

Destructive.

That's exactly what we were.

LOGAN

I COULDN'T SLEEP. I spent the entire night staring at the ceiling of my living room. Whatever I'd thought she might have felt when I left, it was worse than I thought. I knew she'd be upset, sad, hurt—but she was devastated beyond words, which is probably why—instead of talking—she chose to slap me.

I couldn't blame her. I deserved it.

I fucked up. The worst part is that instead of talking to her about it, I practically shoved her out the door and into her car because I was too much of a pussy to deal with things. I should have tried to calm her down, to calm myself down, just enough so that we could actually use words to get through the mess we'd created. But I just bailed, because obviously, that's how I deal with shit.

I cursed under my breath and removed the covers off my pathetic bed. You'd think that sleeping on the floor or tiny fold-out beds would make me want the comfort of a luxurious mattress. It didn't.

I NEEDED TO get out of my head and out of my apartment. No one knew I was back yet, so there was only one place I could go—the bookstore. It was like history repeating itself. Stupid, regretful, lonely boy finds solace in a random bookstore while he pines for the girl of his dreams he fucked up with.

Chantal—the owner of the store—paused mid coffee-pour when she saw me. I had to rush over and stop her from spilling it everywhere. Once she placed the coffee back and handed the cup to her customer, she wrapped her arms around me. "You stupid boy," she whispered in my ear. She pulled back and playfully slapped my chest. "Where the hell have you been? I'm so mad at you."

I laughed and rolled my eyes. "Get in line."

I spent the next hour answering her million questions. I told her about working with Doctors Without Borders for the past year. I didn't offer anything about Amanda, and she didn't bring it up. I respected that a lot.

She stood up when a customer walked to the register. "I know you just got back, but can I ask a favor?"

"Of course. Anything."

"I have a huge delivery at four, can you help out?"

I agreed. It wasn't like I had shit to do anyway.

AT FOUR ON the dot I was back. "It's not here yet," she said, motioning for me to take a seat. Since the first day I'd come into the store, creepily looking for Amanda, I'd always sat in the same spot. "I'm sure it's on its way."

A few minutes later I heard her voice.

Amanda.

A part of me panicked. A part of me was thankful for second chances. Or, in my case, third, fourth, fifth, and sixth chances. "Take a seat at your table. I'll bring it out to you," Chantal told her. I braced myself for when she turned around and saw me sitting here. My hands gripped the sides of the chair. I was half-sitting, half-standing, like my body was ready for a battle.

She froze the second her eyes made contact with me. "Whoa," she said. Then she took a step forward, as if unsure. I found myself sitting back down, relaxing slightly. She bit her lip, her eyes cast downwards, and stopped a few feet away. "What are you doing here?" she asked.

I exhaled loudly. "I can go—"

"No!" she exclaimed, at the same time Chantal came back.

She placed two coffees and a book on the table, then turned to me and said, "You can't go. Besides, that's your chair. It's got your name on it."

I looked at her confused. "What?"

Amanda glared at Chantal, who just laughed. "On the arm. You didn't write it?" She gave Amanda a knowing smirk. "Well. Ain't that something..."

I heard Amanda mumble something under her breath but was too busy looking at my name carved on the wooden arm of the chair. My fingers traced the letters.

"Do you want me to leave?" her voice was so soft I almost didn't hear it.

My head whipped up to face her. "No. Do you want to leave?"

"No." Then she just stood there, her eyes focused on my face. Probably the cut on my lip, and the slight redness on my cheek.

Chantal came back and made an annoyed huffing sound. We both turned to her. "What are you guys doing? You're not twelve." She threw her hands up in the air. "Talk." She placed her hands on Amanda's shoulders and maneuvered her to the seat opposite me. Amanda's gaze never left mine. Chantal pointed at the book and spoke to Amanda. "I got it signed for you."

Amanda finally looked away and up at Chantal. "No, you didn't!" she said, with excitement in her voice.

"Yes," Chantal replied. "Look."

Amanda smiled as she opened the book. Fuck, I miss that smile. "Never regret," she breathed out and then looked up at Chantal in awe. Chantal smiled back. "Never regret," she repeated.

She kept her eyes on the book for a while, her smile getting wider with each second.

"You come here a lot?" I asked her, but then rolled my eyes at myself. *Lame.*

"Why, Logan," she smirked and put the book in her bag. "You've lost your game. That was a horrible pick-up line."

I couldn't help but laugh. So did she. And somehow, in that one moment, the world tilted on its axis and the atmosphere became something closer to normal.

"I do, actually." She fidgeted with a bunch of bracelets on her wrists and then placed them under the table. "Whenever I get a chance, between classes and whatnot."

I nodded, thankful she was speaking to me.

"So," she started, looking around the store. "I assume you're going back to UNC?"

"Yeah," I told her. "Next semester I start back, so I'll be a year behind."

She smiled softly. "How come you moved out here now then? Why not after summer break?"

I felt the tension leave my muscles. She was talking to me; we were talking to each other. Things would be okay. "I wanted to get in early and find a place. I know it becomes harder the closer we get to the school year."

She was about to speak, but Chantal cut her off by placing a bowl on the table: red gummy bears and ice cream.

Amanda's eyes went wide and then a smile formed on her lips. "How did she know?" she asked me, bringing the bowl closer to her.

I shrugged. "No clue."

"Liar."

I laughed.

"What happened to your face?" Chantal asked. I forgot she was standing there.

Amanda choked.

"Nothing," I said.

Amanda coughed some more.

Chantal eyed me and then Amanda. "Nothing?" She raised her eyebrows.

Amanda calmed herself down. "I slapped him," she answered for me.

Chantal placed her hands on her hips. "Well, did you deserve it?" she asked me.

"Yes," I answered, the same time as Amanda said, "No."

Chantal shook her head and walked away.

Amanda put the bowl to the side and leaned forward with her elbows on the table. "You didn't deserve that, Logan. I'm so sorry. I don't know what came over me. I should have never laid a hand on you."

"It's fine. It really—"

"It's not fine. It's never fine." She reached out and pulled on my shirt until my position mimicked hers, our faces so close I felt her exhale of breath against my skin. Then I felt her hand on my cheek. My eyes drifted shut. Her thumb skimmed my lip. "Does it hurt?"

I covered her hand with mine and brought my face closer to hers. I kept my eyes closed. I didn't want to see her pull away. Our noses rubbed against each other.

My heart pounded.

My hand trembled.

"You're shaking," she whispered.

Shit. "Mm," was all I could say.

She placed my hand between both of hers and pulled away. I wanted to tell her to stay. I wanted her to be closer. "Are you okay?" she asked.

"Mm," I said again.

I felt her bring my hand up and press her mouth on my palm. She kissed it once, twice—by the third kiss it'd stopped shaking.

And I knew it then.

I knew she had the power to make everything better. That's why I needed her, but it was more than that. It was so much more than that.

I opened my eyes slowly, and that's when I saw it.

The mark on her wrist.

She must've noticed because she started to pull away. I gripped it and moved her bracelets so I could see it clearly.

And then I gasped. Like a fucking girl.

"What is this?" My eyes left her wrist and moved to her face.

She looked sick, like she was going to puke. She pulled her arm out of my grasp and stood up. "I gotta go."

She rushed for the front door.

I wanted to yell out. I wanted to stop her.

But I didn't do shit.

I just let her walk away.

What the fuck had happened while I was gone?

12

LOGAN

ANOTHER SLEEPLESS NIGHT. I couldn't get her out of my head. Honestly, she was always in my head. She'd only been in my life again for two days. Two fucking days, and this was the effect she was having on me. I had to keep reminding myself that she wasn't mine and that it was my choice.

There was a knock on my door. No one knew I was back. No one knew where I lived. Only Amanda. I stood up and rushed to the door so fast my head spun. Way too excitedly, I opened it, but it wasn't Amanda.

She was pissed.

I grimaced.

"You fucking asshole." She shoved me hard against my chest.

"Nice to see you, too."

"No!" she yelled, hitting my chest a few times.

I tried to block her, but she was adamant on contact. "Fuck, what is with people hitting me?"

She stopped, her fist raised mid-punch, but then narrowed her eyes. "You deserve it this time." She got in a few more hits before she started to cry. "I was so worried about you, Logan. Nobody knew anything, and you've been *here*. Why didn't you call me? Email...anything?" Her body slumped, as she wiped frantically at her tears.

"I'm an asshole, Lucy. I'm sorry. Come here." I brought her in for a hug. She resisted at first but eventually gave in.

"I hate you," she said, and then I heard her sniff. "I missed you so damn much."

TEN MINUTES LATER, after I'd finally settled her down enough, she spoke, "How come no one knows you're here?"

I shrugged. "I just want to lay low for a bit. You can't tell anyone I'm here, Luce. Not even Cameron."

Her eyes went wide. "Well, that's going to be tough."

"Try, okay?"

She nodded.

"How did you even know I was here?"

"I have my ways." She giggled.

I sat on the sofa bed, and she did the same. "How's Cam?"

Her smile was instant. "He's good. We're good."

"That's awesome."

"And you? What have you been doing? Where were you?"

I told her all about Doctors Without Borders and my time in Africa. I told her about Manny and Jamal. She gave me a warning look when I mentioned Rebekah. I laughed at her—she had no idea where my heart and head were. I even told her about Amuhda and her mom. Lucy, being Lucy, cried some more. "But they're okay?" she kept asking.

I kept assuring her they were.

Then I told her about the PTSD meds I was on.

She was quiet for a while and then lifted her chin, as if gaining the courage to speak. "Logan, no one really knows what happened that night. I mean, no one's said anything. Jake and Kayla, they seem to know, but they won't say much. I know Jake's your best friend, but I thought I was your girl?" She grimaced, probably not wanting to bring up Amanda.

I held her hand. Lucy was special to me; she always had been. It's like the moment Cameron brought her into our circle, she saw through my bullshit and just saw *me*. "Ask anything you want, Lucy. There are no secrets between us. Ever."

She nodded, then quietly spoke. "Did you know them? Those bad people who did that to you?"

I laughed under my breath. She spoke like a ten-year-old. "Yes, well, two of them. One of them was my birth dad."

She gasped loudly.

"The other was Megan's ex-boyfriend."

She looked confused.

"Megan, Micky's ex-best friend, the one who cheated with James?" I waited for her to understand. When she did, I continued. "She's my half-sister, from my birth dad's side, and—"

"Hold up." She raised her hand to my mouth. "What the fuck is happening right now?" Her eyes were huge, disbelieving. "Dude." She sucked in a breath and let it out in a huff. "Are you openly telling people this shit? Because you might want to wait until you let everyone know you're back so you can answer the eleventy-three questions we're all going to ask."

I threw my head back in laughter. "Eleventy-three?"

She rolled her eyes. "My brother Lachlan swears it's a thing."

Lachlan—the Amanda date assister.

She must've sensed what I was thinking because she squeezed my hand once and then faced me. "Have you seen her?"

I nodded.

"She give you that fat lip?"

I'd forgotten I had it. "Yup."

She shrugged. "I'd probably do a lot worse."

"Yeah," I agreed.

"You miss her?"

"Every second, of every hour, of every day."

"Okay, Nicholas Sparks," she joked and elbowed me in the ribs.

I pretended to wince.

She paled instantly, panic clear on her face.

I tried to calm her down. "I'm just fucking with you, Lucy. Shit."

Her panicked eyes turned into a glare, directed right at me. "You're an asshole."

I chuckled. "So you've said."

Then all of a sudden, she turned serious. "I'm glad you're back, Logan. I really am. But this time—you better be ready to fight for her. She doesn't deserve anything less."

I FELT LIKE I'd just run a marathon, with weights strapped to me, five times over. I'd thought I maintained my fitness while I was gone, but all I really did was keep the muscle mass. My conditioning sucked ass.

I hopped off the treadmill and prepared to leave. Too busy fucking around with my phone, I didn't see the body I ran into, or the fist coming at my face, or the elbow to my stomach. "Oomph." I held my stomach with one hand while the other tried to hold on to something, anything, to stop myself from falling to the floor. I didn't know what I was holding onto until it was too late. *Boob.* Shit. I quickly let go and tried to find my footing. Then a knee to my junk *ruined* me. I fell to my knees and face-planted. I couldn't breathe. My eyes began to water. I shut them tight. I couldn't let people see me cry. I'm not a fucking pussy.

A loud squeal pulled me from my thoughts. "Holy shit, Logan! I'm so sorry."

Amanda.

I slowly opened one eye, just in case her voice was a hallucination. She was on her knees, bending to look at my face. "Oh my God," she whispered, placing her hand on my cheek. "Are you okay?"

"Ugh," I managed to get out.

She laughed.

Fucking laughed.

"Not funny," I told her.

She grimaced. "I'm sorry. You grabbed a handful of boob. I panicked."

"And before that?"

"I just—I don't know."

Some guy jogged up to her and placed his hand on her shoulder. "Is everything okay?"

"Yes," she told him, but her eyes never left me.

"Is this guy bothering you?"

"What the hell?" I spat out. "I'm the one on the fucking floor here."

He glared at me, his eyes narrowed. "Amanda, you need me to call security on this asshole?"

"Come the fuck on," I groaned, struggling to sit up. "Obviously, I'm not the threat, but please...go ahead and call security on Kung Fu Ninja here." I pointed to Amanda.

Her eyes were huge. She was in as much shock as I was in pain.

Asshole didn't respond, just stared at her tits and asked her if she was okay. She confirmed she was, and he left.

"That asshole was looking at your tits," I informed her.

She rolled her eyes. "At least he wasn't grabbing them."

"Valid."

She held her hand out for me and helped me to my feet. I stood, my body bent at my waist, holding onto my nuts, as if that was going to somehow make it all better. She placed her hand on my arm and led me to a chair nearby where I took a seat. Standing in front of me, she lifted my chin with her fingers. Her thumb stroked under my eye a few times. "Does it hurt?" She bit her lip, anticipating my answer.

My hand reached out to touch her leg. The action was supposed to be soothing, but it had the opposite effect. Her eyes widened slightly and her breath caught. She didn't pull back, and she didn't stop me. I spread my legs and gripped hers tighter, begging her to come closer.

She did.

Her hand stayed on my face as she leaned in close, inspecting it. "Shit, Logan. It's going to bruise."

I shook my head. My eyes never left hers. "It's fine. Don't even worry about it."

"I keep hurting you."

"I keep deserving it."

She smiled. My gaze drifted down to her mouth.

She wet her lips. "Don't you dare kiss me," she warned.

I chuckled. "I wasn't planning on it."

Lie.

I took a chance and wrapped my arm around her waist, pulling her down until she was sitting on my leg. Her arm wrapped around my neck. I breathed out, relieved. She was letting me have this, and I sure as shit wasn't going to question it. I saw her eyes focus on my lips. "You want me to, don't you?"

"Huh?" Her eyes snapped up.

"You want me to kiss you?"

"No." She feigned disgust.

"Fine," I told her. "Can you just sit here with me then, just until my boys get back to normal?" I pointed to my lap.

She laughed and looked away, and her arm around my neck loosened.

She wanted to leave.

Without intending to, the grip on her waist tightened.

"I'm not going anywhere," she said.

"Good," I said. "Neither am I."

She turned to me, an emotion on her face I couldn't understand. Then she leaned in, her face so close to mine I felt her breath on my cheek.

My heart thumped.

My eyes shut.

I waited.

And waited.

Then I felt her lips press on my cheek, just under my eye. "I don't ever mean to hurt you," she said quietly.

SOMEHOW, I PERSUADED her to have lunch with me. We were both in our post-gym sweaty state, so she wanted to shower. "Do it at my house," I told her. "I have to go home anyway; I didn't bring anything to change into."

She hesitated for a moment before agreeing.

I didn't even consider how the thought of her naked in my shower was going to affect me until I was sporting a hard-on in my living room. I heard the bathroom door open and quickly adjusted myself. "All done?" I asked her.

She nodded, looking at the floor. She'd changed into a plain white dress that showed off her legs and her tanned skin. She wasn't as dark as Ethan, but she had that naturally olive skin most girls paid for.

"I'll be done in a little bit. Just make yourself at home."

AMANDA

I'D GONE THROUGH his bathroom cupboard looking for a disposable razor. It wasn't as if I was trying to impress him, but my legs had four-day growth and I really didn't want him to notice, let alone touch it. I didn't find the razors, but I did find a bottle of Xanax prescribed to him.

Now, alone in the living room, I took my phone out of my bag and started researching anxiety medication and its side effects. I didn't get very far before the bathroom door opened. The steam from inside clouded him as he walked out wearing nothing but sweatpants.

No shirt.

I wiped my mouth, positive that I was drooling.

He walked toward me. I stood frozen. He didn't stop until we were face-to-face. His bare chest brushed against my breasts. My breath hitched. A shiver traveled up my spine. "You," he said, licking his lips, "are welcome to grab my boobs whenever you want."

"SORRY WE HAD to come out this far." He bit into his burger and chewed before speaking again. We were at a diner a little ways out of town. "I just still want to lay low for a little bit, you know?"

"Sure."

"So, you didn't keep in touch with Micky and Lucy when I was gone?"

How did he know that? "How did you know that?"

"Through Jake. I called him on your—"

My chest constricted. His words hurt. He must've noticed because he asked, "What's wrong?"

I shook my head and pushed down the pain.

"Amanda," he cooed. "Did I say something?"

He scooted around the booth until he was sitting next to me.

I felt pathetic.

I *was* pathetic.

"What did I do?" he asked. I don't know if he was speaking to himself or me. I heard him sigh and then put his arm on the back of the booth. His other hand reached up, and he used his fingers to turn my face toward his. "Tell me."

My heart broke.

I inhaled deeply and let the words out. "You never called me. The entire year you were gone I got *one* letter from you. I thought that maybe you were cutting yourself off from everyone, but you called Jake? Why didn't you—"

"I called Jake once, because I needed something from him," he explained.

"And your dad?" My voice got louder.

He shrugged. "Is my dad. I owe him that much."

"And me?" I tried to keep it together. "You don't think you owed me something? You don't think that what we had was worth something? You don't think *I* was worth something?"

"That's not it at all, Amanda."

"Then what? Explain it to me, please?"

His gaze moved all over my face and then held it in his trembling hand. I covered it with mine. Then he spoke. "Why are you here with me right now? Why are you talking to me? Why are you spending time with me?"

"I don't know," I said truthfully. "I can't help it, and I can't explain it."

"Exactly," he breathed out. "I can't explain it, either. Not yet, anyway. I just don't ever want you to think that it's because you didn't mean anything to me. You meant the world to me. And if you didn't know that —if you couldn't see that—then that's how I'll start. Every day I'll show you, and every day I'll prove to you just how much you meant to me. How much you *still* mean to me."

13

LOGAN

Logan: I'm doing it. I'm going to fight for her. I can't exist without her. She's my air.

    Lucy: Of course she is.

    Logan: Have you told anyone I'm back?

    Lucy: I told you I wouldn't.

    Logan: Not even Cam?

    Lucy: Not even Cam. Why are you texting me? Are you bored?

    Logan: You know me way too well.

    Lucy: I'll be there in 15.

She stepped in fifteen minutes later, holding a paper bag toward me.

"What's this?" I asked, taking it from her hands.

"We had dinner at Jake's parents the other night. His mom baked cookies."

I got excited. Too excited. I loved Jake's mom's cookies. I pulled out three and shoved them in my mouth.

"Jeez," she said. "It's like you haven't had decent food for a year." She chuckled to herself and then looked around the place. "Your apartment's kind of depressing."

I laughed. "I know. I'm hoping I can persuade Amanda to help me fix it up."

She smiled and tried to sit up on the kitchen counter. On her third attempt, she huffed and motioned for me to help her. I lifted her by her waist and placed her on it. "You're so little."

She snorted. "I know. I have the body of a twelve-year-old boy."

I threw my head back in laughter. "Not true, Luce. You're hot. You just don't care that you are."

"Aw, that's so nice."

I shrugged and leaned against the fridge. "It's the truth."

"Cameron wants us to move in together. Get an apartment and all that."

"Yeah? I'm surprised you haven't already."

She picked at her nails. "I want to, but my dad wants us to wait until we're married, or at least engaged."

"What? Does your dad know that Cam practically lived in your cabin?"

She laughed quietly. "I think he's in denial."

"So what are you going to do?"

She shrugged. "I don't know. I think he wants to do it for the wrong reasons."

"What do you mean?"

She sighed. "Some stuff happened when you were gone, and he thinks this might fix it."

"What stuff?" I straightened a little, paying full attention. "Fix what?"

"Nothing." She shook her head. "Not important. So you and Amanda?"

I couldn't help the smile that took over. "I'm hoping she might want to spend some time with me, you know? Maybe I can try to convince her to give me another chance. I mean—whatever was there before I left—it's still there."

"And you think she feels the same?"

"I can't be sure, but there's always this ... I don't know ... intensity? It's like when we're together, nothing else exists." I paused. "You didn't speak to her at all when I was gone?"

She shook her head. "No. She told us she just needed some time and that she'd contact us when she was ready, but she never did. I miss her, but what can I do? Cam even spoke to her when he dropped off the car; he told her to call me. I guess it was just too painful for her."

I cleared the lump in my throat.

She continued, "Sometimes it's just timing, Logan. Two hearts can beat as one, even if they aren't synced. Maybe that's what it was with you two. Maybe you just need to find the right rhythm, the right timing. Maybe now's that time for you guys."

"Maybe," I told her. "I mean I hope so. I want to be together, like you and Cameron are. I want her to be my Lucy. My forever."

She smiled huge. "Then what are you waiting for?" she jumped off the counter. "Go get her."

I grabbed my keys off the counter.

"I plan to."

AMANDA

"What's gotten into you?" Alexis eyed me from the across the kitchen. We both stood in our pajamas, drinking coffee.

"What do you mean?"

She narrowed her eyes. "Don't play dumb. I've known you since we came out of our mammas' coochies. Who's the guy?"

"What?" I faked ignorance. "I don't know what the hell you're talking about."

She took two steps forward and pinned me against the counter. I waited while her gaze roamed all over my face. "Logan's back, isn't he?"

"What?" I screeched. "I mean—no—I don't know. Is he?" *Smooth.*

"You bitch. When did he get back, and why haven't you told me?"

I sighed, defeated. "I saw him three days ago."

She looked toward the hallway, then back at me. My eyes followed. "What?" I asked.

Her grip on my arm was tighter than necessary when she pulled me into my room. "Talk," she said.

"I don't know. I saw him at a party, and then..." I shrugged. I shouldn't have added anything.

"And then what?" she whisper-yelled, leaning against my door.

"What is wrong with you?"

"Nothing, don't change the subject. And then what, Dim?"

I sat on my bed. "And then we went to a park and talked for a bit."

"What else?"

"Nothing else."

She crossed her arms. "Quit lying."

"Fine," I huffed. "Then we ended up back at his place."

"WHAT?"

"Shut up! Nothing happened; we just talked."

"You just talked?" she repeated, disbelief laced in her tone.

"Yes," I tried to convince her. "And I slapped him."

"WHAT?"

What the hell? I may as well tell her all of it. "And then I saw him at the bookstore and the gym, and I punched him, and then we had lunch…"

"WHAT?" she said again.

I laughed. "Have you finally run out of shit to say?"

"Shut up."

I laughed again.

She sat on the bed and dramatically flung her body backwards. "This is bad," she said.

"What are you talking about? It's fine. Nothing's happened."

"Yet… So, you randomly bumped into each other at all these places; it wasn't planned?"

"No, of course it wasn't planned. I wouldn't do that."

She sat back up and turned her body to face me. "Amanda, I need you to be serious for a second." She spoke down to me, like I was a kid, and held both my hands in hers. "Do you want something to happen?"

I shrugged and looked away. "I don't know."

"It's a simple question. It's a yes or no answer."

I laughed once, but it was bitter. "You should know better than anyone that it's not a simple question. You know how I feel."

Her head fell forward. "I'm sorry," she said.

"Me too."

"Amanda?" She looked up. "You can't tell Ethan he's back. And you sure as hell can't tell him that you've been seeing him."

I reared back, surprised at her words. "What are you talking about?"

"How do you not see it? Ethan hates Logan. Like, *hates* hates him. As in—and these are his words, 'If I ever see that asshole again, I'm gonna lay him out.'"

I looked at her. "He's never said that shit to me."

It was her turn to roll her eyes. "Of course he hasn't. He hates bringing him up with you." She sighed. "Look, I don't say this to hurt you…but Logan—he fucked up. And Ethan—he was the one to pick up the pieces. And not just the last time, but the first time, too. He forgave him once, but that's it for him. He can't do it again." She paused for a few moments. I wondered if she was done, but she kept going. "You know how much sleep he lost over you?"

I opened my mouth to speak, but she stopped me.

"I'm not saying that he blames you or that he's bitter about it. I'm just saying that he cares *that* much. Since your dad left, he's somehow convinced himself that it's his job to take care of you and your mom. You know he used to text me in the middle of the night at random times? He could hear you crying in your room, and he'd ask me what to do—whether or not he should go in and comfort you. You know how many times he called me when you were having nightmares, and he could hear you screaming? You're not the only one who went through that, Amanda. He did, too.

"You don't think he has issues? Or that he doesn't hurt? He walked in on some guy nearly raping you. You know that you blacked out? That he tried to wake you? He thought you were dead, Dim. He thought he lost you that night. And in a way, he kind of did."

My eyes were wide. They'd begun to fill with tears. "Oh my God..." I breathed out. I'd been so selfish. So lost in my own feelings.

She wrapped her arms around me. "I'm sorry I told you."

I lifted my head. "I needed to know."

She nodded in agreement. "You did." She moved the hair away from my face and made sure I was looking at her. "Whatever you choose to do with Logan, I'm going to support you. But just remember Ethan in all of this, okay?"

I swallowed, sniffing back the tears.

Ethan called out for her, interrupting us. She got up quickly. "Are you going to be okay?" I couldn't speak. I lifted my head in a nod. She smiled sadly.

"Babe," he yelled out again.

"Coming!" She patted my head and then left.

LOGAN

I KNOCKED ON the door, ignoring the memories that came with this house. No one answered. I knocked again and looked around. Her car was the only one in the driveway.

After five minutes and four series of knocks, she finally answered the door. The chain lock stopped it from opening fully. "Hey," she said quietly. "What are you doing here?"

"Can you open the door? I can't see you."

She closed it, and a second later I heard her toying with the chain. When she opened the door, I was able to take in her state. She was in her pajamas, her eyes red and her hair a mess. "Were you sleeping?" I asked.

She shook her head. "What's up?" she asked quietly, avoiding eye contact.

"Are you okay? You look like you've been crying."

She looked over my shoulder. "I'm fine," she said. "What's going on? What do you want?" Her tone was flat; it caused me to take a step back.

Honestly, I didn't know what to expect, but I wasn't expecting this. "I, uh..." I rubbed my palm across my jaw and then placed my hand in my pocket. It had started shaking again. "I thought that maybe you might wanna hang out or something."

She bit her lip, her eyes cast downwards. "I don't think so, Logan. Actually, I don't think it's right that you be here—or anywhere, really. I mean—I can't stop you from existing, but I don't think you and me—I don't think it's a good idea that you and I exist together."

"Oh," is all I could say.

"Take care," she said, before closing the door in my face.

No thump.

Just flat line.

14

LOGAN

Four days.

Four.

That's how long it took for me to go insane without her. How I went a year? I have no idea.

AMANDA

You know when you're a kid, and you play hide and seek, but you're too young to fully understand the concept of it? So you stand in the middle of a room and close your eyes and think that somehow, because you can't see anyone, it means they can't see you? Well, that's what I was doing. Only I wasn't a kid, and no one was looking for me. Regardless, I sat in the middle of my bed with my eyes closed and my phone in my hands. Yes, I was hiding from my phone.

Alan had texted me more than an hour ago saying he was looking forward to dinner tonight. I knew that it was our night, but a part of me had wished that maybe Logan had said something to him and that he wouldn't expect me over there anymore.

My phone sounded, pulling me from my thoughts.

Alan.

"Hi," I answered, hoping to sound enthusiastic.

"So, I'm at the store, but they don't have red peppers, only green. Is that okay?"

My heart broke at the excitement in his voice. It'd become a thing—him shopping for the ingredients. After the fourth time I showed up with groceries in hand, he knew to expect me. He asked me to write out the ingredients for the taco casserole and made me promise I'd never buy them again. He said that it was bad enough that I was feeding him every other Sunday; I shouldn't have to be using my hard-earned money to do so.

"Green's fine," I told him. I wanted to ask him if Logan was going to be there, or ask him why he didn't tell me that Logan was back, but all I could say was, "I'll be there soon."

I LET OUT a relieved sigh when I pulled into their house and no other cars were there apart from Alan's. I told myself on the drive over that I would just act as if nothing had changed. Logan wasn't here. He didn't exist. That was the way it'd always been with us, and that was the way it would stay. Yes, we discussed Logan but never in the present tense. It was always about what he was like as a kid.

"Maybe you should look at helping out kids like Logan," Alan once said.

"What do you mean?"

"I know you want to get into nursing, but I see your compassion, your heart, your need to understand why he is the way he is. Maybe you should do something with that."

And that was all it took. Two days later, I'd decided to major in Child Psychology.

HE OPENED THE door before I could knock. His enthusiasm to see me always made me smile. No one knew I came here; we'd even decided not to tell my mom. It might have seemed odd to some people, and I could understand why, but every other Sunday, in the walls of this house, he gave me a piece of my life I never admitted to missing. He also gave me a father when my own seemed to no longer exist.

"I GOT YOU something," Alan said. He sat in his usual spot on the counter, drinking a beer while I made dinner. Just like the first time, only then, Logan was here.

"You don't need to get me things. Don't you think it's bad enough that you guys paid for my tuition?"

He raised his hand and got off the stool. "It didn't cost me anything. Besides, that was Logan's money, not mine. It was his choice what he did with it."

I rolled my eyes.

"Did Logan ever tell you about my Tina?"

I nodded.

He pulled out a wooden box and put it on the counter. "She was my girlfriend, all through high school and college."

I stopped chopping the peppers and wiped my hands on my dress, then leaned forward on the counter. Whatever he had to say, I wanted to give him all my attention.

He smiled at my movements, but it didn't reach his eyes. "You actually remind me a lot of her.," he said. "Not physically, but more...in your hearts. You're both so..." He paused and thought for a second. "Genuine. Your hearts are genuine."

I didn't have the words; I stayed silent, in my own thoughts.

He pushed the box toward me. "This was hers. I want you to have it."

"I can't—"

"Make an old man happy," he cut in.

I took the box in my hands and flipped the lid open. Inside were dozens of bracelets, neon colored plastic ones, thick bangles, bright friendship bracelets, and a few chunky gold chain ones. I couldn't control my smile. "It's like the 80s threw up in here."

He threw back his head in laughter. "She loved them. She always had a wrist full of bracelets, kind of like you." He pointed at mine. He knew I wore them to hide something, but he never asked, and I never offered. That's why we worked as well as we did.

I took a few out of the box and put them on, shaking out my hands to get them comfortable. I had a good twenty on each arm. At first, I did it to hide what was there, and then it became habit to wear them. I was fully aware that they probably bought more attention to that area than if I didn't wear them at all. But like I said, habit.

"Are you sure you don't want to keep them? I mean, the sentiment is so much more valuable to you than if I were to have them."

He shrugged and took a swig of his beer. "What am I going to do with it, Amanda? Give it to my daughter? You're pretty much it for me."

My chest tightened at his words. Looking down at the box in front of me, I cleared the lump that'd formed in my throat. I wanted to tell him how much his statement touched me, and that it went both ways, that he had become like a father to me. I wanted to tell him how much these Sunday dinners meant to me.

I started to speak but got cut off when the front door opened.

His eyes were wide. So were mine. We stood still, frozen, waiting for something to happen.

And then it did.

His voice seemed astronomically loud, but maybe that was in my head. "Dad?"

Alan's smile was instant but disappeared just as fast when he looked at my face.

"In the kitchen," Alan yelled back.

My head dropped, and my eyes cast downwards as I busied myself with prepping dinner.

"What are you doing in the ki—" His word died. He must've seen me.

I inhaled deeply and shut my eyes, slowly building the courage I needed. When I felt I was ready, I opened my eyes and raised my head.

And he was there.

FOUR DAYS.

It had only been four days since I saw him, and already his presence was making me weak.

How the hell did I go a year?

LOGAN

SHE WAS STANDING IN MY KITCHEN.

Why was she standing in my kitchen?

I turned to Dad. He offered no answers.

Why was he not saying anything?

I looked at her. She just stared back. She had a knife in her hand. I took a step closer to see what she was doing; she took a step back.

We paused.

Dad sighed.

"Shit," she said.

"What?" I asked.

Dad sighed again.

"I gotta go." She placed the knife down on the counter.

"What?" Dad huffed.

"Huh?" I said to him.

What the hell was happening?

I instinctively took another step forward, and she took another step back. Her hands were up in a defensive stance.

Dad laughed.

Laughed.

We both faced him.

"What?" he asked, his body still shaking with laughter. He walked over to the fridge, pulled out a soda, and handed it to me. "Welcome home." He patted me on the shoulder. "Looks like you both got a lot of explaining to do."

And then he left.

Just like that.

I turned back to Amanda. "Hey."

She sucked in a breath. "Hey."

I took in our surroundings. "You're cooking dinner?"

She nodded so slowly I almost missed it.

I stepped forward. She stepped back.

"You do this a lot? Come here and cook dinner, I mean?"

She nodded again, but her lips were pressed tight.

"How often?" I stepped closer, and she stepped back, only this time her back hit the counter behind her.

She didn't respond.

"How often?" I asked again, taking another step.

A gasp caught in her throat. I moved again; I just wanted to be closer to her.

Her eyes fixated on the floor as she said, "Every other Sunday."

I let out a breath; it shifted the hair on her head. She gazed up at me, her blue eyes penetrating.

Just like *that* moment. The first time I saw her at Jake's house with blood on her finger and a terrified look on her face.

That was three years ago.

But she had no reason to be terrified. I chanced my luck and closed the space between us. Her hands went up against my chest, but she didn't push me away like I'd expected her to.

"For how long?" I asked.

She swallowed, but her eyes never left mine. "A year."

My stomach tightened. I don't know whether it was the good kind or the bad. "Why?" My hand went to her waist.

Her eyes drifted shut at the touch. "Because he asked me to once."

I lifted her chin with my other hand. "Amanda."

"Mm?" Her eyes were still closed.

I asked her to open them.

She did.

"And you came back here, twice a month, for a year. Why?"

She sucked in a breath, her chest rising with the effort. Her mouth was slightly open. She wet her lips.

"Why?" I asked again, more assertive.

Her eyes intensified. "Because." She lifted her chin. "I felt closer to you when I was here. I missed you less."

Thump. Thump.

"Baby," I breathed out, moving my face closer to hers.

Her hands on my chest became blocks of cement. "Don't you dare kiss me," she said.

I pulled back. Reality set in. "You're going to have to give me something else to do then, because I don't think I can control it."

She pushed off the counter, placed her hands on my shoulders and moved me out of the way.

"Help me with dinner," she said.

So I did.

In dead silence.

DAD PREPPED THE dining table, so it didn't surprise me at all that he set it up the way he did: two settings on one side, one on the other. He was already sitting and waiting for us. You can guess which side he was on.

"I'm starving," he announced once we were seated.

Amanda's bare leg brushed against mine. I wore workout shorts; she wore a loose, blue summer dress. No bra. Not that I was looking.

"Sorry," she whispered under her breath.

I cleared my throat. "It's fine."

"You guys are so awkward," Dad said.

Amanda giggled quietly. I wanted to, but I contained it. Dad didn't talk much, so when he did, it made an impact.

"How are you feeling?" he asked me. There was an underlying tone to his words, but I didn't want to discuss it, not with Amanda here.

I glared at him, hoping he'd understand. "Fine," I ground out.

His eyes went from me to Amanda, and he understood.

It was quiet for a while as we served up the food. After the first mouthful, I swear, my mouth orgasmed. I didn't even wait to swallow before announcing, "Holy fucking shit. This shit is good!"

"Logan Wilbur Matthews," Dad reprimanded.

Amanda's guffaw filled the room. "How funny," she said to herself and then snorted. "Wilbur."

I was about to warn her not to tell anyone or I'd hunt her down and start making out with her in random places, but Dad spoke first. "You could've had taco casserole more often if you'd come back when you said you would."

Buzz. Fucking. Kill.

I sighed. I didn't want to get into it with him. Not now.

"Sorry," Dad mumbled. "I didn't mean for that to come out the way it did."

My shoulders lifted, but I stayed quiet. I reached out for my drink, but my hand trembled. I watched as it attempted to pick up the glass.

"Logan." His voice was strained. "I thought it was getting better."

I didn't speak, just concentrated on my dry mouth and the need for some form of liquid. I gripped the glass, but my hand hadn't improved. A small amount of soda tipped over the lip and onto the table. I cursed under my breath.

I felt her hand first; it brushed against my forearm, then her fingers second, as they slowly linked with mine.

I turned to face her, but she was looking at our hands, her lips turned down into a frown.

In my head, I counted the seconds it took before the shaking stopped. It wouldn't take long. It never did when she was comforting me.

One.

Two.

Then her head raised and our eyes locked. "Taco casserole is pretty amazing," she declared. Her smile was genuine. It wasn't pity. It wasn't forced.

I unlinked our fingers to take the drink. No spillage this time. I thought she'd move her hand away once I'd separated them, but she left it there, palm up, waiting. I didn't hesitate for a second.

She tried to continue eating with her left hand, but it was clearly a struggle. I laughed quietly as I watched her. She glared at me, but a smile played on her lips. She huffed out, as if annoyed, then placed my hand on her leg and released it.

I could feel the warmth of her skin through the material of her dress. I think I moaned; I'm not sure, but she giggled quietly. Then Dad cleared his throat. I'd forgotten he was here.

He stood up, dramatically. "I'm tired," he announced. "I'm going to bed. You should show Amanda your old room and those posters of 50 Cent."

Then he was gone.

"50 Cent?" She laughed.

I didn't even care. I just wanted to hear her laugh.

15

AMANDA

"WHY ARE YOU blushing?" I asked him.

He laughed. "I'm about to show you my room from when I was fifteen."

"Do you have pictures of naked ladies?" I teased.

"Honestly?" He put his hand on the handle and pushed down. "Most likely."

He swung the door open, and I stepped in. "Well," I told him. "This is a total anti-climax. It's just an average teenage boy's room."

"Sorry to disappoint you."

I walked around, looking for something I could make fun of, but there was nothing. Apart from the posters of rappers who were cool more than ten years ago, there wasn't much at all. Surely he had a porn stash. What fifteen-year-old boy didn't?

I walked to his bed and checked under it. Nothing.

"What are you doing?" He followed and looked under it himself.

I went to his nightstand and opened the drawer. Nothing.

"Hmm." I tapped my lip with my index finger. "If I was Logan Matthew's porn collection, where would I hide?"

His laughter filled the room.

I stepped toward his walk-in closet.

"Where are you going?" He blocked me, with a panicked look on his face. One step closer and we'd be chest to chest.

I shrugged. "I told you, searching for your porn collection."

He let me pass. I turned the light on in the small room and looked around. He chewed his lip, his hands going in his pockets.

And then I saw it: a box on the top shelf. I smirked at him. He shook his head. A blush crept to his cheeks.

"Busted," I told him.

I got on my toes and tried to reach for it.

I sensed him before I felt him. The warmth of his hard chest against my back made me tense. "It's not what you think it is." His voice was hoarse.

"Yeah?" I asked, hoping my nerves didn't show. When any part of us connected, it was more than just physical. Or even emotional. It was a collision of comfort and unease. Gut-wrenching and heartwarming. He did this to me. *We* did this to each other. "So, what is it then?"

I heard his shaky breath against my ear. Then his hand settled on my hip as he pressed into me. I let out a moan. It had been a year since I'd felt a guy like this. This close. *This hard.* He reached up with his spare hand and pulled down the box. Then, with the hand still on my hip, he guided me to turn around. He didn't step back and away from me; in fact, he moved closer, and closer, until my body was up against the wall under the shelf. He pulled back slightly, his arm raised, gripping the bar above my head. There were no hangers on it, no clothes; the small space was empty, apart from a few boxes on the floor against the walls. The sleeve of his shirt bunched together, allowing me to see his tattoo again.

"Amanda," he whispered, then opened the box between us. Inside were dozens of pendant glass vials, like the one he'd given me that day in the rain. The day he'd promised me that we would make new memories, ones that I wasn't afraid of. He said that we'd be amazing. We really could have been.

My hand reached in for one. Each vile was in a Ziplock bag with a date and location handwritten. "Every time it rained, I thought of you." He sniffed one. My eyes lifted to his. "I wanted to send you these, but I just— I don't know ..."

"There are so many in here."

He nodded. "There are four more boxes."

"Why?"

"For the same reason you came here every other week. It made me feel closer to you. It made me miss you less."

"Why didn't you just come home then?"

He placed the box back on the shelf and pressed his body against me.

"Because I'm a coward. And an asshole. And I don't deserve to have you in my life, let alone here, in my room."

Wrapping his hand around my neck, he brought me closer to him. "Don't you dare kiss me," I told him. I wasn't ready for it. Not yet. But soon. Maybe once my head was out of the clouds and my heart could handle it.

"Okay," he agreed. Then leaned in close and brushed my lips with his.

"What are you doing?" I whispered against them. I didn't pull back. I let my heart control my head, which made my actions confusing.

"Not kissing you," he confirmed. He moved his lips away from mine, trailed them up my jaw and to my ear. He nibbled gently, just underneath it. Then his lips parted and his tongue darted out as he moved down my neck so fucking slowly. He paused on my shoulder, moving the strap of my dress to the side, and his teeth skimmed along my skin.

My hands flattened on his stomach. I could feel the dips of his muscles. "You said you wouldn't kiss me," I breathed out.

"I'm not." His mouth never left my shoulder.

"So what are you doing?" My voice was strained. My breathing was heavy. I squeezed my legs together.

He pulled away and looked into my eyes. "Remembering you."

My head flung back and hit the wall behind me. I heard him moan from deep in his throat, just before I felt his mouth on my neck, his tongue flicking slowly, gently against my throat. "Oh my God." I sighed. My hands moved lower on him. I couldn't control them, even if I'd tried. They passed the band of his shorts and brushed against his hard-on.

He groaned into my neck, vibrating my skin. I felt it all the way in my core.

My body was on fire, ready to combust. He removed the other strap from my shoulder and licked and sucked there, right before his hand gripped the side of my chest. His thumb skimmed across my already-strained nipple. He placed his knee between my legs and separated them. It was too much. Too many things happening at once. His thumb on my nipple, his mouth on my skin, and his leg between mine—I couldn't take much more.

He pulled away abruptly, and I almost felt grateful. But he just looked at me; his eyes were the darkest I'd ever seen them. They seemed to widen slightly, like something had just dawned on him.

"Fuck," he spat through clenched teeth. I could feel the material of my dress shifting against my breasts with each breath. His eyes zoned in on my chest. In a flash, he'd removed the straps from my arms and was standing there, studying me, as if wondering what to do next. He smirked slightly. His next action had been decided. And then he did it. He yanked my dress down, just enough so that my breasts were free. His breathing was so heavy, so short. He was panting. He rubbed his hand against his dick, just once. But the image of it was enough to drive me insane.

Then his hands held mine, pulling them away from him and raising them above my head. His mouth was still on my neck, licking, sucking. I felt him everywhere. He shifted my hands until they gripped the bar above me. "Keep them there."

And then he moved.

The instant his mouth covered my nipple, my grip on the bar tightened. I cried out in pleasure. But it wasn't enough, not for him. He spread my legs—with his hand this time. I felt his fingers skim my folds through my panties. I could've come. If I wasn't so embarrassed about how wet I was—I would have.

He switched breasts, making sure they both got the same attention. My arms were still raised, gripped tight against the cold metal. Somehow, without me realizing, my hips were moving. His hand on me, moving ever so slightly, was just enough that my clit could feel the friction of his palm.

Then his tongue on my breast stopped moving. I thought we were done. But he sucked on it.

Hard.

I was too consumed with the pleasure of his mouth that I didn't even know how or when it happened. I felt the cold air on my wet sex and my panties around my ankles. He started on the outside, fingering and spreading my wetness, making circles around my nub. One finger slid in and out, replaced by two. He started moving them, slowly.

I got lost in the fog of his actions. I wanted to touch him. I wanted him to feel as good as I felt. "You're so fucking wet." He watched my face as his flattened tongue moved from one nipple to the other.

"I want to touch you," I told him.

"No."

"Please," I begged.

His fingers moved faster, harder, more determined. I felt myself building. I wanted to hold out. It was too soon. I wanted to feel this intensity longer. I'd started thrusting into his hand. It'd only been seconds, not even minutes. There was no slow build-up, no warning. His fingers, his mouth—all of him—were so determined to make me feel. To make me want. To make me his.

And I was. Whether he was around to know it or feel it.

I was always his.

Three years ago to the day—on our very first date—I became his.

His fingers took up a rhythm. He knew I was close. "Baby," he murmured. My legs squeezed tight around his hand and—

"Oh my God," I moaned. I repeated the words over and over as his movements slowed and my vision cleared. When my breathing settled, I opened my eyes, just as he reached into his shorts to adjust himself. I went weak at the knees. I let go of the bar and slid down the wall until my ass hit the floor. "Holy shit." My body was still trembling with the aftermath of the most intense orgasm I'd ever had. My head felt heavy, so heavy. I could barely lift it to see his reaction. He smirked, right before he walked out of the tiny space in the closet. A second later, I heard the stream of water turn on from a shower.

16

AMANDA

I SAT ON his bed and waited while he was in his bathroom. He came out and paused mid-step when he saw me. I wasn't sure why; I didn't know what he was expecting.

"Hey," he said quietly, taking a seat next to me.

I looked at the floor, feeling a little awkward. "Hey."

"I thought for sure you'd bail."

The thought hadn't even crossed my mind. I turned to face him, but his gaze was focused off in the distance. "M ... maybe I should go."

His eyes darted to me. "What? No." He stood up. "I mean—of course if you have to—but I don't want you to." He cursed under his breath and started pacing the floor. "I wanted to ask you to stay with me tonight ... if you wanted to."

"I don't—"

He cut in. "Of course you don't want to. I'm an idiot—"

I got to my feet and stood in front of him. "I was just going to say that I don't have anything to wear."

"Oh." A small smile appeared. "That's it?"

I nodded. My own smile matched his.

"Easy fix," he announced. He led me to the bathroom, shrugged out of his shirt and handed it to me.

When I returned, he was lying in bed with his hands behind his head, waiting for me. I didn't know what we were doing. I don't think he did, either. We didn't discuss it; maybe if we did it would have ruined the moment.

He put his arm out for me, like he used to do every night. I could see the tattoo on it so clearly. I lay down next to him and rested my head where he wanted it. His hand began playing with my hair. "Mm," I hummed. It was so familiar. So perfect. I moved closer and nuzzled into his neck. My leg covered his. I placed my hand over his heart; I could feel it pounding through his chest.

All of a sudden, I was crying. I wasn't sobbing or weeping, but the tears fell silently onto his shoulder. His heart thumped faster, harder. "It's going to be okay, Amanda." He kissed my head. "I promise," he said. "I'm going to make it okay."

I let out a small sob. He had no idea. It wasn't up to him to make things right. We were both to blame. It wasn't just him. It was me, too.

"Shh," he soothed. He continued to stroke my hair until the tears subsided and sleep overcame me.

HE WAS CRYING. He was asleep, but he was crying. He mumbled something, and it sounded like my name. His head thrashed from side to side. I sat up and turned on the night light. I didn't know what else to do. His face was pained. It broke my heart. "Stop," he quivered, still asleep. And then tears fell from his shut eyes.

"Logan!" I shook his heavy shoulders. "Wake up."

He didn't. I shook him harder.

Then, with lightning-fast speed, he gripped my wrist tight, making me wince in pain. "Logan," I cried out.

His eyes snapped open. He sucked in a breath, as if he'd just come up from drowning. His eyes were glazed.

I tried to pull my hand from his grip, but he didn't loosen his hold. "Logan, it hurts."

"What?" he croaked.

I started to pry his fingers from their death grip.

"Shit!" His fingers straightened, releasing me instantly. "Fuck, I'm sorry." His breathing was loud, heavy.

"It's okay." I massaged my wrist, trying to recirculate the blood.

He held it in both his hands and did it for me. His thumbs massaged the area I'd tried so hard to hide. He pulled it toward his lips and kissed it once, twice, then placed my palm over his heart.

He sighed. "I'm sorry," he repeated. "How bad was it?"

I shrugged. "I have nothing to compare it to."

He nodded, picked up my hand again and looked at my wrist. "I'm not going to ask you, but you'll tell me when you're ready, right?"

"Yes," I said truthfully.

"Good."

"Does it happen often—the nightmares?"

He nodded again.

Sweat had built on his hairline; I wiped it away with my fingers and sat cross-legged next to him. I knew what he was feeling. The aftermath of nightmares was painful. The images plagued in your memory overshadowed the relief that it was just a dream. He blew out a breath and rubbed his hand against his jaw. "I forgot to take my meds," he admitted quietly.

"Xanax?" I asked.

His eyes narrowed.

"I saw them in your bathroom. I wasn't snooping, swear it."

He looked up at the ceiling. "Yeah."

"Can I ask you about it?"

He eyed me now, a look on his face I couldn't decipher. "Of course," he said. "I'll never keep anything from you. Come here." He held out his arm again, but I chose instead to lie on top of him. He didn't complain.

My forearms rested on his chest, my head only inches away from his. "I researched it—Xanax—treatment for anxiety...you have anxiety...or panic attacks?"

He nodded slowly.

"And it causes the pounding in here." I placed my hand over his heart again.

"Yes," he confirmed.

"And you were supposed to take it tonight, but you were here?"

"Yes," he said again.

"What causes it?"

His eyes became uneasy, but he still answered. "I have flashbacks. Not just when I sleep. Sometimes things can set them off."

"Of that night?" I swallowed the knot in my throat. "Do *I* set it off?"

"No." He was quick to respond. "Not all." He placed his hand under my shirt and started rubbing slow circles on my back. "And not just of that night," he continued. "Even stuff from when I was a kid that I'd suppressed. I'm still working through it, or trying, anyway."

"I'm so sorry," I told him.

He licked his lips. "Not at all your fault."

"Have you spoken to her—Megan?"

He inhaled sharply. "No. I know she's okay, that's all that matters. But I don't want to see her, not until I get my shit together."

"I get that."

"Any more questions?" He smiled at me. Those damn dimples. My fingers traced the dips. His eyes drifted shut. "I missed you so much," he said.

I wanted to tell him that I missed him, too. Every day. But it wouldn't heal us completely. It wouldn't change the past.

My gaze caught on his tattoo, and my fingers moved on their own, tracing the words. When did he get it? I wish I could've waited until he was ready, but the words were out before I could stop them. "What does your tattoo mean?"

He threaded his fingers through my hair and moved it away from my face. "It means *shadow passes, light remains.* You're my light, Amanda. In a life full of shadows and darkness and monsters, you're my light. When the blackness fades and the memories subside, you'll be there. You're always there." The corners of his lips lifted. "You know, the first time I saw you at Jake's, at the wake—that's what I called you. In the most horrible of circumstances, that's what you were to me—a light in the darkness. That's what you became, and that's what you stayed. In my head. In my heart. *My light.* Forever."

My heart beat out of my chest. I wanted to pick it up and hand it to him, tell him that it belonged to him and that I had no right to possess it.

But I couldn't do that. So I did the one thing I could do.

I kissed him.

And just like the very first time, and all of the times after that, I lost myself in his touch and in his kiss. I completely lost myself in Logan Matthews.

I didn't want the kissing to lead to somewhere it wasn't supposed to go, and even though I felt him hard against my stomach, he must've felt the same way, because we pulled apart after a few minutes. He licked his lips and moaned in approval. I moved to get off him, but he held me there. "Stay right here, please?"

"Am I not hurting you?"

"No," he said quietly. "You're healing me."

LOGAN

She wasn't in bed when I woke up. A panic settled at the pit of my stomach. I kept my eyes shut, not wanting reality to set in, but then I heard movement and her footsteps coming closer. I prayed that this wasn't one of my usual dreams. Last night felt too real. I think I'd die if it wasn't.

I felt the bed dip and her fingertips on my cheeks. Only then did I feel it safe enough to open my eyes. She hovered above me, her hair curtaining her face.

"Hey, handsome," she greeted me. It made me smile like an idiot. Her smile matched mine, and her fingers poked my cheeks. "I missed these dimples."

Pulling her down and under the sheets with me, I whispered in her ear, "I wanted to tell you something last night, but things got a little... um...out of hand?"

She giggled into my chest and wrapped her arms and legs around me, getting as close as she could get. "Yeah? What's that?"

I lifted her face and kissed her on her lips quickly. Once. Twice. A trillion times over. I couldn't get enough. She laughed into my mouth. Then I said it. "Happy three-year anniversary."

"No way!" She pushed against my chest. "You remembered?"

"Of course I remembered." I kissed her again. "How could I forget the day I found my person?"

She wanted to take all the glass vials with her. I didn't argue. They were hers, anyway.

The smell of coffee wafting in from the kitchen convinced her to stay a little while longer. We walked in, hand in hand, just as Dad rushed in to gather his things. He tried to hide his smile, but it was clearly impossible for him.

"Morning," he greeted Amanda and kissed her on the cheek.

"Hands off my woman," I joked.

Amanda laughed. "Woman need coffee from crazy caveman."

Dad chuckled and shook his head as he left the room.

I rubbed my hands together. "Looks like it's just you and me. What ever shall we do?"

She leaned her back on the counter and crossed her arms. "I told you. Your woman needs coffee. Get on it."

"Jeez," I rolled my eyes. "No wonder they call you Demander."

Of course I did what she asked. She still had my balls in her pockets.

After handing her a coffee, I placed my arms on the counter, on either side of her. "I wish we could spend the day together." I sounded like a desperate asshole of the extremely whipped variety, but I didn't care; it was the truth.

She took a sip of her coffee and set it back on the counter and then brought me closer with her arms around my neck. "I know, me too." She sighed. "But I have classes, and then I have to work."

"Tomorrow?"

She grimaced. "Classes and then gym."

"You can't skip gym?" I started kissing her neck. "I'm sure we could find a way to work out together."

She started to laugh, a low build-up from deep in her throat. "I can't. I have self-defense classes."

I pulled back. "So that's how you learned to attack me."

She nodded, grinning as she did.

"Well, I'm glad you can hold your own." I kissed her again. I could kiss her my entire damn life and it wouldn't be enough. "Can I come with you?"

Her eyes widened. "You want to?"

"I'll do anything to spend even a second of my time with you."

She smiled. And it was all I ever wanted.

I kissed her again.

And again.

And then some more.

Over and over.

17

LOGAN

I WALKED OVER to her car when I saw it pull into the gym parking lot. She stepped out, one tanned leg first, then the other. All leg, upon leg, upon leg. It's all I could see. Leg. Then she came to stand. Her gym shorts barely covered her ass. Her tight tank ... I don't even know. Words can't— they don't—

"Hey," she said, her smile huge.

I couldn't speak. All functioning neurons fled my brain and travelled straight to my dick. I didn't even know how I ended up with my body pressed against hers, pushing her into her car and kissing her like she was my oxygen, my water, my food, my goddamn everything.

She laughed into my mouth and tried to pull away.

No.

Just no.

I needed more of her. I'd missed her so much in the day we were apart.

Somehow, I managed to pull her off the car long enough to open the back door and get us both inside.

She laughed again. "Logan, what are you doing?"

"Shh," I told her. My tongue swept into her mouth, and my hand went to her breast. She gripped my wrist and then laughed. Hard. "It's the middle of the day. Control yourself."

I grunted.

She laughed again.

I pounded my chest with my fist. Then in a low caveman voice said, "Me, Logan need his woman. Woman look too damn sexy."

She laughed. But then her eyes darkened. She shifted until she was straddling my waist. I don't think either of us noticed how uncomfortable we were in the tiny space. She ran her top teeth against her bottom lip. Her hand moved down and rubbed my hard-on over my shorts, her fingers curling around it. "Mm," she moaned. "Looks like caveman Logan is happy to see me."

I chewed my lip and nodded. Her hands flattened under my shirt onto my bare stomach. She kissed my neck, moving her tongue in slow circles, so fucking slowly. It made me insane. Her hands went lower, and lower, until they were under the band of my shorts. "I wonder if caveman Logan would be happy to *feel* me."

My dick twitched.

She kissed me once. "Too bad we have to get to that class."

Then she was off me, out of the door and walking toward the gym entrance.

"Blue balls!" I yelled out.

Fuck.

WHEN MY DICK had finally settled down, I went inside the gym. She sat at a table opposite the juice bar with a smug look on her face.

I shook my head at her. She laughed at me.

The guy who was there the day Amanda decided to go kamikaze on my entire body was her instructor. Of course he was.

"Jordan," he said as he shook my hand. I didn't miss his extra-strong grip and his over cockiness as he watched Amanda talking to some girls. "So that's your thing, huh?" he asked, lifting his chin at me. "You get girls' numbers at the gym after pretending they hurt you?"

Fucking. Asshole. "Not at all what happened, but maybe you should watch your mouth."

He let go of my hand so he could raise his arms in surrender. "Buddy," he said. I wasn't his fucking buddy. "It's all good. I'm just messing with you."

And that's what he decided to do for the entire session: mess with me.

"Logan has volunteered to be the attacker," he announced. I hadn't but what-the-fuck ever. I wasn't going to let him win. He watched me with amusement in his eyes and a smug smile that matched Amanda's earlier one.

I squared my shoulders and stood next to him. Amanda grinned at me.

"Who wants to be first defender?" Jordan asked.

All at once, every single girl in the room raised their hands.

Amanda's face changed instantly. It seemed like she simultaneously glared at each of them, one by one. Her glare seemed to intensify when her eyes landed on me and my newly-developed smirk.

One girl stepped forward. She was hot. The Heidi kind of hot. She wasn't Amanda, so she wasn't my type. "I'll go first," she informed. She stood in front of me with her back turned and pressed against me. Then she grabbed my arm and placed it over her shoulder. I chanced a peek at Amanda. Her arms were crossed over her chest, her eyes narrowed to slits.

I couldn't help the grin that took over. "Blue balls," I mouthed at her.

Her eyes widened. She got my message. Payback was a bitch.

For the next twenty minutes, I let girls beat on me, all the while watching Amanda's unamused reaction to it all. It was good times—until it was her turn.

I ended up limping away from the class.

I couldn't be mad. I deserved it.

SHE SAT AT a small table opposite the juice bar while I got us some drinks.

"Hi, Logan." I heard from next to me. "Do you remember me?"

The girl looked familiar, but I couldn't place her. "I'm sorry," I told her. I spent my freshman year screwing around, so it wouldn't surprise me at all if she'd been a one-night stand.

"Kellie," she said, as if that was going to help me. "Kellie I E."

"Oh." Now I got it. "Kellie I E. Sad face emoticon?"

"Huh?" She looked taken aback.

"Nothing."

The guy behind the counter handed us our drinks.

"Shoot," Kellie I E huffed, looking in her bag. "O M G. WTF. I totes don't have my purse. Lol." She slapped her palm against her forehead. "I left it in the car."

I have no idea what the fuck she'd just said, but I handed the guy a twenty and covered her drink.

"Aaaww," she cooed. She had that annoying baby voice I hated so much. "You totes didn't have to do that. Soooo sweet."

"It's no problem." I started to walk away, but she grabbed my arm. "Maybe you could give me your number, and I could pay you back some time."

I looked over her shoulder at Amanda. She was watching but quickly looked down, paying attention to her phone when she caught my eyes.

"Not necessary," I replied, walking away from her.

Amanda stood when I reached the table. She took her drink from my hands and started to lift all her bags. "I gotta go." Her voice was firm.

"What?" I blocked her path. "Is something wrong?"

Loud, shrill giggling filled the room. We both turned to see Kellie I E, Heidi-hot girl and a few others all watching us.

"I don't really feel like being patronized by a bunch of hot mean girls because I'm here with you," she mumbled.

My eyes narrowed at the girls and then at her. "Did they say something to you?"

She shook her head. "They don't need to use words."

Amanda was amazing; she really was. Her confidence and carefree attitude was one of the things that drew me to her, but there was this part of her that seemed to turn into this young, insecure little girl at times like these. I never knew what caused it or why she was like that. I never asked. I should ask.

"I just want to go," she repeated. The girls giggled again. Her lips turned down at the corners.

"Amanda?"

She fixated on the floor. "Yes?"

"Are you jealous?"

She nodded. She looked so damn cute.

The group of girls got up and started walking toward us. She dropped her bags, stepped forward and wrapped her arms tight around me.

My shoulders shook with silent laughter. "What are you doing?"

She didn't look up from the floor. "Bitches need to know you're mine."

I lifted her chin with my finger and let my eyes roam her face. A slow smile formed on my lips. And then I said the words I'd wanted to say, ever since I saw her at that party. "I love you."

Her eyes went huge. "What did you say?"

"Don't act surprised. You know I love you. You know I've always loved you."

She grinned. "Say it again."

"I love you."

"Okay," she breathed out. "Now don't say it until I do."

"Yes, Demander."

The giggling girls got even closer.

"I love you," I yelled, loud and proud.

And then I kissed her.

It wasn't just to prove a point to those girls; it was to prove a point to her. She needed to know that she had nothing to worry about, at all. She was my person. She was it for me. Always.

WE WALKED TO her car, but she didn't get in. Holding both her hands in mine, I asked her, "Are we really doing this? You and me?"

She nodded. "Being amazing, you mean?"

I kissed her again. I couldn't stop fucking kissing her. "Yeah."

She looked down at the ground again. "I want to," she confirmed. "If you do."

I released her hands and held her face instead, making sure she was seeing me, really, truly, seeing me. "I want to. More than anything. You know how I feel."

She removed my hands from her face and placed them on her waist. Her arms curled around my neck, bringing us chest to chest. Heart to heart. "I just—I want to, I really do...but maybe—can we just keep it on the down low for a bit? Just until..." She blew out a breath. "Just until people get used to the idea."

I knew exactly what she was saying. I tried to pull away, but she held me closer. "You mean just until people won't judge you for taking me back?" Saying the words hurt more than her kick in my gut earlier. I knew she'd have some barriers to overcome, and I'd overcome them with her. I wasn't lying when I told her that I'd fight for her. It's the least she deserved.

"Yes," she said quietly.

"I don't like the idea of us sneaking around."

"It's not sneaking around," she said, unconvincingly.

I ignored her and held her in my arms. "Stay with me tonight."

She laughed. "You're not sick of me?"

"Never."

"I have to work."

"Fuck work."

She laughed again.

My head dropped to her shoulder. "I just want to be with you *all* the time." Seriously, someone needs to put an APB out on my balls. She started stroking my hair like I was a scared, sad, lost little kid. Maybe that's exactly what I was.

She kissed the side of my head. "Baby, I have three more days of classes, and then I'm all yours."

I hugged her tighter. "Mine?" I said into her shoulder.

"All yours."

AMANDA

I FINISHED WORK at midnight and waited for Tony to be done so he could walk me to my car. Sitting on the bar stool, I pulled the phone out of my bag and checked the messages.

Unknown number: *I know you're working, and that's fine. But just FYI— I'm up. You know, in case you're not tired and feel like hanging out...*

Unknown number: Or not...

Unknown number: *I mean, you're welcome to come over, regardless of time.*

Unknown number: *Fuck, I'm spamming your inbox. Either way. You don't have to, but the invite is there.*

Unknown number: *Shit. This is Logan.*

Unknown number: *Fuck, ignore all my previous messages. I'm going to sleep.*

Unknown number: *I lied. I'm wide awake. Offer stands*

Unknown number: *Did I say it was Logan?*

I couldn't help the grin that took over my face. He answered first ring. "I know what you're thinking. Maybe a fifteen-year-old girl had stolen my phone and was texting those things to you. I'd love to say it's true, but I'd be lying. Please don't think I'm crazy. I mean I am. Over you. Shit. I just really want to see you. Bad. Wait. Do I sound like Nicholas Sparks?"

My laugh interrupted his rambling. "Logan, stop. Let me just call E and tell him I won't be home ton—"

"Wait." It was his turn to interrupt. "I just invited you to come over." His tone switched to amusement. Cocky, even. "I didn't say anything about spending the night. It's a little presumptuous of you, isn't it?"

"Yeah," I teased back. "Plus, I've kind of triple booked with my other boyfriends. They might get upset."

"Shut up; don't even joke about that," he said playfully, then, in a more serious tone, "Call me when you're nearly here. I'll wait out the front. Don't get out of your car unless I'm there, okay?"

I agreed.

Amanda: *I'm going to a late-night study session at one of the dorms. I'll probably just crash there.*

Ethan: *Is your phone charged? You got mace? Is the building secure? Have you got gas?*

Amanda: *Yes, Dad. I'll be fine. I love you.*

Ethan: *Call me in the morning.*

Ethan: *Please.*

Ethan: *You know I worry about you.*

A knot formed in the pit of my stomach. I hated lying to him. I hated the sneaking around. I stared at my phone, deciding whether or not to call Logan and cancel. It chimed and vibrated in my hand.

Logan: *I'm out front waiting. Can't wait to see you.*

WE WALKED UP the five flights of stairs hand in hand, but we didn't speak. Not until we were in his apartment. He closed the door behind us and checked the four locks at least three times. Then we just stared at each other awkwardly. Kind of like the first time you're alone with a boy and you want to do so many things at once, but the idea of it makes you hold back, and you just stand there and do nothing.

"So." That was him.

This was me. "So."

Smooth, right?

He closed the space between us and loosely linked our fingers together. "How was work?" There was a slight mocking in his tone, as if the question had been asked a thousand times in the past or a thousand times in our future. My chest tightened at the thought. This could be our future.

I tried to hide my smile. His teeth clamped around his bottom lip, doing the same. There was a certain energy around us: excited, anxious, nervous, terrifying. He lifted our hands and placed my palm flat against his heart. It thumped so hard, so fast against my skin. He sighed. "I know I saw you this morning, but shit, I miss you so damn much."

My eyes drifted closed at the same time his lips found mine. I sucked in a quick breath on contact, let my body relax, and let it out in a moan into his mouth.

I felt myself falling. Again.

He released his hold on my hands and placed one on the small of my back, the other in my hair. He deepened the kiss. His tongue brushed against my lips, my teeth, and then my mouth. I gripped onto his shirt. I needed to hold onto something so it would hurt less when my feet landed back on earth.

He pushed me backwards until my back hit the door. He never pulled away from the kiss. Not once. My hands went under his shirt. I needed to *feel* him. My nails dug in when his mouth moved to my neck, kissing and biting gently. I inhaled deeply, needing the air in my lungs as much as I needed *him*.

His hands went to my thighs, bringing my legs up and around his waist while he pinned me to the wall. I didn't stop him. I didn't mind. Not at all. The need in my body caused a buzzing in my brain.

He cupped a breast with one hand and my ass with the other. A deep, guttural moan escaped him, right before his mouth met mine again. These kisses, they were different. They weren't fueled by lust. They weren't demanding. It was passionate, but slow. So slow. As if he were taking me in for the first time. Treasuring me.

Suddenly, he pulled his face away and cursed under his breath. I slowly dropped my legs to the floor while he took a step back and away from me.

"I'm so sorry," he said. "That's not why I asked you over. I lost control. I'm sorry." He shook out his hand.

"Hey." I cooed. "I didn't exactly try to stop you." I placed my hand on his face, but he pulled away.

"I know. It's just—" He blew out a breath. "I just don't want you to think that that's all I want, you know? That's not—I mean—fuck." His eyes shifted, glaring at his shaking hand. He covered it with the other. Agony consumed his features while his chest heaved.

"Logan." I took his trembling hand between both of mine and kissed it a few times. It seemed to help when I'd done it in the past.

His breath becomes steady, and after a few seconds, his hand settled. "What's going on?"

He chewed his lip but refused to look me in the eyes, instead opting to look past me. Then he was off and walking to the kitchen.

I followed.

He pulled out two beers from the fridge and offered me one. I declined, so he exchanged it and handed me a bottle of water. His head tilted back to take a swig, but his eyes focused on me. When he was done, he placed the bottle on the counter, but then dropped his head forward. He rubbed his palm against his jaw. "I just don't want to fuck this up." He said it so quietly, I didn't know if I'd heard right.

I stepped forward so I was right in front of him. His hand went to my waist. "What?"

His eyes lifted to my face, darting around, taking me in. "You know, the time I was gone, I never stopped thinking about you. I knew that coming home would mean maybe running into you. I swear, I hoped you'd just talk to me." He swallowed loudly and shook his head. "I just hoped you'd talk to me, maybe get a meal once or twice. But I never thought—I mean—never in my dreams did I even want to imagine that we could be this." He pointed his finger between us. "I never thought that you'd want *us* again, not after what I did. And now we're here. You're here. And I don't want to fuck it up. I can't, Amanda. I can't fuck this up." His eyes started to glaze over, but he wiped at them before I could grasp what was happening. "You can't let me fuck this up, Amanda. Please." He was pleading with me. Begging.

And then I felt a tear drop on my arm. It was mine. I hadn't even known I was crying. I sniffed back my emotions, but he must've heard. "Don't cry," he said, wiping my cheek with his thumb. He kissed me once. "Please don't cry." He kissed me again but didn't pull back. "I can't be the one to keep making you cry."

WE WENT UP to the rooftop; both of us needed some air. He sat on the outdoor sofa with his beer, and I sat on the table in front of him. "I heard you weren't supposed to drink while you were on your meds," I told him. I'd studied the shit out of Xanax, just so I knew what to expect if things ever got really bad.

He smirked and raised an eyebrow at me. "You've been doing your research."

I nodded, trying to keep the stern look on my face. "And research showed that you shouldn't be drinking."

His smile got wider. "Yes, ma'am." He offered me the beer, but I declined. He placed it on the table and then pushed it away. "You don't like beer anymore?"

I shook my head. "No, I don't drink anymore."

"What?" His eyebrows bunched. "At all?"

"Yup." I waited for the questions I knew were coming.

"Why not?"

I had to choose my words carefully. The only person who knew the reason was Alexis, and she couldn't really understand it. She hadn't been there. "I just think that maybe, if I was more clear-headed that night, things might have ended differently."

He sat up now, leaning forward and in between my legs. He still had the same confused look on his face. "What are you talking about?" The words came out low, slow, as if he couldn't comprehend what I was saying.

I shrugged. "I don't know. Sometimes I think if I wasn't so buzzed I'd have had better judgment that night. Maybe it—"

"Amanda." His tone was harsh. Biting. *Final.*

I reared back in surprise, but his arms wrapped around calves, stopping me from going far.

He apologized instantly. "I didn't mean for it to come out like that, but you can't think like that. You can't blame yourself for what happened."

"Why?" I lifted my chin, ready for a fight. "You did."

His eyes widened slightly, probably at my direct approach. We locked eyes for what seemed like forever, until he sighed, and his features relaxed. "Baby," he said quietly, causing my defenses to back off. He pulled me down off the table and onto his lap, straddling him, the way he always wanted me. Moving my hair away from my face, he kissed my nose once. "I want to talk about this stuff, I really do. But not now. Now, I just want to be with you. I want to hold you. I want *us*. Together. Can we just do that? Tomorrow I'll give you all the answers. I'll give you everything." He started playing with my hair but paused mid-stroke, only for a second, before continuing. He remained silent, but I could sense something wasn't right.

"What are you thinking?" I asked him.

"You can't even see me. How do you know I'm thinking?" he replied.

"I don't need to see you to feel you."

He kissed the side of my head but waited a while to speak. "What did Ethan say when you told him you were here?"

I tensed.

He felt it. "You lied?"

I pulled back just enough to look him in the eye. Biting my lip, I nodded once.

He shook his head. "I don't like that."

"I know," I whined. "But what do you want me to do? Don't you think it's better that we just have some time together at least? I mean, how do I know you're not just going to lea—"

My words died in the air when I saw the heartbreak on his face.

"I won't," he whispered. I could tell he was disappointed. With me—or himself—I wasn't sure. "Do you want me to talk to him?" he asked, his voice louder.

I shook my head frantically. "No. Not yet, okay?" I tried to calm the thumping against my chest. The knot in my stomach rose to my throat. I tried to clear it. "Look," I started, "you don't want to talk about what happened that night, and I don't want to tell Ethan. You have your reasons. I have mine. Let's just agree to leave it alone for now, okay?"

He held me tighter. "We got a lot of shit to work through."

"Yeah," I agreed. "But once we do, we're going to be amazing." I felt his smile against my face.

I FLOATED DOWN onto a soft surface.

"Shh," he said. "You fell asleep."

"Logan?" I whispered.

"Yeah, baby. I'm here."

"You're here," I repeated his words.

He was here, with me.

It wasn't a dream.

Not this time.

19

LOGAN

SHE'S COMING OVER today. It's the first day of summer break for her, which means she's all mine. Her words, not mine. I'm not really a caveman. Much.

We hadn't seen each other since the night she fell asleep in my arms up on the roof. I can't even count the amount of times I dreamed about that exact thing when I was away. And now—it was happening.

We were as honest as I think we could be. We knew there were situations to overcome, issues we had to deal with, things to talk about. We weren't dumb. We weren't naïve. Sooner rather than later, we'd have to face them. But right now, we just wanted each other. Maybe we needed each other, like air.

Logan: *Hurry up and get your ass over here.*

Amanda: *I just pulled up.*

I ran down the stairs so fast, I almost twisted my ankle on the final landing. I slowed down just before I opened the door to outside. It wasn't like I was some pathetic asshole who'd been waiting all day just to see her or hold her hand or kiss her. Nope. Not me. *At all.*

Her smile widened when she saw me. She was a good twenty feet away, but the distance between us was too much, and she must've felt it, too. Her pace picked up as she started toward me. It was just like in the fucking movies when she jumped up and wrapped her legs around me. I caught her and spun us around. "We're so lame," I told her, half-laughing.

"Shut up. You're ruining the moment. Keep spinning," she demanded.

"You're going to get dizzy and throw up."

"Am not."

I spun twice more before she made me stop; she said she felt sick and dizzy.

I wanted to say, 'I told you so' but I left it alone. I was just happy to see her.

"Did you miss me?" she asked.

"You have no fucking idea."

I walked us to my shitty old truck and opened the door for her.

Her nose scrunched in disgust. "This is yours?"

I couldn't tell if she was serious or not. Squaring my shoulders, I said, "Yeah. So what?"

She lifted her shoulders dramatically with her nose up in the air. "Nothing, I guess." She was teasing me. "I'm just used to dating guys with expensive cars."

I picked her up and threw her on the bench seat of the truck. "Whoever you dated before is an asshole," I told her, getting into the driver's seat. "You should tell him that."

NINE. FUCKING. HOURS.

That's how long it took to buy furniture at Ikea and set it up in the apartment. She made me buy a bed for the bedroom. I told her I probably wouldn't use it. She understood but said I should have one anyway.

By the time it was all done, we were exhausted. "Let's order take-out and go to bed," she suggested.

"Sounds perfect."

It really did.

A half hour later, the food arrived, and we sat at my new dining table to eat. She placed her feet on my lap and pointed her fork at me. "Tell me more about Doctors Without Borders," she said.

I smiled at her. We hadn't talked about why I'd left yet, and she hadn't asked. It was almost as if she didn't want to know, or maybe she knew already and didn't want to bring it up. Maybe she'd moved on, and like me, just wanted to be together. I knew it was bad, living our lives like this, in our little bubble, far away from anyone that could take us away from each other. Soon enough, something would cause it to burst.

But it'd only been a week. Surely we had time.

I started telling her all about my time in Africa, then thought I'd do one better. I walked over and picked up my journal. I emptied the content from the pages. Dozens of pictures fell out. I started sorting them so I could show her, but her eyes were fixated on the book. I cleared my throat; her gaze lifted and focused on me. "It's my journal," I told her.

Her eyes narrowed slightly. "Oh."

I weighed up the options of my next words in my head, but nothing seemed to be able to stop the sentence forming. "You should read it, maybe—"

"Oh no," she interrupted. "It's personal. I can't do—"

"Nothing's personal. Not when it comes to you and me. I don't want to keep secrets from you. You want to know about my time away—it's all there. You read it, or you don't. It's up to you. But I want to lay it all out for you. Maybe it'll help you understand some of it."

She nodded, took the journal in her hands and slowly flipped through the pages. A single picture fell out. It was beyond worn but still visible. She picked it up carefully, like it was an antique and might disintegrate it her fingers. "What's this? How?"

"That one phone call I made to Jake, I asked him to send it to me."

She inhaled deeply, her chest rising with the motion.

"It kind of saved me." Truth.

"What do you mean?"

"Read it." I got up and started clearing the table.

When I'd finished cleaning, she was still fixated on the picture.

"Babe." I tried to get her attention.

Her head lifted. "Huh?" she said, but her mind was elsewhere.

"You're staying, right?"

She nodded and got off the chair, placing the picture carefully on the table. I walked to the sofa to convert it to the bed, but she pulled on my hand to stop me. "What's up?" I asked, turning to face her.

She looked uneasy. "Um. Maybe you—or we—maybe we could try the bedroom. I mean, you don't have to...but I thought—if it doesn't work we can just come out here, right? Or not. We don't have to." Her words came out shaky. She was nervous. "I don't want to push you, Logan. I just..." She shrugged. "I want to help you."

My eyes shut tight. I wanted to rewind time and unhear her words. It was the last thing I wanted.

Maybe because it came from her. Or it was just my damn pride. I opened my eyes and stared her down. "You think I need help?" I yanked my hand out of her hold. "I don't fucking need help." I turned and started adjusting the sofa.

"Stop it!" she almost yelled. "I knew you'd get like this." She moved so she was in my way. I tried to ignore her and the aching in my chest. "Logan!"

I straightened to full height. "What? What the fuck do you want from me? You think I need saving? Fine. You can save me from the comfort and safety of your own damn bed."

She pushed hard against my chest. "Quit it," she bit out. "Don't fucking talk to me like that. I don't fucking deserve it, and you know that. You want to treat me like shit? Go ahead. It's not like I expected anything more from you anyway!" She was crying. Fuck. She pushed me again to get me to move out of her way. The aching in my chest got worse. My heart pounded against my ribs. I was expecting it to explode out of there at any second.

"Move!" she yelled it so loudly, I swear the neighbors could hear.

I gripped her wrists and pulled her closer, then wrapped my arms around her. "I'm so fucking sorry, Amanda. Please," I said. "I'm fucking up, again. I can't lose you. Please." And then it hit me. "You're right," I told her. "I need you. I need your help. I'm sorry. Just please, please be patient. Please." I was begging, but it was all truth.

I felt her shake her head against my chest. "I know things are hard for you, and I shouldn't push it, but I'm not your enemy."

"I know. You didn't push anything. You didn't do anything. I'm just an asshole."

I walked us over to the front door, hand in hand, while I triple-checked the locks. She wiped her face on my arm; I felt the wetness from her tears. Sighing, I faced her. "I really am sorry, baby. I don't ever want to be like that with you. Swear it. I don't ... I don't even know how to explain what just happened, but I hate that it did."

"I know. I forgive you."

"You shouldn't."

"I do."

"I got you something."

"A present?" Her eyes lit up, and any sign that she was upset only minutes ago had disappeared.

"Yup."

"Gimme."

I laughed and led her to the bathroom. Opening the cupboard under the counter, I handed her a toothbrush. She laughed the instant she saw it. "Hello Kitty?"

"Yup." I kissed her on the forehead. "Just for you."

"Aww," she cooed, holding the toothbrush to her chest and faking dreaminess in her voice. "You're the bestest boyfriend ever."

SHE LEFT THE bedroom and came back seconds later with the journal. She set it on her nightstand, walked to my dresser and started opening and closing all the drawers until she found what she was after. I watched her remove her jeans, then her shirt. I tried not to jump her when she stood in nothing but her bra and panties. She pulled out an old baseball jersey and shrugged it on. I walked over to her, wanting to touch her, just a little. "I missed seeing you in this." I curled my arm around her waist and brought her as close as she could get.

"Not as much as I missed wearing it."

I grinned from ear to ear. "I love you."

Her eyes drifted shut. "Stop it. You're not supposed to say it until I do."

I shrugged. "Too bad. You deserved that one."

She pulled back and walked to the bed, undoing her bra at the same time.

I gazed at her, then at the bedroom door. Panic set in. She must've noticed because she said, "I always sleep with the door open. If that's okay with you?"

I turned off the lights and got into bed. She pressed her body against mine. Our limbs were a tangled mess. "Good night, pretty girl."

AMANDA

HE FELL ASLEEP almost instantly. I freed myself from his hold, turned on my night light, picked up his journal and flipped to the first page.

Five weeks post-Amanda.

There are no dates here. Only time passing with each moment.

Dear Diary—says the twelve-year-old girl in me.

Manny, one of the guys in the field with me, told me I was depressed...

LOGAN

IT TOOK ME a while to work out what the sound was; she was sniffing, sobbing quietly. I'd fallen into such a deep sleep that it took longer than I'd hoped to get even one eye open, but when I finally did, I kind of wished I hadn't.

She was sitting up in bed with her knees to her chest and my journal resting on them. Her hand covered her mouth while tears streamed down her face. I wasn't sure what part she was up to, so I did what I thought was best: I closed my eyes and pretended to sleep through it. I wanted her to have this moment—the time to read what she wanted, learn what she needed, and accept what had been done. Still, it took everything in me not to reach over and comfort her somehow.

I don't know how long I lay there, listening to her laugh, sigh and sob. I heard the pages turn, almost like clockwork, every few minutes. Eventually, I heard the slapping of heavy pages as the book closed. Her weight shifted on the bed, the covers moved, and the warmth of her body enveloped me.

"Logan," she whispered.

I pretended to ignore her.

I felt her breath against my lips. She must have been close. "I love you so much, Logan."

My eyes snapped open. Her smile grew. "What?" I croaked out, my voice scratchy from sleep.

She nodded slowly. "You heard me. I love you, so damn much." She moved closer until we were chest to chest.

It was like that day—the dream—her words. She must've read it. She must've known what those words would mean to me. "Yeah?" My voice broke. "You're not just saying that bec—"

She shook her head, interrupting me. "I'm saying it because you never let me say it before. I'm saying it because I've wanted to say it ever since you took me to that bookstore. I've wanted to tell you since you got me this." She pulled out a gold chain from around her neck and showed me the vial. "When you kissed me out there in the pouring rain and told me that we'd make new memories. You took something that I was afraid of and turned it into something amazing. That's what you are to me, Logan. Amazing. I want you to know that, and if it means telling you that I love you over and over and over, then I will. I love you so much, Logan." She kissed me once. "I love you." Another kiss. "I love you." Another kiss, deeper this time. "I love you."

"Stop," I told her. "You're going to waste them."

She pulled back. "I can't waste them, Logan. You're my person. I'll never run out of loves for you. Ever."

20

LOGAN

THE SUN WAS coming up by the time we'd decided to go back to sleep. She'd asked her million questions, like I'd known she would. I answered everything as truthfully as possible.

Some things were harder than others. Amuhda was a hard one to try to talk about, but she held my hand and helped me through it. The only thing that wasn't serious was when she got to Rebekah. "You swear you guys didn't do anything? She just kissed you, right? And you stopped it immediately, right?" she'd asked, pacing around the room. "Swear it," I'd assured her.

"You don't have to lie to me," she'd said, almost like a warning. It made me laugh. That made her pissed. Her eyes thinned to slits as she clipped, "I don't care, Logan. It's not like you and I were...you know...whatever!" She threw her hands in the air. She got so flustered and so annoyed at my laughing at her that I couldn't help laughing harder. Typical asshole boyfriend move.

Then it was my turn to question what she'd done with other guys while I was gone. I'd been trying hard not to bring it up. A part of me wanted to know, and another part of me felt too sick at the thought. Actually knowing, mentally being able to picture it, I think I'd puke. When she promised me she hadn't even touched another guy and no hands had been on her...I lost it for a little bit.

We fooled around for so long, I swear my dick was about to snap off. We got to the point of me almost being inside her before I stopped it. We both agreed that we wanted to wait. Neither of us really knew why; we just wanted to take it slow, savor it.

Now, there was an incessant, loud banging at the front door. We both shot up and out of the bed quickly. She pulled my jersey down over her thighs, a panicked look on her face. "W...what's happening?" She moved closer to me.

I pulled on sweatpants as she made her way over. "I don't know." My heart thundered frantically against my chest. I hadn't been this scared since I was seven.

She hugged my arm tightly, and I turned to face her.

She flinched when the banging started up again.

"It'll be okay." I tried to keep my voice even, but I failed. "You need to stay here, okay?"

"No," she whined, gripping my arm tighter.

"Babe, come on."

I freed my arm from her grip, opened the drawer in the nightstand, and pulled out the handgun.

I heard her gasp.

I tried to soothe her. "It's just..."

She shook her head, her eyes never leaving the gun in my hand. "I get it."

I covered the few steps between us, ignoring the banging, not just at the front door but in my chest and in my head. I kissed her once. "It's probably just my neighbors, it's fine," I lied. It wasn't them; they knew better. They'd done it once and had me answer the door with a gun in my hand. Never again.

She returned my kiss. "I love you."

I wanted to tell her I loved her, too, but the banging started again. "You *have* to stay here. No matter what you hear, okay? If you think you need to, call the cops."

With each step toward the front door, my feet felt heavier. By the time I was there, they were lead. The trembling in my hand against my leg caused the gun to sway from side to side.

Thump. Thump.

The blood rushed to my ears.

Thump. Thump.

I looked through the peephole.

Assholes.

I opened the door.

"I swear it, I tried not to tell him, but he knew I was keeping secrets. I don't like to keep secrets, Logan."

Cameron stepped in. "You asshole." Then he saw the gun in my hand and took a step back. "Shit, dude."

After my mind and body had caught up to each other, I placed the gun on the new entry table next to the door.

"Shit," Cam said again. "Sorry, man. The loud knocking and—" He cursed under his breath. "I didn't even think." He put his fist out to bump.

I did, but I couldn't speak yet. My heart was still racing. I walked to the kitchen for a drink. They followed.

"I'm sorry," Lucy squeaked, as I ran the water to fill my glass. I drank like my life depended on it. They watched in silence.

"It's fine," I finally said. "Just don't do that shit again."

"Seriously," Cam started. "We were at this barbecue on campus and Lucy started drinking, then she told me about how you were going to fight for—" He cut himself off, conscious of the fact that I may not want to hear her name. "Anyway," he continued. "I got it out of her that you were back and then she spilled. I just had to come see it for myself. Honestly, I'm a little pissed you both kept it a secret. If I was an asshole, I'd probably accuse you two of screwing around."

Lucy started to giggle. Then hiccupped. Then giggled some more.

"She's drunk," he informed me. "It's good to see you. You're good?"

"Yeah, man," I started for the living room. "I'm good." I threw my body onto the sofa the same time as Lucy opened the curtains. The room filled with sunlight. I squinted at the sudden change.

"Dude, were you asleep? It's, like, three in afternoon. You look like shit." Cam. So observant.

"Logan?" We all paused and looked to the hallway when we heard her tiny voice.

Both their heads whipped to me. "You have a girl in here?" Lucy all but shouted.

Cameron grinned like the Cheshire cat. "Yeah, you do!" He stepped closer and raised his hand for a high five. I sat up, rolled my eyes, and gave him what he wanted.

"Logan?" Amanda said again, louder this time.

Lucy's eyes went huge. "Who is it?" She was still yelling. Standing next to Cameron, she got on her toes and whispered in his ear, "Logan has a girl in here."

Cam shook his head, his eye-roll matching mine from only seconds earlier. "I know, babe, I'm right here."

"Who is it?" she asked him.

He sighed but didn't answer.

I chuckled to myself and yelled, "Babe, you can come out." Then a second later, "Put pants on."

Cam grinned again. "You mad dog." He was amused. I'm glad someone was.

Amanda walked in wearing a pair of my sweats and my baseball jersey.

Lucy gasped loudly when she saw her. It made Amanda stop in her tracks. Lucy's gaze went from Amanda to me to Cameron. "Is she real life?" she asked Cameron.

"Yes, babe. She's real." He patted her on the head.

Lucy slowly took steps closer to Amanda, as if she were a wounded animal and Lucy was her savior. Amanda's eyebrows bunched as she watched Lucy slowly approach. Cam sat down next to me, but both of us watched the girls. Then, when Lucy got close enough, she poked Amanda on the arm. Amanda flinched but stayed silent. Lucy hiccupped and then narrowed her eyes. "Are you real life?" she whispered.

Amanda smiled, but it didn't reach her eyes.

Lucy yelled, "You are real!" Then she hugged the shit out of her. "Oh my God," she said, pulling back. She touched Amanda's face with both hands. "I've missed you." Hiccup.

Then Cameron from next to me, "You guys should totally make out. That would be hot."

Amanda and Lucy snorted in unison, then walked toward the sofa. Amanda sat on the other side of me, grabbing my arm and placing it around her shoulders.

"Ooooooooooohhhhhhhhhh," Lucy crooned, looking around the apartment. "Now it makes sense. You have actual furniture."

Amanda rubbed her nose on my bare chest. I still hadn't put a shirt on. "Are you okay?" I spoke into her ear.

She smiled at me, but it was forced. I lifted her chin so I could look at her properly. She still looked scared.

"We're gonna jet," Cam announced, standing up. "I just wanted to see you with my own eyes."

I stood, too, thankful he knew well enough to leave us alone. I walked them to the door.

"Look," Cameron started. "I get that you want to lay low or whatever, but Jake doesn't even know you're here. And I mean—I don't want to tell you what to do or whatever, but if I were him, I'd be pissed if I found out you were here and didn't even bother telling your best friend. I just think it's gonna get worse with time, you know?" He ran his hand through his hair. "And you know Jake. He doesn't get pissed. He freezes you out, and that shit's not cool."

He was right. Jake didn't do openly angry or pissed often, but you knew if you'd upset him.

I nodded.

"Oh, I know," Lucy screeched. "My bonfire tomorrow night. Come! At the cabin, like old times! Remember, Logan? Remember?"

Cam cut in. "Okay, Drunky McDrunkface. Time to get you home. Let's leave Logan and Amanda alone, all right?" He picked her up and threw her over his shoulder. Then to me, "It's not a bad idea—the cabin tomorrow night. You guys should come. It'll be a welcome home, you know?"

"Maybe," I answered.

"I mean it, Logan; it's really good to see you." His tone was serious. He looked over at Amanda, who was still on the sofa. "You too, Amanda. I'm glad you're both *safe.*"

"I SHOULD GET home," she said.

I sat down next to her. "Why? You don't have to leave." I laid down and pulled her body on top of mine.

"I just need to. Ethan will start to get worried."

Stroking her back, I let out a sigh. "You should just tell him you're here."

She was quiet for a moment and then said, "You're not the only one who has things to overcome, Logan."

I don't know what she meant, but whatever it was, I wasn't going to push her. She got off me and walked away. A second later, I heard the shower running.

I waited, watching the trembling in my hand slowly steady itself, and then I got up and made my way to the bathroom, too.

"I think I should talk to Ethan," I said, loud enough so she could hear me over the sound of the shower.

The pipes made a clanking sound as the water turned off. "Towel." Her hand was out, waiting.

I handed her one. "Maybe it won't be so bad. Maybe you're exaggerating it—I don't know—maybe if I talk to him it'd be okay."

She stepped out with her hair tied up messily, the towel around her, and an annoyed look on her face. "A. I'm not exaggerating. B. It won't be okay. C. Trust me. I know Ethan."

"Fine." I looked down at the floor. It felt like a rejection.

I heard her sigh. Her feet invaded my vision. She stood inches in front of me. "Are you mad that we're lying to Ethan, or are you sad that I'm leaving?"

"Both," I answered quietly, still staring at the floor.

"Which one more?"

"The second," I sulked.

She laughed quietly before wrapping her arms around me. She brought my head down to her chest. "I'm going to miss you," she admitted.

"Then don't go yet."

"You're going to get sick of me quick."

"Not possible."

She made a humming sound when I hugged her tight.

And that's how we stayed.

Seconds turned into minutes.

"I was so scared, Logan."

I wanted to assure her that it would be okay. I even opened my mouth to let the words out, but they died in my throat, along with my pride. Instead, I looked her in the eyes—truth time. "So was I."

21

AMANDA

I DIDN'T WANT to leave him, but I didn't want us to suffocate each other, either. We'd spent so much time together already, and it'd only been days since we were back in each other's lives.

It wasn't just about spending too much time with him. It was also about Ethan. The fact that I was lying to him was bad enough; I didn't want to give him more reason to worry. And he did. He worried way more than he should.

Which is probably why he was sitting on the edge of my bed, staring at his phone when I got home.

"Hey," I said quietly, taking a seat next to him.

He sucked in a breath and let it out in a huff. "Hey," he responded, lifting his head to face me. "Where have you been?"

I shrugged and faked a calmness to my tone. Deep down, I was wrecked with guilt. "Just out with friends."

He nodded.

"I'm sorry. Were you worried?"

"A little."

"You could've called. I would have told you where I was."

He sighed and looked back down at his phone. "Yeah, I know. I just feel like I need to give you some space, you know?"

I didn't respond. I just let the silence fill the space between us.

"Actually," he said, "I wanted to talk to you about something real quick." He flung his body back on the bed and covered his face with his hands. Classic nervous Ethan. He did that to hide the redness in his face when he said or did something that embarrassed him.

"This'll be good," I teased and then copied his position on the bed. "Out with it."

He removed his hands from his face but continued to stare up at the ceiling. "I want to ask Alexis to move in."

"What!" I sat up, paying full attention.

He laughed once. "So I take it she hasn't brought it up with you?"

I shook my head, a disbelieving laugh bubbling out of me. "No, not at all."

He cursed under his breath. "It's probably too soon, huh?" He almost looked sad.

"No," I said truthfully. "I don't know. Maybe it is too soon, but who gives a shit, right?" I smiled, remembering how I'd felt the first time I said those words to Logan.

He faced me now. He was so serious. "You think she'd say yes?" His knee started bouncing. He was stupidly nervous.

"I think she'd—"

"I've looked around for jobs and stuff for her," he cut in. A grin slowly developed on my face. "She doesn't want to go to college, so she'd just have to work. I mean—I can probably take up a few more shifts and support her, but I don't think she'd be into that. Do you think she'd be into that?" he mumbled, his words coming out all at once.

Then it hit me. "Ethan, calm down. You're just *in love* for the first time. Don't question it. Just let it be. She loves you, too. She'll say yes." I stood up to use the bathroom, but his grip on my arm stopped me.

"Honestly, Dimmy. Do you think she would? Because I'm not going to ask her and get rejected. I don't know if I could take it."

I turned around and laughed at him. I couldn't help it. "You're so desperate and cute."

He reared back in surprise. "Shut up! Only Lexie gets to call me cute." I started to walk away, but he caught me again. "Promise me she'll say yes," he demanded.

I rolled my eyes. "I promise she'll say yes."

"Spit-swear on it."

"What? No! Gross. What's wrong with you?"

I tried to get to the bathroom, but he swiftly blocked my path. "Spit-swear," he said again, trying to contain his laugh. He spat on his palm and held it out.

"Yuck, Ethan. That's disgusting."

I tried to get past, but he blocked me again. "Do it!" He waved his spit-filled hand in front of my face. I started dry-heaving. Pushing him out of the way, I tried again to get past. He continued to block my path. His shoulders lifted with his laugh.

Then he did it.

He smeared his hand across my face.

"You asshole!" I squealed, but you couldn't hear me over the sound of his laughter.

I squared my shoulders and narrowed my eyes at him. He understood. "Oh shit," he muttered, his features evening out.

I raised an eyebrow. "Game. On."

"Fuck." He bolted, jumping over the bed and running out of my bedroom.

I chased him, but somehow I started laughing, too. He ran down the hallway and straight into Tristan. "Whoa," Tris said, lifting his hands to block me. Ethan hid behind him. Coward.

I tried to pass him to get to Ethan but he, too, blocked me. "What the fuck is going on right now?" he scolded. "This is just like the Epic Missing Cookie Battle of 2003." He was laughing, too. We all were. "By the way," he continued. "I totally ate that cookie."

Ethan and I stopped laughing immediately. Shit just got real. "What?" we both asked.

His laugh became silent when he saw how serious we were. We blamed each other about that missing cookie for a good five months and froze each other out completely. Meals with two non-speaking twelve-year-olds were not good times. "You ate it?" Ethan deadpanned.

Tristan swallowed loudly, looking from Ethan to me and back again. He nodded once, his eyes wide. "Yes."

"Swear it?" Ethan asked him.

He nodded.

"Spit-swear it?" I said.

"What?" He scrunched his nose.

Then in unison, Ethan and I spat on our hands and offered it to him. "Do it," we both insisted.

Tristan's face contorted to a look of disgust. "No. Fucking. Way."

Ethan's eyes met mine. "Game on," I announced, lifting my chin.

Then, simultaneously, Ethan and I wiped our hands across his cheeks.

He squealed. Not a manly one, either. Ethan's head threw back with the guffaw that took over him. "You sound gay," he yelled.

Tristan wiped his cheeks with his sleeves. "I *am* gay, asshole."

"Soooo," TRISTAN MOCKED in a high-pitched girl voice. "Who's the boy?"

He'd walked in just as I opened the bathroom door after I'd finished showering and frantically scrubbing my face of Ethan's spit. His question made me stop in my tracks. For a moment, I wanted to tell him all about Logan. Instead, I lied. "I don't know what you're talking about."

"Bullshit," he said calmly, taking a seat on my bed. "I know you too well, Dim. Who is he?" He smiled eagerly, waiting for my response.

I couldn't lie. I'd been doing it too much already. Slowly shutting my door, I faced him. "You can't say anything to anyone, Tris. Swear it."

He laughed. "As fun as it was to pretend we were kids just then, we're not. We're grown-ass people. I don't need to swear on anything. You know you can trust me."

"Fine." I paused, thinking of my next words. I felt the corners of my lips turn up, and before I knew it, I was grinning.

Tristan sighed. "How long's he been back?"

My eyes went wide. "What? How do you know?"

"I'm not an idiot. You shutting the door, keeping secrets, that goofy look on your damn face." He blew out a breath. "I take it Ethan doesn't know?"

I shook my head slowly. The guilt slowly developed into a knot in the pit of my stomach.

He made a frustrated noise as he rubbed his face with his hands. "This is not going to end well, Dim. Especially with you keeping it from him."

"I know," I said quickly. I sat on the bed next to him and did my best to persuade otherwise. "It's complicated, Tristan. We know we have stuff to overcome and issues to deal with, but we just want some time. We just want to be together without the world judging us. We just want to be happy, even if it's for a little while." I felt the sob rising up my throat and swallowed it down. I hated this. I hated thinking about what might happen. Not even about when we went public, just Ethan's reaction. He was the only one who mattered to me. "I know it's hard to understand—"

"Wait," he cut in. "You do realize I'm gay, right?" He laughed once. "If anyone knows what it's like to be afraid of judgment, it's me."

"Valid," I agreed.

"Dim, there's a reason I came out to you first."

"Yeah? What's that?"

"Because. You don't judge, you don't ask questions, you just accept things for what they are. You accept people for *who* they are, regardless of who they *love*. You understand that you can't help who you fall in love with.

"I think, deep down, Ethan's the same. But it goes both ways, Dim. You can't help being in love with Logan, just as much as Ethan can't help loving you. And either way you look at it, you and Ethan—you're both trying to protect the people you love."

LOGAN

A STUPID GRIN took over my face. I couldn't stop it, even if you paid me. Placing the phone to my ear, I said, "Hey, pretty girl." I'd been on the roof for twenty minutes, contemplating whether or not I should call her. I knew she said we should spend some time apart. I didn't get it. That's not what I wanted at all. She thought I was going to get sick of her. As if that was possible. Luckily, I didn't have to call—seemed like she was the first to break.

"Hey yourself," she replied. "I'm sorry for calling."

"You never have to apologize for that."

She sighed. "What are you doing?"

"Honestly?"

"No, lie to me."

I chuckled under my breath. "I'm sitting on the roof thinking about how much I miss you."

"It's only been a few hours." She sounded sad.

I tried to lighten the mood. "Hey, you called me, remember?"

"Yeah," she said softly. Something was wrong.

"What's going on, Amanda?"

She sighed again. "I don't know. What are we doing?"

My heart started to pick up pace. "What do you mean?"

Another fucking sigh. "I mean—what are we doing? You and me. Us. Together?"

My heart sank. I wanted to slap myself for believing that things could be so simple with us. I sat down, my knees too weak to hold myself up, my head lowered. It was my turn to sigh. "Baby, I don't know what you're saying, but if you don't want to be with me, just say so."

It was quiet for so long I thought for sure she'd hung up, but then I heard her intake of breath. "I don't think it's a good idea that we keep sneaking around. I just have a feeling it's going to blow up in our faces, you know? I want to be with you, like, *all* the time, and I feel like there's this knot in my gut whenever we do it—guilt or something—and I shouldn't feel like that. I shouldn't feel guilty for wanting to be with the person I love."

The tension in my shoulders disappeared. "So you're not breaking up with me?"

"What?" A quiet laugh escaped her. "Not at all." I blew out a breath, relieved. She must have sensed it. "I'm sorry, babe. I didn't mean to scare you," she assured.

"It's fine." I wiped my sweaty palms against my shorts. "Actually, I wanted to talk to you about that. I think I want to go to Lucy's bonfire thing tomorrow. I mean—Cam's right. It's just going to get worse with time. Band-Aid effect, right? Just rip it right off?"

I heard movement from her end, like she was shifting around in her bed. "That's good. I think that's a good idea."

"Obviously you'd be coming with me." I assumed she would, but I'd never asked. "If you want to, I mean."

I could hear the smile in her answer. "Yeah, that sounds perfect."

"Yeah," I agreed. "So, it normally starts around six-ish. I guess if we take into account the two-hour drive there, that means you should get here...say...as soon as you wake up in the morning?"

She snorted with laughter. It made me smile into the phone. "What are you doing, pretty girl?"

She sighed again, differently this time. "Lying in bed, missing the shit out of you."

"Yeah?" I smirked to myself. "What are you wearing?"

22

AMANDA

WE FELL ASLEEP on the phone to each other. It was close to four in the morning. He told me I should've just stayed there; he was right.

I decided to call before I knocked, just in case it freaked him out. But he didn't answer; instead, it was a girl's voice on the other end. My stomach dropped. I held the phone tighter. "Hello?" she said. I hung up. What was I supposed to say? I wanted to leave, run out of there, but my feet were lead, glued to the floor. Then his door swung open, and there he was. No shirt, sweatpants hung low on his hips and the band of his boxers peeking through. He had that perfect V, you know, the one that drives women crazy. His abs. His stupid abs. When I finally got to his face, he had a twinkle in his eye and an amused smirk. I wanted to lick him and punch him all at the same time. Apparently that was the general consensus when it came to my dealings with Logan Matthews.

"What are you doing here?" he asked through his now-huge grin.

I raised an eyebrow.

"This is a nice surprise," he said, opening the door wider, right about the same time Blonde Dreadlock Barbie exited, her hair wet, dressed in a skirt-suit. "Hey, Amanda," she greeted me, brushing past and giggling. "I'm sorry I answered your call. I had his phone looking up the bus schedule. I didn't even think." She was too perky for this early in the morning. Or maybe I was just grumpy. Or both.

Logan laughed.

Fucking laughed.

He waited for me to enter before closing the door behind him. Leaning back against it, he eyed me. He opened his mouth to speak, but a chuckle came out instead. He shook his head. "You're so damn cute when you're jealous. I can't even handle it right now." He took the steps to cover the space between us and then wrapped one arm around my waist, bringing me closer to him. He placed his thumb between my eyebrows and smoothed out the creases. "You're pouting," he said, kissing me once. "And you're crazy."

My eyes narrowed at him.

Sighing dramatically, he picked me up and flung me over his shoulder. He walked us to his bedroom, placed me down on the edge of the bed, pulled out a jersey from his dresser and came back. Kneeling in front of me so we were eye to eye, he spoke. "You're crazy to think that I'd ever want any other girl, ever. Their water got cut off this morning; she came in for a shower before work. That's all. Swear it."

I nodded but stayed quiet. Truth? Once I'd let the initial shock of him having some random girl in his apartment sink in, I knew there'd be a valid explanation.

"You're still pouting," he said. I didn't know I was. He sighed again, softer this time. "Are you being grumpy because you didn't get enough sleep?"

He knew me too damn well. I nodded again. He chuckled lightly under his breath. "Let's get you to sleep then, pretty girl." He pulled me by my arms until I was standing and then slowly unbuttoned my jeans and slid them past my hips until they were down to my ankles. He didn't wait for me to kick them off before he started removing my top. He let it drop to the floor before raking his eyes all over my body, slowly, so fucking slowly, from head to toe.

I swear, time stood still. I closed my eyes and balled my fists at my sides. I did everything I could to not cover myself. I wanted to give him this moment, give him time to remember me, just like he said in the closet of his dad's house.

He blew out a breath. My eyes snapped open. He was no longer there. But then I felt his arm snake around my bare stomach, pulling me down until I was sitting on his lap. I could feel his hardness against my ass. He started kissing my back, his lips soft. He nibbled lightly on my bare shoulder before moving up to my neck. My nipples ached against my bra. I wanted it off, but he beat me to it, the material falling down my arms and onto the floor in front me.

I moved on him, my ass grinding against him. He cursed when his fingers brushed against my nipple. They were stiff with arousal. Cut-through-glass type stiff. Just like his dick beneath me. He gently cupped my breast with one hand, and the other moved down my stomach, under my panties. Exactly where I wanted him. He cursed again when his finger ran between the folds, my wetness coating it.

I panted. My mouth was dry. I needed water. Air. *Logan.* I needed Logan. Turning my head and wrapping my arm around his neck, I brought his mouth to mine. It was the exact same moment his finger slid deep inside me. Our teeth clanked together with the roughness of our kiss. We were rushed, needy, and desperate for each other.

"Fuck, baby," he moaned into my mouth. Then he pressed up against me, just once, but it was all I needed to lose control. I started grinding harder into him. His thrusts became faster. I wanted more. I wanted him. *All of him.*

I released his neck and shifted my hands to the band of his boxers and sweats.

"Stop." He pulled away, cursed again, and then moved me to the side. Standing up, he rubbed both his palms against his jaw. "Fuck," he spat. He eyed me again, that same fire in his eyes from earlier. His jaw was tense, and the muscles kept moving, like he was contemplating something.

Then, it happened. Something in him snapped. A decision was made. He stood between my legs, put two fingers from each hand against my shoulders and slowly, carefully, pushed me until my back was flat on the bed with my legs hanging off the edge. I closed my eyes. My body shook. The idea of what was about to happen was too overwhelming. I was too turned on.

The throbbing between my legs magnified. I felt the warmth of his fingers curl around my panties, and then cold air hit against my warm center. I gazed down over my body to see him at the end of the bed, his palms flat against my thighs, spreading them further for him. I must have made a sound because his eyes snapped to mine. "Do you know how many times I got off thinking about you? Exactly like this."

I sucked in a breath but didn't say a word. I had none. He stood up now, his huge, hard dick tenting his boxers. "No," he said. He was talking to himself. He reached down, grabbed both my hands and placed them on my breasts. I tried to swallow, but my mouth was too dry. He stood between my legs again, his eyes roamed from my spread legs up to my breasts, lingered there, then up to my eyes.

"Squeeze," he whispered softly, but it was an order. It turned me on more. I dropped my head back onto the bed and did what he said. I heard him grunt, right before I *felt* him. My hips jerked at the instant pleasure of his lips on me. His fingers moved inside me, his tongue made laps, back and forth, up and down, in and around. I felt myself building. It was too soon.

Then his fingers slowed, and his mouth was gone. I lifted my head, wanting to see what was happening. His eyes were trained on my hands: one hand squeezing, the other pulling at my nipple. I didn't know I was doing it. I cleared my throat. His eyes locked with mine, only for second, before he went back to business.

Seconds later, it happened. The climb was just as mind-blowing as the fall. He never stopped, not until the last shudder had vibrated through me.

When my body stopped trembling, my mind cleared, and the buzz had faded, I opened my eyes. He was standing again at the edge of the bed with his hand down his pants. My eyes travelled up his body. A sheen of sweat coated him. "Hey." He smirked at me. Then he started to walk away. I sat up and pulled on his pants to stop him. "What's up?" he asked, his eyebrows drawn in.

I dropped to my knees and yanked down his pants and boxers in one swift move. His eyes widened when he worked out what was about to happen.

It didn't take him long at all. When we were done, we showered and brushed our teeth. We climbed back into his bed, naked and exhausted. His arms circled me. "You haven't even said hello to me yet," he said. It's true. I hadn't spoken a single word since I'd gotten here.

23

LOGAN

"OUR SLEEP PATTERN is going to be screwed," I told her. We'd slept until three in the afternoon.

We'd planned to stay overnight at Dad's house after the bonfire. She'd packed an overnight bag, so she'd changed from her jeans and top into a dress. I told her she didn't have to dress up. She said she wanted to, not because she was seeing my friends, but because she was seeing me. I told her I loved her regardless, clothes on or off. We started to make out again but stopped ourselves before it got too far. My dick was still hard. She knew it, too, because her bare feet kept rubbing against it.

We were in my truck, driving to Lucy's cabin. Amanda sat sideways, her long, tanned legs covering the entire bench seat. She chewed her lip with a smirk on her face as she felt my dick get harder and harder. "Stop it," I warned, running my hand up the inside of her thigh. "This can quickly turn into a two-player game."

She squeezed her thighs tight, trapping my hand between them. Giggling, she removed it and sat up straighter. She moved to the middle of the seat, pressed her body against me and maneuvered my arm around her shoulders. "I love you," she said.

You couldn't wipe the grin off my face.

"What?" she asked, watching me.

"Those words—leaving your lips—I don't think I could ever get enough of it."

She kissed my cheek and then moved to my ear. "I love you," she whispered and nibbled gently there, at the same time running her hand over my dick.

I pushed her away. "Quit it," I warned again.

She laughed, that all-consuming, stomach-holding, head-thrown-back laugh. I pulled over, just so I could watch it. Remember it. Savor it. When she finally settled down, she wiped at her eyes.

"Are you done?" I asked. Honestly, I didn't care if she was. I could watch her like that for the rest of my life and it still wouldn't be enough.

She nodded, but then, seriousness took over her features. "Are you nervous, babe?"

I pulled back onto the road. "What do you mean?"

"Seeing your friends again? I mean Jake—he's your best friend. You only called him once. You didn't even tell him you were back. You think he'll be pissed?"

I hadn't even thought about it. "If he is, I'll talk to him. I need to talk to him anyway, tell him all of it, you know?"

She nodded and placed my hand on her leg. "If I were him, I'd just be glad you're here. Back *home*. Where you belong."

Home, I thought to myself. I looked down at her hand, now covering mine. "You're my home," I told her. Truth.

"NO. FUCKING. WAY!" Was Jake's reaction. He basically threw Micky off his lap and stomped toward me. His eyes were huge, almost as big as his grin. He kissed Amanda on the cheek first and then stood in front of me. "Wait," he said, looking around the bonfire. He eyed Cam. "You knew he was back?" He sounded pissed.

Cam grimaced as his shoulders lifted in a shrug. Then Jake's gaze came back to me. "I don't even fucking care; I'm just so glad you're home." We did that one-arm bro-hug-handshake thing. When we pulled apart, he faced Amanda. "Mind if I borrow him for a while?" he asked her.

Amanda shrugged. "He's all yours. I'm kinda sick of him, anyway."

That got laughs.

Jake and I walked near the private dock, closer to Lucy's main house. I couldn't even remember the amount of times we'd come here during summers once she and Cameron had started dating. "Remember that time Cameron did that back flip and smacked his head on the edge?" Jake asked.

"Yeah." I laughed. "Remember how Lucy panicked because we'd all been drinking, and she didn't want to tell her dad?"

Jake laughed, too, and then mimicked Lucy's voice. "If Papa comes out and sees y'all been drinkin' he's gon' whoop your be-hunds, that's if he dun get the shotgun first."

I laughed harder. Jake continued, "Luce always turns into a hick when she's anxious."

"I know, right?"

We waited until our laughter died down before choosing to speak.

"Sorry," we said at the same time.

"What? Why?" Again, both of us at the same time.

He motioned for me to go first, and so I did. "I'm sorry I didn't tell you I was leaving."

"I get it," he responded. "I mean—no, actually, I don't really get it. But I'm sure you have your reasons."

"Jake," I paused, waiting for the right words to come. I wanted him to know that it wasn't personal—me keeping things from him.

"I'm sorry," he said, pulling me from my thoughts. "I'm sorry I was a shitty friend to you all those years."

His words surprised me. "What?"

"Yeah. I should've been around enough to know what was going on with you. We were boys, best friends—well, at least you were to me. I should have paid more attention. Not made shit about me all the time."

"Stop," I said quietly. He didn't need to apologize. He'd done nothing wrong.

"I mean it, man. Seriously, fuck my life. I have a great family, an amazing girlfriend, the major leagues knocking on my door. I have nothing at all in my life to worry about. I've never had to deal with anything. Ever.

"I always just thought you were this cocky asshole, gifted with brains. You never let it show, you know? How hard you worked or the fact that your birth parents used to beat the shit—" He cut himself off with a grimace. Maybe he didn't mean to go that far.

I pulled us away from the awkward silence that would have ensued. "Yeah, my birth parents were assholes, Jake, but that has nothing to do with you or our friendship. It didn't show because I didn't let it. I could've easily told you—told the world. But that's not me, and you know that."

We kept on with the damn stones and the water. We weren't trying to skip anymore. Now, we were just throwing the fuckers in there.

"I dunno, man." He stopped with the stones and turned to me. Removing his cap, he rubbed the back of his head and then replaced it, adjusting it until he was comfortable. "I just think I could've been a better friend. I shouldn't have just left when you didn't answer the door. I should've kept going, kept knocking, and kept coming back until you had no choice but to speak to me. I could've stopped you from leaving. I should have made you stay.

"Instead, I had to hear a week later from your dad that you were gone. I was a shit friend to you, Logan. But not anymore. You need to know that. I don't care where I am or what I'm doing; if you ever need anything from me, tell me. I'm not going to let you disappear again."

I let his words sink in.

Silence filled the space around us.

"I appreciate it, man. I really do. The past is my past, though. I'm done with it. I just want to move on. Move forward."

He nodded once, and a slow smile developed on his face. "With Amanda?"

"Yup."

"How long have you been back?"

"A few weeks."

"Did she know where you were?"

"Nope."

"So you've been back a few weeks, and you already got the girl?"

I smirked at him, the cockiness in me returning. "Well," I puffed out my chest like the dick I was feigning to be. "I'm still Logan Matthews. That shit hasn't changed."

He laughed, shaking his head. "Fuck, I've missed having you around."

AMANDA STOOD UP when I returned to the bonfire; she'd been sitting on an abandoned log with a bottle of water in her hand. She'd told me that her not drinking wasn't a vow of any sort; it just wasn't something she was interested in right now. I respected her decision and never questioned it, even though I disagreed with the reasoning behind it. "Did you miss me?" I asked her, taking her newly-emptied spot and bringing her back down on my lap.

She nodded, the corners of her lips lifting.

"Good," I rubbed my nose along her jaw. "I missed the shit out of you."

Lucy piped up, "Alright, Nicholas Sparks. Leave the girl alone." She lifted a can of beer in the air as an offering.

"It's okay, I'll drive back," Amanda said.

I nodded at Lucy, right before she threw the can right at my head. My catcher reflexes took action. "Holy shit, girl, you got a good arm." I shook out my hand from the pain caused by catching it.

Lucy shrugged. "Jake's been coaching me."

I looked over at Jake, who shrugged. "I needed something to do while you were gone."

Micky laughed. She sat on the ground in front Jake as he rubbed her shoulders. "He kind of went a little crazy without you, Logan. Don't disappear again."

"Yeah, asshole." That was Heidi. It was the first time she'd spoken since we got here.

"Nice to see you, too," I greeted.

She had a beer in her hand, her eyes half-closed. Her head tilted back against the seat.

And then it hit me. No Dylan.

"Where's Dylan?" I asked the group, but my eyes never left Heidi.

She laughed. It was bitter. Kind of like the one Amanda uses. "Afghanistan," she deadpanned.

"What?" I looked around at everyone else. "What's he doing there?"

"Marines," she stated, just as flat.

"Huh." Amanda spoke. Everyone turned to her, even Heidi.

"What do you mean 'huh'?" Heidi asked her. Her tone was cold, icy. Not at all the Heidi I know.

Amanda seemed to shrink into herself. "Just—I mean—he actually decided to go ahead with it." I wanted to ask her what she meant, how she knew this, but Heidi beat me to it. She stood now, her eyes narrowed at Amanda. My arms tightened around her. It was instinct. "You knew?" Heidi spat. "How the fuck—wait—I don't care. You knew, and you didn't stop him?"

Amanda's body tensed, but her words didn't show it. "I'm sorry, Heidi, but I don't know you or Dylan all that well. I just bumped into him once, and he told me he was thinking about it. That's all."

Heidi took a step closer. "So what? You encouraged him?"

"I just listened to him. That's it."

Then Heidi exploded. "He's in fucking Afghanistan! He broke up with me, joined the Marines, and is in fucking Afghanistan! And you knew!" She took another step toward us. Jake and Cameron both stood. "You knew and you just fucking let him go." She was yelling now, her face red with rage.

Amanda tried to stand, but I held her down. Whatever was going on with Heidi, she needed to leave it alone.

Amanda slowly pried my fingers and hands off her so she could get to her feet. She took a few steps forward until she was toe to toe with Heidi, her fists balled at her sides. "I didn't do shit. I told you, all I did was listen to him. You knew where he was, right?" Her voice was calm. Smooth, almost.

Heidi nodded. If she was surprised by Amanda's actions, it didn't show.

"So he told you he was leaving? He told you where he was going? He kept in touch? Told you how he was? Wrote to you?"

Heidi's eyes were huge now, but she nodded again.

"Good." Amanda said. "That's fucking great." Her voice got louder, her initial calmness all but gone. "That's a hell of a lot more than I got from Logan. You at least got to say goodbye. You get to know that he's *safe*." Her voice changed. She was holding back a sob. I stood up and placed a hand on her shoulder, trying to soothe her. She jerked away from my touch. "You get to write to him. Occasionally, get a phone call from him. I got nothing. NOTHING. He could've been dead, and I wouldn't have even known." She wiped her face.

"Amanda." I tried to get her attention. I wanted her to turn her around so I could see her. I wanted her to stop talking. Her words weren't just hurting her or Heidi—they were hurting me, too.

Eventually, she turned around, but she was still pissed. "No, Logan," she ground out. "She got to say goodbye. Her boyfriend—or whatever the fuck he is—is out there, serving our country, doing something he believes in. And he keeps in touch. She can write. He can call. It's so much more than I got. And I won't stand here and be blamed for that shit." She turned around and faced Heidi. "Just be fucking thankful that he loves and cares about you enough to let you know he's safe. Because it's sure as shit a lot more than I fucking got."

Heidi stepped back and wiped at her eyes. I don't know who she was crying for—Amanda or herself.

Amanda turned back to me. "I'm sorry," she said, before brushing past me and walking away. And I just stood there, not knowing what the fuck just happened.

Then I heard Lucy. "Bitch, you best go after your girl. You better fight for her, like you promised. You ain't lettin' her go again. Nuh-uh, I ain't letting that shit happen no more."

Then I felt a full can of beer smack into my stomach. "Oomph," I grunted.

"Fuck, baby," Cam whined. "Quit throwing beers around."

"Go, Logan!" Jake yelled.

It pulled me out of my daze. "Shit!"

24

LOGAN

I FOUND HER sitting in the bed of my truck, her knees up against her chest and her head in between them. Her soft cries filled the night air. I climbed up and sat next to her. I didn't touch her or comfort her. Honestly, I wasn't sure if she was pissed at me or not.

"Hey, pretty girl."

She sniffed once and then lifted her head. Her blue eyes glistened with tears. She wiped at her cheeks. "I'm sorry, Logan."

"What?" I said. "You have no reason to be sorry."

She moved in closer to me and leaned her head against my shoulder. "I shouldn't have let all that stuff come out, especially in front of your friends. I embarrassed you—"

"Babe," I cut her off. "I don't care about my friends or what they think. I just care about you."

She looked up at me, her eyes huge.

"Will you play a game with me?" I asked.

She nodded.

"Two truths for fifteen?"

"Okay," she answered quietly.

I stretched out my legs in front of me and tugged on her hand until she got the hint. Straddling my hips, she placed her arms on my shoulders, her excessive amount of bracelets clanking against each other. "So, you hate me?" I asked her.

She rolled her eyes. "I don't hate you."

"But you're mad at me?"

She sighed loudly as her body slumped. Nodding slowly, she let her words come out in a rush. "I am. I mean—you know I love you, and I've tried not to be mad, I really have. But I can't help it. I'm glad you're back. I'm glad we've found each other, but that doesn't change the fact that you just left. And I know that you have your reasons, and that's fine. But you could've said goodbye. I was right there, that day when I came to see you. You could've told me you were leaving.

"I spent a year worried about you, wondering if you were okay, if I was ever going to see you again. I got that one letter from you, and that's all. A whole year, Logan. Surely you would've known that I'd worry about you. What you did—leaving like that, that wasn't fair to me, and you know it."

"I know," I said quietly, looking down between us. "And I'm sorry. I guess I just thought you'd forget about me soon enough, you know?"

She lifted my chin with her finger, the way I'd done to her so many times. "I don't know what would make you think that. We weren't just some boy and girl who fell in love. What we had—we were *more* than that. At least, that's how it felt to me."

I swallowed down the lump that'd formed in my throat. "It was that way for me, too, babe." I brought her in closer. "I guess I should've known better. Looks like I have a year's worth of mistakes to make up for."

"Hm," she said, tapping her index finger against her lips. She eyed the sky. "How ever shall you start?"

I pinched her sides. She squealed and squirmed. "Show me your boobs and I'll show you where I'll start."

"You're a pig." She giggled.

Chuckling, I started to kiss up her neck, across her jaw, to her lips. "I love you," I whispered against them. "You're my heart, Amanda. And one day soon, I'll give you the world, just like I said I would in that letter."

She pulled back slightly. "I don't need the world, Logan. I just need you."

BY THE TIME we got back to the bonfire, Heidi was gone. She'd called a friend to pick her up but wanted to make sure Amanda knew how sorry she was for the way she'd acted. She'd told the others that she'd call me. I wasn't too fazed. It wasn't me she had to apologize to.

"It's fine," Amanda told them.

"It's not fine," I said. "She *should* apologize to you."

"Logan." She said my name like I was a kid who needed calming down. "Her heart's in the right place; she just let her emotions take over."

Cam raised a beer. I nodded. He threw it, but it landed a few feet in front of me. Amanda stood to pick it up the same time Lucy quipped, "Weak, babe. I'm so ashamed of you right now." She shook her head.

"So," Jake started. "I take it you're back for good?"

"Yup," I answered. "Or, for as long as this little lady will have me." I kissed Amanda on the cheek.

"Oh no," Micky laughed, then looked at Lucy. "He has turned into Nicholas Sparks."

"Right?" Lucy all but yelled. "I told you."

Amanda's body shook with her giggle.

"Who the fuck is Nicholas Sparks?" Jake asked.

"*The Notebook*?" Cam answered, his tone serious. "How do you not know *The Notebook*?"

Jake huffed, "What the fuck is *The Notebook*?"

Cam gasped like girl. "*The Notebook!*" he yelled, as if repeating the words would somehow make Jake understand what the fuck he was talking about. "What is wrong with you?"

We laughed.

"It's really good to have you home, man," Jake said. "But if you leave like that again, I'm getting on every plane possible and finding you, and when I do, I'm gonna beat your ass. I'm not even close to kidding."

You could always tell when Jake was angry or serious; his accent got stronger.

"If I ever do it again, I give you permission to do so. But trust me, there's no way it'll happen." I held on to Amanda tighter. "I have way too much to lose. I won't go through that again."

WE ENDED UP leaving before midnight. Lucy and Cameron had promised they'd take her brothers to a carnival the next day. They invited us along. I knew Amanda would want to. She couldn't say no to the food or the Ferris wheels. Jake and Micky had to leave; they were flying out early the next morning to see Micky's non-aunt's new baby—or something.

"Do you miss your old car?" she asked from the driver's seat of my truck on the way to Dad's.

I shrugged. "Not really. When I was sixteen, a Mercedes was the greatest thing in the world. Now, I just want to be able to get from one place to another. Money could be much better spent on other things."

She grabbed my hand and placed it on her leg. I loved it when she did shit like that. "Yeah?" she asked. "Like what?"

"Like...I dunno, for example, malaria. It's the fourth leading cause of death in third-world countries. For ten dollars you can buy a net that helps prevent it, maybe save a kid's life, you know? Do you know what that means? That means the money spent on my *first* car could've bought ten thousand nets. That's ten thousand potential lives I could've saved. I'm not saying that I'm not thankful to my dad for buying the car or that I don't appreciate how hard he works for that monetary success. And, I mean, you know my dad as well as I do. He doesn't do it for the money. I don't know, I just don't think enough people our age know about shit like that."

She didn't respond, just continued to drive in silence. The occasional street lamp lit up her face. Her brows were drawn, her mind deep in thought.

I squeezed her leg once. "What are you thinking?"

She glanced over at me, as if she'd forgotten I was even here. "It feels like I've fallen in love with you, for the first time, all over again."

"THIS PLACE BRINGS back memories," she said quietly. We were lying in bed in the pool house, side by side, on our backs, holding hands.

"Yeah, it really does."

She turned on her side to face me. I did the same. "Good or bad for you?"

"A lot of good, a lot of bad. Both, I guess."

She nodded slowly. "Me, too."

I moved closer to her and then flipped us so she was on top. She sat up, her legs folded on either side of me. Her fingers traced the dips of my abs. She had her wrists full of bracelets. I examined each one carefully. "Surely you can't sleep with eleventy-three bracelets on?"

She giggled. "Eleventy-three?"

"Lucy's brother Lachlan swears it's a thing."

"Is Lachlan the one who got me to go out with you?"

I laughed. "Yup."

"Good kid." She started removing the bracelets and setting them on the nightstand.

"He's my favorite." I watched her remove them one by one. The last one stood out; it was brighter and thicker than the rest. I'd seen it before. "This looks familiar."

She took it off and examined it quickly before placing it with the others. "Yeah, your dad gave it to me. It was Tina's—his high school sweetheart."

Now I remembered. I'd seen it in pictures of her.

I picked up Amanda's hands and ran my thumbs on the inside of her wrists, right over the marks. I gazed up at her, her eyes intently fixated on where my thumbs were skimming. I lifted them and placed a kiss on each one. Her breath caught. I felt her body tense above me.

"Do you want to know about them?" she asked.

Of course I wanted to know. I'd wanted to know since the day I saw them at the bookstore. "Yes." My voice cracked. I cleared my throat.

She sucked in a breath and then let it all out. "I got it the day of your birthday. It was meant to be a surprise. I was going to show you that night."

My heart dropped. I felt it fall to my stomach.

She placed her forearms on my chest, palm up. "See?" she said, tracing the letters of the tattoo. "LM on one side, AM on the other." She shifted her arms, so the tattoos were half-connected. "When I do this, the letters form a heart. Because that's what you were to me." Her voice broke. "You were my person, Logan. The other half of my heart." I pulled her down so I could hold her closer. Tighter. Her body began to shake. "Those fucking monsters stole our moment. They stole all our moments." She lifted her head; her tear-soaked eyes penetrated mine. "They stole you away from me."

I held her head in my hands and kissed her hard. "No one stole me away from you. I told you that you own me. You've always owned me. I was always yours."

I lifted her wrists to my lips and kissed them again. Closing my eyes, I took a breath. I wanted to savor this moment—with her in my arms and our forever in front of us. "Did you ever think to get them removed?" I asked.

"No," she answered quickly. "Never. The year you were gone, I could look at them and remember the feelings I had when I got them, and all those feelings I had for you. The way you made me feel alive, and the way you made me feel loved. The way you made me feel like I was the only girl in the entire world. And how you'd do anything and everything for me. You took my nightmares and turned them into dreams. If ten, twenty, thirty years from now, I look down at them and can still feel all those things, still remember the way I felt—the *love* I felt when I was with you, then it was worth keeping."

"And you still feel that way about me?"

"No." She shook her head, but her eyes stayed on mine. "Now, I feel *more*."

"And what if I didn't come back? What if you'd married some other asshole?"

"Then that other asshole would always know that I belonged to you first."

I inhaled slowly as I let her words sink in. "I love you so fucking much," I told her, right before I kissed her. I needed her to know how I felt; I wanted this kiss to represent it, but I don't think it even came close.

She smiled down at me. "I love you, too, babe."

"Ha." I swallowed down my nerves. "No, Amanda, I don't think you get it." I held her tighter and brought her head to my chest. "I don't just *love* you. It's like the word I want to use hasn't been invented yet. Maybe it's because no one's ever felt this type of love before. Maybe I'm the first to feel it. I don't know. I can't explain it. But those words—I love you—they just don't seem like enough. Not anymore."

I gripped the back of her shirt with my hand to try to hide the trembling. It didn't work. She felt it right away, like she was a part of me. "Your hand's shaking." She placed her hand on my heart. I'm sure she could feel it.

Thump.

Thump.

"What's going on, Logan?"

I tried to level my breathing, let my body settle down, but it wouldn't change what was happening. It wouldn't change how I felt or what I wanted to say. So I told her the truth. "I'm trying really hard to stop myself from asking you a really, really stupid question."

Her head lifted again. "What stupid question?"

"*The* question." I wanted to ask her to be mine forever.

A gasp escaped before she could stop it. "Oh," she said, her eyes wide. Then it was silent.

We both stared at each other.

Waiting.

Wanting the other to speak first.

She cleared her throat. "I would've said yes," she whispered.

"I know," I said honestly. "That's why I didn't ask you. It can't be like this. Not now. Not yet."

"I would've if you'd asked me in Vegas, too."

My eyes narrowed. How did she know about that? Then it hit me. The journal. "I thought it would be okay, but it's not. I want to give you everything. The world, remember? When we do—it needs to be right. We have to have everyone's support."

She knew what I meant. We had to tell Ethan.

"I have an idea," she said, kissing my neck softly.

"Mm?" Within seconds, the trembling in my hand had ceased, and my heart rate had settled, "What's that?" My hand went under her shirt, the other on her ass; she'd started to move her hips, rubbing herself on my dick. It only took a second before I was hard as a rock.

"I think..." She trailed off. Her mouth sucked harder as it made its way up my jaw.

She drove me crazy. My hand went under her panties, gripping her bare ass. I squeezed hard. She moaned into my skin, pressing harder onto me. My other hand went higher on her back, through the neck hole of my jersey she was wearing. I laced my fingers in her hair and curled them, gripping and pulling softly until she lifted her head. "You think what?" I breathed out.

She sat up, her palms flat against my stomach. She wet her lips, closed her eyes, and moved on me. Just once. But it was all I fucking needed. My cock rubbed in between her legs. Our only barrier: our underwear. I wanted them gone. I wanted nothing between us.

She opened her eyes. They landed where we connected. Her hips moved back and forth a few more times. "I think..." She trailed off again. She lifted her gaze and looked around the pool house. She chewed her bottom lip as she took in the space, then finally, they rested on me. She removed her top, her breasts out in the open, waiting for me. I sat up on my elbows and took one in my mouth. Slowly making circles. Savoring this moment. "Oh God..." she moaned.

She pulled back, and her fingers curled around the band of my boxers as she pulled them down, freeing my raging hard-on. She ran her palm across the head. It jerked against her hand. Her eyes went wide. Then she shifted again until she was back grinding on me, my bare dick against her panty-covered pussy. Her head was thrown back, her eyes closed. She started to moan. I wanted more. Slowly, lightly, I ran my hands on the inside of her thighs. She didn't stop me. Not even when I got to where we joined. I slid my finger under the material and moved it to the side. We both moaned when it was skin on skin contact. She was so fucking wet. I was so fucking hard.

"You think what?" I asked her again.

She started moving harder, faster.

I cursed under my breath.

"I think..." She stopped moving and opened her eyes.

Then she slid off me, pulling my boxers down with her. I lay naked on the bed with my dick standing up in the air. Her eyes raked me from head to toe, resting longer than they needed to on my junk. I placed my hands behind my head and let her take her time. I could never get sick of her reaction to my body. Ever.

"I think you and I need to make new memories in here." She pushed her panties over her hips and let them fall to the floor.

I tried to speak, but her standing naked at the end of my bed, offering herself to me, was too much. I'd failed the first time, and the second. By the third, I'd finally gotten my shit together. "I think that's a really great idea."

25

AMANDA

HE CAME TO a stand next to me. His breath warmed my cheek, but I kept my eyes straight ahead, focusing on the bed in front of me. One of his fingers brushed against my lip, down my chin and in between my breasts. He kept moving it lower and lower until I felt it between my legs. I let out a gasp.

"You want to make memories?" he said into my ear. His voice was scratchy and oozing with lust.

I sucked in a breath and held it.

"Close your eyes," he ordered. It was soft but demanding, just like his touch.

I did what he asked. He still had that power over me.

Then I heard his footsteps moving around the room. I exhaled loudly, just as I felt his hand on my breasts. He cupped them both, then ran his thumb over my nipples. I whimpered and squeezed my legs together. "You trust me, right?" His thumb on my nipple was replaced with his mouth, his tongue making circles around it. My hands fisted at my sides, and my back arched, pushing my breasts further into him.

I wanted to open my eyes. I wanted to see him. My breaths became heavy, my mouth dry. Then he was gone. My eyes snapped open, and he was right there—in the small space between the bed and me. "Pretty girl," he sighed, shaking his head slowly. "I told you to close your eyes."

I opened my mouth to speak, but he cut me off with a kiss. "It's okay," he said into my mouth, and then he pulled back, smirking, right before lifting his hand to show me a tie. "Now I'm going to have make sure of it."

He took a step forward, his hardness pressed against my stomach. He made a show of blindfolding me, knotting it tightly at the back of my head. He moved behind me, making sure it was secure, and then he growled over my shoulder. "I want you on your hands and knees, crawling on the bed."

I whimpered. "Logan," I whined, covering my breasts and sex with my hands.

"Amanda," he scolded. "What's wrong? Are you self-conscious?"

I swallowed my nerves, chewed my lip and nodded once. Then he was in front of me. "Are you kidding me?"

I stayed silent. He removed my arms and exposed my breasts. Kissing my neck slowly, he directed my hand to his dick, encouraging my fingers to wrap around it.

"Does this feel like you have any reason to be self-conscious?"

I let out a moan as he slowly pumped into my hand.

Then he pulled away, moving behind me again. His palm splayed flat against my stomach as he pushed me forward. "Hands and knees," he repeated.

I did what he asked, climbing onto the bed and slowly crawling forward. I tried to stay confident, remembering his words and how he'd felt under my touch. "That's it, baby, keep going." I felt the bed dip as he climbed on behind me. His hands covered both my ass cheeks as he squeezed them, tight. I was wet, so fucking wet I could feel it dripping down my leg. "Stop," he said. I did. Then, lifting my hands slowly, he guided them to the top of the headboard. "Don't let go." I felt the bed shifting again; he was moving away. "Spread your legs," he ordered.

Ho. Lee. Shit.

I'd been with Logan before; he was always alpha in bed but never like this. The effect it had on me must have been evident when his finger slid effortlessly inside me. "Oh fuck," he mumbled. And that's when I felt it: his warm breath blowing against my wetness. I didn't have time to ask him what the hell he was doing before his mouth covered me. My hips jerked instantly when his tongue made contact with my clit. "Holy shit, Logan."

I started thrusting slowly, encouraging his mouth and his tongue to fuck me and bring me over the edge. It only took seconds, my body already prepared for the buildup. My thrusts came faster, jerkier. He grabbed handfuls of my ass, pulling me down onto him. And then he sucked. Hard. It was all I needed. I screamed his name—louder than I'd thought possible. I tried to move off him but he kept going, his mouth insistent on getting everything out of me. I rode out every wave, every shock, with my throbbing sex on his face. He never let up, not until the last wave hit and my body became limp. "Holy shit," I breathed.

I tried to open my eyes to get my bearings, but the blindfold was still on. The bed shifted again as he pulled out from underneath me. Moments later, I felt his hardness against my ass, his chest against my back and his breath against my ear. "We can't go any further."

"What?" My chest heaved. "Why?" I panted, trying to fill my lungs with much-needed air. "But I need you."

He bit my earlobe gently. "I need you, too, baby. But I don't have anything."

"Huh?"

"Condoms—I don't have any."

"Oh." I took a few more breaths. "Did you get tested when you got back?"

"Yes—for everything."

"Then we're good, I'm safe."

He let out a breath. "Thank fuck."

I felt the air hit my back when he straightened up. He slid his dick between my folds, spreading me open for him.

"You have to go slow, babe. It's been a while. I need to get used to your size."

He grunted as he slowly slid inside me, inch by inch, letting me get comfortable.

"Okay," I assured, once I'd taken all of him. I felt his hand flatten on my back as he pulled out almost all the way and then thrust back in slowly. He did this a few more times, coating his dick with my juices.

"I fucking love watching you take me like this. Your ass is incredible."

His words turned me on even more. I started meeting him thrust for thrust. He was so slow, so gentle.

I wanted more. I needed more. "Logan?"

"Mm?"

And I don't know how the words were formed or how I let them leave my mouth. "Fuck me," I begged.

He moaned. Then one hand cupped my breast, the other rubbing my clit.

"Are you sure, baby?" He kissed down my spine.

"Please, Logan." I needed him.

"Hold on tight," he ordered, right before he moved.

Within minutes, I exploded again. It was stronger this time, and I felt myself throbbing around him. He pulled back, released my breast and splayed his hand against my back again. He kept pumping into me, harder, faster, just the way I wanted it. "Fuck me!" I demanded.

Then I felt him get bigger inside me, right before his body stilled and a growl escaped him.

26

LOGAN

"Why did we agree to be up this early?"

I heard her low chuckle from next me. "Because we didn't plan on staying up half the night."

I turned to face her. "Mm," I hummed as I took her in. Short shorts and a tight tank covered just enough of her perfectly tanned skin. Her long legs kicked out in front of her, crossed at her ankles. We were sitting on a bench just outside the entry gate to the carnival.

I ran the backs of my fingers against her thigh, flipped my cap backwards, and moved in to kiss her neck. She chuckled again. "What are you doing?"

"Just remembering last night."

She turned her face toward me and skimmed her lips against mine. "Yeah?" she whispered, kissing me once. "Are you remembering that part where I asked if I could finger your a—"

I cut her off with a kiss and then deepened it. One of her hands fisted into my shirt, the other curling around my neck, bringing me closer. I pulled back slightly. "Don't bring that up ever again."

She chuckled into my mouth. "Fine, just keep kissing me."

So I did.

She moaned when my hand went under her top and rested on her waist. My fingers dug into her skin when her tongue brushed against mine. I'd started to get hard.

"Hey, assholes!"

We instantly pulled apart and turned to see a kid standing in front of us.

It was Lachlan, Lucy's brother. He was older now. Not the same four-year-old who helped me get Amanda to agree to a date back when she worked at the diner.

He turned around and looked at a bunch of boys standing a few yards behind him—the rest of Lucy's brothers. They all wore goofy grins.

My eyes went from the older boys to the kid in front of me. "What's up, little man?"

He looked from me to Amanda and back again. "Do you guys give each other blowfish jobs?"

Amanda snorted with laughter. "Oh, jeez."

"What?" I tried to hide my own amusement.

"Not blowfish," one of the older boys said. I'm pretty sure it was Little Logan. "BLOW JOB!" he yelled. Then all the boys started yelling, "Blow job! Blow job!"

Lachlan just shrugged but stayed put.

"Blow job!" The other boys kept shouting.

"What the hell?" Lucy shrieked, walking toward them. "Why are you all yelling blow job?"

The boys fell into a fit of laughter.

Then Lachlan stepped in front of Amanda. "You're pretty," he told her, then wriggled his way to sit between us. He put his tiny hand in hers. She grinned from ear to ear. "And you," she said to him, "may just be the most handsome boy I've ever seen."

I rolled my eyes. "Gee, thanks."

Lucy and Cameron headed toward us, and we all stood up. Lachlan held onto Amanda's hand. Lucy introduced us to all her brothers. "I don't expect you to remember them all," she quipped.

Once we'd paid and entered through the gates, Cam pulled out his wallet and handed them all some money.

"I want to stay with pretty girl," Lachlan told them.

I had to laugh at his name for her. "Dude," I teased. "You're stealing *all* my game."

He growled at me with a sneer on his lips. I took a step back in shock, and Amanda laughed.

"Let him go with them," Little Logan insisted. "Then we can all go on the bigger rides, and we don't have to worry about him."

"We don't mind," Amanda spoke up. "We'll take him. You guys have fun."

"OKAY, BUD," I spoke quietly into Lachlan's ear. "I'll aim, you hold down the trigger, okay?" His eyes were huge. It matched his smile. He sat on my lap as they reset the little ducks with the targets on them back to the starting line. It was one of those water pistol aiming games.

Our winning celebration was a little over the top. It was all fine until we were handed a panda soft toy, and the little girl next to us started crying. Lachlan pouted when he saw her and then walked to her side. "Here you go," he said, handing it to her. "My uncle, Logan, will win more things for me, so you can have this one." Then he hugged her.

"That was a good thing you did, bud," I told him.

He shrugged. "Now you have to win me more, otherwise I lied, and liars are bad."

TWO HOURS LATER, we all met back up to eat. I laughed when Amanda told me to get her one of everything. My features straightened when I realized she was dead serious. "Are you sure?" I asked cautiously.

She pulled out the girl card. "Are you calling me fat?"

I walked away without a word. I wasn't stupid.

WHEN I GOT back—after the third fucking trip—I noticed one of Lucy's brothers, Leo, fixated on a girl a few yards away.

"Leo!" I tried to get his attention. "What's up? You into her?"

This made the other boys look up and follow his gaze. "Oooh," one of them said. "Double D Debbie."

"Shut up," he spat through clenched teeth.

I ignored the funny nickname and asked, "Why don't you go talk to her?"

He shrugged. "She's with her boyfriend."

I looked back over at her. She was standing by herself, shifting on her feet and looking at the ground. I scanned the area around her. There was a group of guys a few feet away, chatting up a bunch of girls. "Where's her boyfriend?" I asked, not bothering to look away.

"The one at the front of the group, talking to the blonde."

I faced him again, my eyebrows drawn in. "You mean her boyfriend's letting her stand there alone while he tries to get on with another girl?"

He shrugged.

"What a dick."

Cam and Lucy laughed. My attention went to them. "What's funny?"

Cam spoke first. "That *dick* is classic high school Logan."

"Gross," Amanda muttered.

I couldn't say shit; they were right. I went back to Leo. "You know what you should do..."

"What?" He was all ears.

"You should go over to her, tell her that her boyfriend's a dick, and that you'd treat her so much better. Because you would, right?"

"Oh no..." Lucy groaned.

Leo nodded.

"Then, without giving her a chance, hold her hand, and move in for the kiss. If she doesn't knee you in your junk—" I paused to let Amanda's laugh fill my ears. "If she doesn't push you away, and she kisses you back, bring her over here."

"Her boyfriend's gonna kick your ass," one of the brothers said.

I shrugged. "If he tries, you got me and Cameron." I looked at Cam. "Right?"

He leaned forward and jerked his head in a nod. "Go for it, dude," he told Leo. "You'll never know if you don't try."

Leo looked over at her, then at us. He blew out a breath and stood. Running his hands over his shirt, he nodded. "Okay, I'm going in." He wiped his palms on his shorts. I knew that action. He was nervous. Hell, I was nervous for him.

We all watched as he made his way over to her.

"No way he's gonna do it," Little Logan said.

He stood in front of her and must've said something, because her eyes lifted to his. We could see his mouth moving, and then she smiled. He reached his hand out, gripped hers, took one step forward, and then leaned in for the kiss.

We all sucked in a breath, the anticipation of her reaction killing us. "Get it," I heard Cam say.

We waited.

And waited.

Then her arm came up and curled around his neck, bringing him closer.

We all cheered and then laughed at how stupid we were.

We must've been loud, because it caused them to pull apart. He turned around and shook his head at us. His mouth started moving again. She nodded, her smile huge. They walked toward us, hand in hand, and then her boyfriend called out. He broke through his little group and followed them. By the time he reached them, they were already at our table. Cameron stood up and placed his fisted hands on the table. He glared at the kid. "Problem, you little punk?"

The kid halted. I stood up. He raised his hands. "No problem."

He walked away.

"Great," Little Logan said. "Now he's gonna beat the shit out of you when Cam's not around."

"No, he won't," Cam said. He eyed me and jerked his head toward the kid who'd just left. "We'll take care of it."

AMANDA

"Neanderthals," Lucy stated.

I laughed. "They mean well." I watched as Logan and Cam caught up with the kid. Logan placed his hand on his shoulder and spoke down to him. He could be intimidating when he wanted to.

He could also be ridiculously hot.

I turned back and looked at the spread of food in front of me. Hot dogs, funnel cakes, nuggets, burgers, fries, corn dogs, you name it, it was all on the table. "Okay, Lachlan. What do you think we should get into first?"

"All of it," he yelled, clapping enthusiastically.

"Okay, then."

He giggled as I started giving him portions of all the food Logan had bought. "He's okay to have all this?" I asked Lucy. "He's not allergic to anything?"

She shook her head. "The kid ate dog poop when he was three. He's good to go." Leo's girl giggled next to him. He watched her with a small smile on his face, just like Logan did with me.

"Hey, bud," Logan said. He stood behind me with his hands on my shoulders, but he was talking to Lachlan. "You think maybe I can have my girl back? Maybe I can sit next to her for a bit?"

He shrugged. "Maybe later."

I contained my laugh while I continued making his plate for him. Logan muttered something under his breath but took a seat on the other side of him. "You planning on stealing her?" He winked at me, his dimples on full show. I couldn't help but smile.

"Maybe," Lachlan shouted. "Probably not. I love her."

Logan choked on his soda.

"Actually," Lachlan started. He eyed the sky, contemplating. "Will you be my mommy? I don't have a mommy. You can be her, right?"

I sucked in a breath as his eyes locked with mine, the intensity in them so much more than his years should allow. He waited anxiously for my answer. I opened my mouth to speak, but the words caught in my throat.

Then Logan spoke, "Hey, buddy."

Lachlan turned to him.

I let out the breath.

"You know," Logan said, glancing at me quickly, "I don't have a mommy either. But it's cool, because my dad—he's pretty awesome. I bet your dad's awesome, too, right?"

Lachlan nodded enthusiastically.

"And you have a lot of awesome brothers and sisters, as well."

Lachlan's head turned as he looked around the table. "Yeah." Then he faced Logan again. "Do you have brothers and sisters?"

Logan smiled, but it didn't reach his eyes. "Yes and no," he answered. His head bent down so he was speaking only to Lachlan. "I mean—your sister, Lucy, and our friends Mikayla and Heidi, they're kind of like sisters to me. And our friends Jake and Dylan and even Cameron—they're my brothers."

Lachlan nodded slowly. "Cameron's my brother, too," he announced. "He's my brother... in...lawn? No! Low? No! No!"

The corner of Logan's lips curled up.

"Um..." Lachlan looked up to one of the eldest boys. "What did you tell me he is? Brother in...?"

"Law," his older brother confirmed. "Brother-in-law."

Lucy smiled and Cam placed his arm around her shoulders, bringing her in to kiss her on the temple.

"Yeah. Brother-in-law." Lachlan turned back to Logan now. "So does that mean we're brothers?"

"Yeah, dude, we can be brothers. I'd like that."

"But you'd be a good brother, right?" Lachlan's tone was low, serious. "Not like them." He jerked his head in the direction of his brothers. "They all told me to eat dog poop."

Everyone laughed.

Logan raised his eyes to me. *I love you,* I mouthed. He smiled, but it was sad.

"C'MON, LACHY. LET'S get you cleaned up," Lucy said. Everyone stood and started clearing the table.

"Okay!" he agreed. He stood on the seat and smacked his lips on my cheek, leaving a wet stickiness when he pulled away. "Wait up, guys!" He jumped off and joined the rest of his family.

Then it was just Logan and me. I heard his deep chuckle from next to me. He picked up a napkin and wiped my cheek. "I can't take you anywhere," he joked quietly.

I turned my head slowly, kissing first his palm, and then his lips. "Are you okay?"

He shrugged and looked away.

"Do you think about them?"

"My mom or Megan?"

"Both."

His shoulders lifted again.

I sighed. "I love you." I didn't know what else to say.

He was distracted when he replied, "I love you, too."

I pulled out the vial pendant and held it in my hand. "You know, one day, baby, I'm going to take your nightmares and turn them into dreams."

He glanced at my hand holding the pendant, and then our eyes locked. "You already do, Amanda. Every damn day."

My lungs filled with his breath as he kissed me. It was slow, needy, and passionate. He was remembering me. Savoring the moment.

A tiny throat clearing interrupted us. We both turned to see Lachlan, his hands behind his back and a cheesy grin on his face.

"Buddy," Logan teased. "You keep killing my game here."

We stood up, just as Lachlan wormed his way between us. He held each of our hands in his. "Ferris wheel," he squealed.

So that's what we did.

———

"I LOVE LIVING here," I told him. We were almost at the top; you could see the town and the city from where we were.

"Yeah?" he asked. "You plan on staying around?"

I shrugged. "It depends, I mean—eventually, I think so."

He waited a while before he asked, "Eventually?"

I glanced at him quickly, but then turned back to the view. "After we live wherever you go to med school, maybe travel for a bit, come back here, create a home..." I trailed off.

"I was hoping you'd say that."

———

LACHLAN PASSED OUT within two minutes on the Ferris wheel. I texted Lucy and told her we'd meet her back in the parking lot. Logan carried him to the bed of his truck and laid him down gently, trying not to wake him. We sat on the edge, his arms wrapped tight around me. "I finally got you all to myself."

I laughed into his chest. "You're so needy."

His body bounced with his chuckle. "I know. I just miss the shit out of you. You're kind of my drug." It was quiet for a moment. "I think you need to tell Ethan, and I think you shou—"

"I'm telling him tonight," I cut in. "I decided this morning that the first chance I got, I had to. I hate lying to him. I hate sneaking around."

"Good," Logan said. "And then maybe after that, once he's okay with us, maybe—I mean, you don't have to—but maybe we could stop missing each other and you could just move in."

My head tilted back so I could look him in the eye. "Seriously?"

"Or not." He shook his head, his confidence waning.

"I'd have to wait until someone could take over my rent and room. I can't just leave right away."

A huge grin overcame him. "But that means 'yes', right?"

I bit my lip and nodded.

His hold on me got tighter. "Oh my God," he mumbled, a disbelieving laugh erupted from him. "How the fuck did I get so lucky?" He held my face in his hands, his grin still in place. He kissed me once, twice. Eleventy-three times. Then he pulled back, his gaze roaming all over my face. "You and me," he said. "We're going to make so many damn moments worth remembering."

27

AMANDA

"BABE." I COULD hear Logan's voice, but he sounded far away. "You're home."

I opened my eyes slowly and took in my surroundings. We were in his truck in the driveway of my house. It was dark outside. We'd hung around and had takeout with his dad after the carnival. I must've fallen asleep on the way home. "My car's at your house."

"Yeah, I know. I didn't want you driving home this tired." He chuckled. "You fell asleep as soon as we got on the highway."

"Oh," I said, still trying to gain my bearings.

"I know you're working tomorrow night, so I was thinking maybe I could pick you up for lunch and we could spend the day together?"

I sat up straighter and rubbed my eyes. "Okay."

He smiled. "So you're still going to talk to Ethan tonight?"

I nodded through a yawn. "Yeah." I looked to the house. The lights were still on.

"Okay," he sighed. "So just call me when you wake up, and I'll come and get you."

I scooted closer and put an arm around his waist. "I'll miss you tonight."

Laughing, he lifted my chin with his finger. "You have no idea how much I'll miss you, pretty girl."

"Thank you for today. I had fun." I kissed him once.

He returned it. "Thank you for all my days."

I kissed him again, deeper this time. Pulling away slightly, he whispered, "I'm kind of crazy in love with you, you know that?"

His words made my eyes drift shut. I'd never get sick of him telling me. Ever. I kissed him again, but he cut it short. "You better go. This is going to make me miss you more."

I hugged him and smiled into his arm. "You know what this feels like?"

He laughed quietly. "Our first date?"

"Uh-huh." I nodded.

"I didn't want to say goodbye to you then. I don't want to say goodbye to you now." He turned his entire body to face me. Chewing his lip, he linked our hands between us. "It was the hardest thing to do, saying goodbye to you. Not just that night, but the night I left." His voice broke. "It was the hardest and stupidest decision I've ever made."

"It wasn't stupid," I told him. My eyes dropped to where his thumb skimmed over my tattoos. "Maybe it needed to be done. Who knows? Maybe it wasn't our time then. Maybe we needed that time apart to grow up. Maybe now's our time. Maybe—"

The front door slamming cut me off. "Amanda!"

Ethan.

He walked toward the car, his hand out, blocking the headlights from blinding him. "That better be you."

"Shit," I muttered.

Logan held my hands tighter. "It'll be okay." His words were shaky. He didn't believe it, either.

Ethan got close enough so that the headlights were no longer in his way. Looking into the car, his eyes widened when he saw us. "What the fuck?" he mumbled.

Then something in him switched.

Rage filled his eyes. His jaw clenched. His fists balled.

"Get the fuck out of the car, Amanda!"

"Ethan," I tried to calm him down.

He swiftly moved to the driver's side, opened the door and pulled Logan out. I didn't even have time to react before his fist met Logan's jaw.

"Stop," I screamed. "What are you doing?"

I jumped out and went straight for Logan, but Ethan held on to my arm and pulled me back. "Get in the fucking house, Amanda." His tone was as loud as it was harsh. I heard the front door open and footsteps, but my eyes were fixed on Logan. He stood with his arms stretched and his hands against the side of his truck. He spat blood.

I stepped forward, wanting to go to him.

Ethan blocked my path. His chest heaved with his breaths. "I'm not fucking around, Amanda. Get in the goddamn house."

"Fuck you, Ethan."

"No!" he yelled. "Fuck you, Amanda."

Logan raised his head now, his lip busted, blood pouring from his mouth.

Ethan continued, "Do you know how fucking worried I've been? I've been calling you all fucking day. Your phone's off. I called everyone. Mom's in a fucking panic. I even called Dad!"

I sucked in a breath. The guilt took over. He stepped closer. "The whole fucking day I've been tearing my hair out, and you've been fucking around with him? HIM!" He pointed to Logan but kept his glare on me. Logan's hands went in his front pockets. "You've been fucking around with him—and behind my fucking back. You knew how I'd feel, because you kept it from me. You knew I'd be pissed, and you still fucking did it!" His voice got louder. I took a step back, not wanting to feel the full wrath of his words. "I'm gonna tell you one more time," he said, his voice lowered. "Get. In. The. Fucking. House. NOW!"

"Babe," Logan spoke from behind him. He spat out more blood. "Go," he said quietly. "We're just gonna talk."

Ethan turned to him. "Don't you fucking tell her what to do." He shook his head and moved closer to him. "Don't you fucking *dare* talk to her. Your opinion doesn't count anymore, asshole."

Logan just nodded, but his eyes were on me. Pleading.

Then a hand wrapped around my elbow. "C'mon, Dim." *Alexis.* "Let's just go inside. They have a lot to talk about."

I looked at Logan. He raised his chin slightly.

I walked backwards toward the house, my eyes never leaving them. They stood, toe to toe, neither moving, neither talking.

Alexis closed the front door once we were inside. "It's okay," she assured me. "They're just gonna talk."

LOGAN

As soon as the door shut, his fist was in my stomach. I was expecting something, but not that. It made me fall to my knees. "You can't just fucking come back and pretend like everything's fine!" He kicked the same place he'd just punched. My body fell forward, but my arms held me up.

"Get up," he yelled. "Take it like a man."

I used my truck to get back to my feet. The pain in my body was nowhere near the pain in my heart. I knew Ethan. I knew him as the cocky asshole who never took anything too seriously. But this—this was not Ethan. At least, not the one from a year ago.

"Oh, wait," he mocked. "I forgot. You don't do things like a man." He punched me again. My face this time. My head flung to the side, but I took it. I'd take anything he gave me. I deserved it all.

"Your girlfriend almost got raped, and you bailed, right? That's your thing. You just fuck off?" Another punch. They were getting weaker. I'd be able to take a few more before my body failed me. "You fucking left. It was me that was there for her. I had to listen to her nightmares, her screams at night." I lifted my head to face him. I didn't know she'd had nightmares. "Oh." He nodded slowly as understanding dawned. "Of course she wouldn't tell you about that. Poor you, right? We better protect your fucking feelings." I let his words sink in as I took in his state. His knuckles were bleeding, or maybe it was my blood. Who the fuck knows? His shoulders lifted with his heavy breaths, but he could barely get a lungful before he hit me again. Another gut shot. Weaker again.

I let the pain consume me. I needed to feel it. I deserved to feel it.

"You've got nothing to say to me?" Another punch to the face. The blows hurt less, but the pain was constant. "Did she tell you she couldn't be home alone? Or that she slept with the light on? I bet she didn't fucking tell you any of that shit!" I tried to swallow the knot in my throat. She didn't tell me, but I'd never asked. I should have asked. He pushed against my chest, too weak to do anything else.

Thunder clapped and rain poured down.

Maybe it was a sign. Maybe she had every reason to be afraid of it. I couldn't just turn her nightmares into dreams, not when I didn't know they existed.

He fisted my shirt in his hand, the rain soaking us both. He got right in my face.

I waited.

Then I heard her voice.

"Stop," she yelled.

I lifted my chin.

"Stop it!" she yelled again.

My head pounded, the beating finally catching up. I tried to square my shoulders.

Ethan's voice was quieter now, intended just for me. "Do you know what it was like to walk in and see some guy on top of her like that? I got him off just in time, but she'd blacked out." His voice broke. He could've been crying, but the rain hid it. "She blacked out, and I thought she was fucking dead. I thought she'd died, Logan. I thought I'd fucking lost her."

I shut my eyes tight. The mental image of that night came back to me. I'd locked it away—with the rest of my nightmares. And now it was here. His body on top of her, holding her arm. Her scream as he pushed it against the floor, breaking it. Me, pathetically crawling to get to her. Her tears flowing. Her body slack. She'd given up.

And then darkness.

"Do you know what that was like for me?" Ethan yelled again.

And then it happened.

The walls I'd built to block out that night, the heartache, and the turmoil—it all came crashing down around me. I pushed him away. "How the fuck do you think I feel?" I shouted back. I pushed him again, my emotions taking control. "I was right fucking there, and I couldn't stop it."

I heard her say my name, but I ignored it. "I couldn't do a fucking thing to stop any of it. It's my fault they were there! It's my fault they hurt her! You don't think I fucking know that?"

"Stop," she yelled again.

I kept my eyes on Ethan. "You don't think I have to live with that guilt every day? Ethan, I was right there! It was on me. I couldn't fucking save her!" I was crying, sobbing like a fucking baby.

"Fuck you," he yelled, pushing against me again.

"I couldn't fucking save her," I repeated. "I fucking hate myself for what I let those assholes do."

"STOP IT!" Her high-pitched scream sliced through the night air. We both turned to her. Tristan was holding her back. She wrenched herself free and stepped toward us. "It's *my* fault."

"What?" Ethan and I spoke at the same time.

She glared at both of us before speaking. "It's my fault," she said again. "I should have stayed outside like you'd asked." She turned to me now. "The first thing you did when you knew we were in danger was get me out of that house. You picked me up, threw me out and locked the door. You told me to call the cops. That's all I had to do," she shouted over the sound of the rain. Her voice was strained from her withheld sob. "All I had to do was call the police and wait. But I couldn't even do that. I had to go back in...and for what? To save you? How the hell could I save you? *One minute.* One fucking minute and the cops would've been there, and everything would've changed. I'd be *safe,* just like you'd intended." She turned to Ethan now. "You would've never seen me in that position. I would've never even been in there. And Logan, he would've never left." She faced me again. "It's my fault. You think you're to blame for it all? You're so wrong. It's me. It's all on me." She collapsed to the ground. Her head fell in her hands.

I tried to speak, but the lump in my throat prevented it. I wanted to tell her she was wrong. She was beyond fucking wrong.

"And now you're here." She lifted her head. Her eyes met mine. "Now you're here, and Ethan blames you." I knelt down, so we were face to face. She placed her hand on my cheek. I did everything I could to stop from wincing in pain. "I'm sorry," she said. "I should've told you it was my fault, but I was so—"

"Stop." I kissed her once, ignoring the sharp ache. "You can't ever think like that. Ever. Promise me?"

She shook her head, her sobs taking over.

"The neighbors are watching. Let's get inside," Tristan spoke up.

Amanda's head turned as she looked around at us. Then her eyes met mine. "I'm coming with you," she whispered.

I shook my head. "You can't. You need to stay here. No more running. No more hiding." I kissed her forehead. "We'll get through it together, okay? Swear it."

"But I want to stay with you." She ran her thumb under my eye. It'd started to swell.

Tristan picked her up off the ground. "No one's going anywhere." He held his hand out to me. "You can't drive; your eye is about to swell shut." He helped me up and the same time looked around us. "Y'all can get back inside; everything's fine. There's nothing to see here." He chuckled to himself. "I've always wanted to say that."

28

LOGAN

I SUCKED IN a breath with a hiss.

"I'm sorry," she grimaced.

"It's fine." I ran my hands up her thighs. She sat on the counter in her bathroom. I stood between her legs while she tried to clean my face and the mess that Ethan had created. "You're not freaking out over the blood. It doesn't bother you anymore?"

She shook her head and quietly repeated, "I'm sorry. He had no right to do this to you."

"Yeah, he did." Truth. "We fucked up, Amanda. We shouldn't have been sneaking around behind his back. We wanted to live in our own world—our own little bubble—it had to burst at some point. This was the bursting point."

She sighed. "He didn't have to hit you."

"I would've done the same." I moved her hand away from my face and kissed her wrists. "I mean, I knew he'd be pissed, but not like that. But you—you knew, didn't you?"

She swallowed and nodded slowly.

"What the fuck did you expect would happen, Lexie?" Loud shouting from the hallway caught our attention. Ethan's voice echoed through the house.

Amanda's eyes went huge. "Oh no..." she muttered.

Moving me to the side, she hopped off the counter and tiptoed to her closed bedroom door, putting an ear to it, as if we actually had to strain to hear them.

"Fuck you, Ethan. You think acting like a dick is going to make me want to move in with you? No fucking way." Her footsteps got louder as she got closer.

"Baby, come on." Ethan was right in front of the door now. "You already said you would; you can't just take it back."

"Bullshit," Alexis snapped. "Watch me. And you can watch me walk out of your fucking life, too."

"What?" he yelled, the desperation clear in his voice.

I moved Amanda out of the way and opened the door. They were right there, with his hand gripping her elbow stopping her from leaving.

I cleared my throat. They both turned to me.

"Look what you've done to his face, you asshole." She pointed to me, but she was talking to him.

"It's fine," I cut in. "It looks worse than it feels."

Lie.

I tried to smile. "How are you, Alexis?"

Her eyes narrowed in confusion. "Um, I'm okay?"

"Cool." I placed my hands in my pockets and leaned against the door-jamb, faking a calmness that didn't exist. "So you're leaving?"

"Uhh ..." She trailed off.

I chanced a glance at Ethan; his eyebrows were bunched, waiting for me to speak.

"Look, I don't want to get in the middle of your shit, but if you're leaving because of me and what happened tonight, then don't. It's not worth what you guys have going. *I'm* the dick. *I* deserved it. Truthfully, I'd be kind of pissed if he didn't react the way he did. He's just looking out, protecting her, you know? It kind of makes him the good guy. The best kind of guy, actually." I felt Amanda's hand on my back. "I don't know." I shrugged. "I just think it'd be the wrong decision if you were to walk away. And trust me, I know all about wrong decisions."

BY THE TIME we went to bed, Alexis had calmed down and decided to stay. We could still hear them talking from where we lay in bed. They weren't arguing or screaming at each other, so at least there was that.

"That was nice of you—saying that shit about him." She reached over and held my hand.

"I didn't do anything. Besides, how many more people need to be caught up in our mess?"

She leaned up on her elbow and looked down at me. Raising an eyebrow, she spoke quietly. "You think we're a mess?"

I glanced at her quickly before looking away. Squeezing my eyes tight, I tried to ignore the pounding ache in my head. "I think that we fucked up. Obviously we can't help the way we feel about each other, but this sneaking around, lying to people—this shouldn't have happened. We should've waited. And now it's out, and I'm gonna have to work five times as hard to get him to understand." My eyes began to drift shut, the exhaustion of the day finally catching up to me. "I think I just need to—"

"Go to sleep, babe." She kissed me softly. I barely felt it. "I love you so much, Logan."

29

AMANDA

I woke up the next morning in an empty bed. "Logan?"

He made a grunting sound from the bathroom.

My breath came out in a whoosh when I saw him. I didn't see him for a week after what had happened the night of his birthday, so I never had to deal with the aftermath of him physically. Now, it was staring me in the face. He stood with his arms stretched out, hands flat on the bathroom counter. His back was to me, but I could see his reflection in the mirror.

"I'm fine," he said.

"Don't lie." I stood next to him.

He turned and curled his arms around my neck, kissing my head once. A sheen of sweat covered his body. "I'm good." His voice was low, shaky. "I didn't take my meds last night, so I'm just a little out of it."

I went to hug him back but barely got an arm around him before he winced in pain. I pulled back and looked at his ribs. Bruises that had just started to show last night were now completely formed. "How bad is it?"

He swallowed as his eyes roamed my face. He hesitated before he answered, "Bruised ribs, that's all. Definitely not broken, though. So that's good."

I didn't even know what expression was on my face, but it made him chuckle. "I just need to get some painkillers. I'll call Dad later."

"No! What are you going to tell him? That my brother beat you? You can't tell him that. I'd be so embarrassed."

"Quit it. He won't care."

"I do!" My voice rose. "I care."

"Okay," he tried to soothe me. "I'll work something out. It'll be fine."

"Great." I rolled my eyes. "Now you're comforting me when I should be the one comforting you."

"Quit being sulky."

I pouted.

Then he smirked. "Caveman Logan want some breakfast."

I stared down at his junk.

"Not *that* Caveman Logan." He shook his head, but his tone was amused. "Jeez, you're such a dirty girl."

I tried my best to lighten the mood. "I could be a dirty girl."

He eyed me up and down, inhaled deeply, and then winced.

I grimaced.

"Sorry, babe." He held his side. "I think I'm going to be out of commission for a while."

I pouted. "Well then, last night was all for nothing. You're kind of useless to me now."

LOGAN

TRISTAN SUCKED IN a breath with a hiss when he saw me sitting at the dining table. Alexis followed it up with a loud gasp. I didn't think it was that bad, but then again, they didn't see me the days after my last beating. This was nothing.

"You look like ass," Alexis said, flopping down on the seat next to me.

"Did someone say ass?" Tristan chirped. "I like ass."

The girls laughed. I spat out my cereal.

Ethan walked into the room.

Dead. Fucking. Silence.

The sound of my spoon repeatedly hitting the bowl broke through the quiet. I watched my hand shake uncontrollably. "Fuck." I dropped the spoon and straightened my fingers. My breathing became erratic. I tried to calm it, but it just made the pain in my ribs worse. I cursed again and folded over myself.

Amanda's voice was quiet. "You broke his ribs, E." She linked her fingers with mine.

I heard Ethan curse.

Looking up at him, I tried to keep my face straight. "They're not broken. Just bruised." It wasn't important, but I didn't want him thinking he'd done more damage than he had.

Then Amanda moved. Her chair scraped against the floor as she stood up. "C'mon, baby," she said to me. "I'll drive you home. I need to pick up my car anyway, I gotta work tonight."

"No you don't," Ethan spoke.

All eyes went to him.

"I called in. You got lady cramps. We're going minigolfing tonight." He kissed Alexis on the cheek and took a seat next to her. "We all are."

"WHAT THE HELL is with minigolf?" I asked her.

She stood next to me and helped me remove my shirt, then did the same with hers. "It's his way of apologizing without actually saying the words. You know E. He's stubborn. And stupid."

"Okay, but why minigolf?"

She pulled down my shorts and did the same with her sweats. "It's this thing he and Tyson and I used to do."

"Tyson?" I raised an eyebrow.

"Yeah, when he lived here." She turned to check the water temperature in the shower and then removed her bra.

I reached out and cupped her breast. She didn't even flinch. "Nothing happened between you and Tyson, right?"

She shrugged and yanked down my boxers. Her eyes widened when my dick was exposed. Like she didn't expect to see it erect. She was standing in front of me topless...what else was going to happen?

"We kissed once," she said nonchalantly.

Her thumbs curled around her panties, ready to push them down, but I stopped her with my free hand on her shoulder. "You kissed?" I wanted to puke.

"Yeah." She laughed out. I don't know why she was laughing. This shit wasn't funny. "It was so gross, I could've been kissing Ethan." She shuddered and dropped her panties to the floor.

Then she just stood there with her arms at her sides and a boob in my hand. I let out a grunt, annoyed that we couldn't go any further.

Logan: I'm going to need a script for some painkillers.
    Dad: Is everything okay?
    Logan: Yes, but I can't drive to see you. Can you come here?
    Dad: I'll be there in a few hours.
    Logan: I'm at Amanda's, my old house.
    Dad: Should I ask what happened?
    Logan: Everything's fine. I'm safe.

Sometimes, you live life searching for moments to remember. Then there are moments you'd rather forget. His face when he saw me was one of them. I thought I'd gotten used to it. When I was a kid and he tried everything to get me to speak, that face was a constant. For years afterwards, it never showed. Not until the night of my twenty-first birthday. And now. Now he was looking at me with that same pained expression.

"I'm fine."

He stepped into the house without responding.

I watched as he scanned the halls, probably trying to forget the memories that came with it. And then his eyes lit up, and a smile overcame him. "Pretty girl," he greeted.

She moved slowly toward him as if unsure. "Alan," she responded, hugging him quickly.

We sat at the table while he examined my injuries. He studied my face injuries, but I pulled away. "I'm not worried about my—"

"Logan." It was said with finality. "You have a bruised jaw, black eye and fat lip. I don't know what happened, but either way, I need to check you out. Your vision might be damaged, your jaw could be fractured, and knowing you, you'll take the pain before telling anyone how bad it is."

I felt like a kid who'd just been schooled. "Okay."

Amanda hugged my arm and used it to hide her face. Then, so quietly I almost didn't hear her, "I'm so sorry."

Dad's eyes narrowed slightly. He looked from her to me, searching for a reason why she would say that. I subtly shook my head.

"Quit it," I said quietly into her ear. "You have nothing to be sorry for."

He spent the next few minutes going over my injuries and taking notes. I knew what he'd do. He'd go home and compare them to my previous injuries—the ones from when I was a kid—just to make sure he didn't miss anything. "Your ribs?" he asked knowingly.

I nodded. "Not broken. Just bruised."

He motioned for me to stand up and remove my shirt.

I stood. Amanda helped with my shirt. He didn't say anything about that.

"Breathe in," he ordered.

I tried. He noticed immediately how much pain it caused.

"Hm," he murmured, scribbling down more notes.

I sat back down, grateful for the reprieve.

The living room door that led to outside slid open. Ethan, Lexie and Tristan walked in. Dad smiled at them, but it wasn't genuine. I wondered if anyone else could tell. He greeted them by name quickly and went back to his notes, his mind too preoccupied to keep up with conversation.

I wanted to ask him how he knew them, but Amanda answered my unasked question. "He met them in my hospital room after..." She trailed off.

I had no idea.

I searched his face, wondering why he'd never told me. "And your anxiety pills? You're still taking them? You'll need another script soon."

My eyes darted to Ethan and the others. They sat on the sofa, pretending not to listen.

"He didn't take them last night," Amanda chimed in.

I glared at her.

She shrugged. "That's two nights in two weeks he hasn't taken it. That's bad, right?" She pulled her phone out of her pocket. "Should I set a daily alarm to remind him?"

That made Dad smile. Genuinely, this time. "Maybe you might have to do that, sweetheart."

"Okay," she said quickly, frantically typing on her phone.

I pulled it out of her hands. "You don't need to do that. I'm a big boy."

She yanked it back from me and continued tapping. "And he shouldn't mix drinking with the painkillers, right?" she asked him.

I rolled my eyes and sat back. I had no say in this conversation at all.

He reached over and squeezed her hand once. "That's right."

Ethan spoke up, "No drinking at all?"

Dad faced him now. "No. Not once he starts on the painkillers. It's a bad combination. Can knock him out."

"There goes minigolf," he mumbled.

"Huh," Dad said, coming to a stand. He handed me the scripts and started packing his shit.

"Thanks for coming all the way out here," I told him.

He shrugged. "You're my son, Logan. It's what I do."

Then he turned to the others. "Ethan?"

Shit.

I waited for him to say something. Reprimand him in some way. Talk to him like I was a kid and Ethan was the bully. Instead, he took the few steps toward him and looked down at him on the sofa. "You need me to look at your hand, son?"

Ethan's eyes went wide. He opened his mouth to speak, but the words caught. He cleared his throat and shook his head. "Um. No, sir. It's fine. Thank you."

Dad nodded once. "If you're sure."

"I'm sure," Ethan confirmed.

Then Dad turned to me. "If you can deal with the pain for a night, maybe you boys should have a drink together, talk some stuff out. Clear the air. Start the painkillers tomorrow."

Two minutes later he was gone.

"So, minigolf?" I said to everyone.

Ethan got up. "If you can deal with the pain for one night, let's do it."

"Dude, your dad's my hero," Tristan declared.

Yeah. He was mine, too.

30

LOGAN

"WHAT'S IN IT?"

The others laughed while Ethan shrugged. "It's magic."

I warily took the flask from his hand and sniffed.

He rolled his eyes dramatically. "It won't kill you. You have to do it; those are the rules of minigolf."

I looked at Amanda. She just smiled and nodded her head. "Have you had this before?"

She shook her head and raised the car keys. "Designated driver, remember?"

Ethan made a huffing sound. "Just drink it, asshole," he teased. "What? Did you turn into a pussy the year you were gone?"

I took a swig. It tasted like gasoline. My face contorted.

Ethan laughed.

And that's how it went.

Apparently, the rules of minigolf were this: For every putt, you drink. That's it. After the third hole, I could barely feel the soreness in my body. "This shit's better than painkillers," I announced loudly.

Amanda snorted with laughter.

"Yeah, buddy!" Ethan yelled, then put his putter between his legs and started humping it.

"Oh my God," Amanda muttered next to me. "You're so mature."

He winked at her, right before Tristan mimicked his actions. So there they were, side by side, humping their putters. Amanda's laugh bubbled out of her. I loved hearing her laugh. I turned around and kissed her, probably longer and deeper than what's publicly acceptable.

"Get a room," some dick yelled.

Then Lexie spoke up, "Fuck off, asshole. They've been apart for a year. Let them make out."

"Dude, that's my sister." Ethan made a disgusted sound.

"Could be worse," Tristan stated. "At least it's not Alexis again."

We pulled apart from the kiss, but not each other. My hands gripped her waist, her hands fisted into my shirt. "Does he know?" I whispered.

"I don't know," she whispered back.

Then we slowly, and simultaneously, turned to face Ethan.

He smirked, sauntered over to Lexie and put his arm around her shoulders. "Luckily, she's moved on to *bigger* and better things."

BY THE TENTH hole, we were plastered. Beyond wasted. I couldn't feel my body, let alone how sore it could be. Everything was numb. Amanda had to hold me up. "It wears off real quick," Amanda told me.

"I just want to make out with you all the time."

"What?" She laughed.

"Your ass."

She laughed again. "You're not making much sense, babe."

I shrugged as we watched Tristan take his eleventy-third shot, all whilst Ethan and Alexis pointed and laughed at him. Then I felt her hand curl around my arm, and all of a sudden, I was being dragged away. She took me to a spot hidden by a palm tree and a mini windmill. "Oooh, I like your thinking," I told her. She pressed her body lightly against mine and tilted her head to the side, allowing me access to start kissing her neck. Her fingers curled into my hair.

"I'm sorry." She sighed. "I feel bad, like I should be really pissed at Ethan for what he did to you, not be out here laughing and hanging out with him. He hasn't even said sorry yet."

"It's fine." I sucked lightly on her shoulder. "It could be worse. He could've just beaten the shit out of me and forbid us to see each other."

She snorted. "Forbid? What is this? The 1800s? Besides, you really think anyone can stop us from seeing each other?"

I pulled back and watched as her face searched mine, waiting for an answer. I wanted to tell her that they could. That I respected Ethan enough that if he said we couldn't, then I wouldn't. But I couldn't lie to her. "Truth?"

"No," she answered. "Lie to me."

"I don't think anything, or anyone, is ever going to keep me away from you. I love you way too much. You're my heart, my world, *my light*."

AMANDA WAS RIGHT. Whatever Ethan had in the flask was killer, but it did wear off quick enough. By the time we'd gotten home, my body was still numb, but my mind was sobering up. It was the same for all of us, which meant only one thing.

Beers in the backyard.

The girls stayed inside, something about catching up on TV. I heard them giggling about some guy who got cast in that *Fifty Shades* movie. Whatever.

Half an hour later, we were a mess again.

"I can't believe the shit Amanda said last night." Ethan's cap was pulled low on his head as he eyed the night sky.

"What part?" Tristan asked.

I sat up and waited for Ethan to speak.

"That shit—you know, how she blames herself for what happened that night."

I kicked my legs out in front of me. "I know, right? Like it's anyone's fault but mine."

"Psshh," he replied. "Dude, it's not your fault, either."

My eyes narrowed at him. "How is it not—"

"You know what I think?" Tristan cut in, putting his finger up in the air like he was preparing to enlighten us with a piece of wisdom. "I think it's human nature to blame yourself. When things fuck up in life, you always want to find a reason for it. There *has* to be a reason, right? Bad things don't just happen, especially to good people.

"So we sit around and try to make sense of it all, and the only sense we can make is that we probably deserved it, so we make up these ideas in our heads." He linked his fingers behind his head and stretched out. "Like, maybe if I didn't eat that cookie when we were thirteen that caused my best friends to fight for months, then maybe I wouldn't have turned out gay." I didn't miss the knowing look he gave Ethan before continuing. "Like that night—for months I blamed myself, too."

"What?" Ethan asked.

I just sat there and let his words sink in.

"Yeah, remember how I asked the cab driver to pull over so I could take a piss? What would've happened if I didn't? Maybe we would've gotten here on time, maybe the same time as them. It could've all been prevented."

"That's stupid," I said.

He shrugged. "About as stupid as you thinking that you being related to assholes is your fault."

"Agreed." Ethan raised his beer.

"Wait." I turned to Ethan. "You don't think it's my fault? The shit that happened that night? You're pissed at me. There must be a part of you that blames me."

He shook his head and looked me like I was stupid. "I never blamed you for that night. I'm pissed because you left. I mean—I'm sure you have your reasons, but to me—you took the pussy way out. It's not just that you left Amanda, but you and me—we were friends, we were housemates, we saw each other every day. When you left her, you left me, too.

"And it's not just about me having to take care of her, dealing with her crying about missing you, or her being scared or whatever. I'm pissed at you because you should've been there, too. You should've been the one to help her heal. I didn't know what to do half the time. And I was bitter as fuck because I knew you'd know what to do. You always knew what to do with her. Fuck's sake, you got her to quit being afraid of the rain. I'd been trying for years, and then you show up and make it all better. You could've made it all better for her, and I didn't know how to. That's why I was pissed.

"Then one day I open the mailbox, and there's a letter from you—and I could tell right away, just from the look on her face, that she was still in love with you. That pissed me off more. And then you come back and she just forgives you, like she forgot all the shit you put her through...but I get it now. Lexie talked to me about it last night. Dimmy—she doesn't see it that way. She doesn't blame you for any of it—even the leaving part. And I get it. She remembers things differently. While I was trying to get her to stop crying from missing you—she was doing exactly that—just missing you. When I thought she was having nightmares about what those assholes did to her—truth is—she was dreaming about what they did to *you*. We experienced things differently. She's crazy, stupid in love with you, and I wouldn't have understood it, not until I started dating

Lexie. Now I'm crazy, stupid in love with her, and it all kind of makes sense."

I stayed silent, replaying his words verbatim in my mind. I looked into the house to where Amanda was in her Hello Kitty pajamas, laughing with Lexie. I turned back to Ethan and opened my mouth to speak, but his hand in the air stopped me. "You don't need to say anything. I get it."

I'm glad he said that, because I had no idea what I was about to say.

Tristan sighed, his body slumping further down in his chair. "You guys are making me want to turn straight."

We laughed quietly.

"You think it's funny. If I could get girls like Dimmy and Lexie, I probably would."

Ethan sat up now, paying full attention to his best friend. "I'm sure there are plenty of guys interested in you."

Tristan raised an eyebrow.

"Fine," Ethan conceded. "I really don't know shit about your love life. Is that weird? Do you want me to ask you about it? I mean..." He shrugged. "I just don't know how open you want to be about it all."

The living room door slid open, and Amanda stuck her head out. "You guys coming to bed?"

"Yeah, in a minute," we said in unison, then laughed.

Lexie snorted. "It's like we're nagging housewives and they're forty."

They closed the door, and Tristan continued. "I wish I was straight."

"Don't be gay," Ethan joked. "You can't choose that shit."

Tristan belched. "I know. But sometimes I'll be sitting on the sofa and Amanda will walk in, in her tight gym shorts and her sports bra, and her goddamn perfect ass—"

"Whoa," I said, at the same time Ethan said, "Gross, dude."

Tristan laughed. "Just bear with me here. I'm trying to prove a point." His eyes were half-closed, the alcohol clearly affecting him. "So she walks in wearing barely anything with this killer body, and I look down at my dick," he lowers his head to look down at his junk, "... and I stare at it, thinking, *just get hard, just once, if she can't do it for you...then there's no hope*."

By now, I've started laughing.

He kept on, getting more animated. "I'm like, *Come on, kid!*" he shouted. "*Get. Hard.*" He got louder. "GET A FUCKING HARD-ON!" He was screaming now. Ethan was on the ground laughing. I held my ribs, trying to ease the pain. The image of a twenty-two-year-old jock like Tristan yelling at his dick to get hard was just too fucking much.

"I'LL GIVE YOU A DOLLAR! JUST GIVE ME A BONER!"

I WAS STILL laughing when I got into bed with Amanda.

"What's funny?"

I shook my head, containing my laugh.

"What?" she asked through a smile.

"Just Tristan—trying to get hard when he looks at your ass."

"What?" she squealed.

"Nothing, babe." I was still buzzed. "I can't even explain it right now."

She didn't press further, just pulled the sheets up to her chin and got more comfortable.

"You didn't take your Xanax again."

I shrugged. "I'm fine, babe, honestly."

She scooted closer, resting her head on my chest. "Will it hurt if I hug you?"

"Not sure, try it."

She did. "Does it hurt?"

"No." Lie.

"What did you and Ethan talk about?"

"A lot of stuff."

She kissed my chest once. My fingers played with her hair. "Are you going to tell me, or is it some kind of guy code or something?"

"It's not a guy code. It's just something between me and Ethan, and I think I'd prefer it to stay that way."

"Okay," she said suspiciously.

"It's nothing bad. You just mean a lot to both of us, that's all."

She sighed. "So are things going to be okay with you two? And with us?"

"Yes." Truth.

31

LOGAN

I waited for her at the bar while she finished up her shift. We'd spent every spare second together since the blow up at her house. That was a week ago.

"All done." She untied her apron and threw it in the air dramatically. "I have the weekend off and I'm going to spend every single second of it attached to you, and you better not complain." She pointed her finger at me with her lips pursed. As if I'd ever complain about that.

"Shit," I teased. "I kind of planned on seeing my other girlfriends at some point."

She gasped in mock horror. "Well," she said, her nose up in the air as she made her way to the exit. I watched her ass as she did. "You better tell them to go easy on you. You should be healed well enough to let me do..." She spun around and started walking backwards. "...some really dirty, dirty things to you."

I grunted.

Legit, grunted.

I quickened my pace to catch up to her. "What kind of dirty things?" I asked, putting my arm around her and bending low so only she could hear.

She shrugged. "I dunno," she said, then pinched my ear. Hard. "Tell me again about these so-called other girlfriends?"

I pulled back, laughing. She let go of my ear. "I love when you get jealous. It's such a fucking turn on."

We got to my truck, and I opened the door for her. She turned around to face me before getting in. "Seriously, how sore are you?" She pulled at my shirt until my chest touched hers.

I shook my head. "Not sore at all."

She wet her lips with fire in her eyes.

I drove home, completely distracted by her hand on my dick.

We were there no longer than a minute before our clothes were off and I was inside her. We had to go slow. I'd lied. I was still a little sore.

"DOES MICKY NEED me to bring anything tomorrow?"

"No." I spoke into my pillow. I was half-asleep when I turned my head in her direction. "I don't even know what it is. I hope it's just the gang, you know?"

She moved in closer so we shared the pillow and her nose touched mine. "It's a good reason to celebrate, though. You being home and all."

I couldn't help the smile that formed. "Yeah? You know what else is a good reason to celebrate?"

"What?"

I put my arm around her waist and pulled her closer. "You."

"Me?"

"Yup. Just you. I love you, Amanda."

She kissed me softly. "I love you so much, Logan."

And just like when I dreamt it, her voice, her words replayed in my head, over and over until sleep consumed me.

"WAKE UP," SHE whispered against my lips. I opened my eyes slowly, letting them adjust to the morning light. She hovered above me on her hands and knees, her hair loose and curtaining her face.

I lifted my hand to move it so I could see her clearly. "Jesus Christ ..."

"Why are you smiling like that?"

I hadn't realized I was. "I'm just happy."

"Why?"

"Because." I paused, searching for the right words. Moving her to the side of me, I kissed each of her wrists. "Because you're here. You're real. And you're mine."

She grinned from ear to ear. "I have a present for you."

"What?" I reared back.

She rolled her eyes. "Okay, not really a present. But..." She sat up and reached over to the nightstand and came back with a plate. Five cupcakes. Two with candles. "I missed out on your last birthday, and you didn't get cake the birthday before. So..." Her voice was strained as she lit the candles. "Happy birthday, baby. I love you."

I sat up, so we were face to face. I couldn't tear my eyes off her if I'd tried. I took my time, wanting to remember this moment. Savor it. Because ten, twenty, thirty years from now—when I told our kids the moment I knew my nightmares were over and that my dreams had come true—I'd have every detail clear.

"Babe." She smiled softly. "The candles are going to burn out. You need to make a wish and blow them out."

I didn't need to wish for anything. I had everything I'd ever needed right in front of me. "I love you," I told her, before taking a deep breath and exhaling. Licking the icing off one, I asked, "Why five cupcakes?"

"Oh." She shrugged. "Two are for me."

My eyebrows bunched. "And the other one?"

Her smile grew. "That's for this." And faster than I thought possible, she'd picked it up and smeared it all over my face. I froze. My body had not yet caught up with my mind. Her giggles got louder and louder.

"You are in so much trouble," I deadpanned, throwing the covers off me and lunging for her. Her high-pitched squeal filled the room, but it was cut off quickly enough when I pinned her body with mine against the floor.

She licked the icing off my face. "Mm," she hummed.

My nose scrunched. "That's kind of gross." I laughed. "I have another place you could lick it off." And like an asshole, I thrust my dick into her leg.

Her eyes widened. "That, Mr. Matthews, is an amazing idea."

And that's how we spent the next two hours. Licking icing off each other.

Best. Non. Birthday. Ever.

———

WE WERE LATE showing up to Jake's. Who would have thought it would take so long to clean icing off naked bodies? Not that I was complaining. At all.

"So, you've missed out on Lucy versus Jess, Battle of the Brains." Cam laughed. They'd spent the last hour catching me up on shit that had happened the year I was away. It was just the gang, like I'd hoped. "So tell me about this so-called battle." I stretched my arms out and settled one behind Amanda's chair. Her lips turned up at the corners. She did this—noticed the little things I did that came naturally, and she took the time to appreciate them.

"She's a fucking whore," Lucy snapped.

We all laughed.

Cam began the story, "So, this girl is epic pissed at Luce because she's —without fail—top of the class—every time—which is right, because you know Luce. My girl's wicked smart." He put on a Boston accent for the last two words, mimicking *Good Will Hunting.* "But this Jess girl—"

"Whore," Lucy cut in.

We laughed again.

"Anyway," Cam chuckled. "We were at this club a few months back—"

Lucy intervened. "She's just a fucking whore, Logan. That's all you need to know. Whore. She's been boning the professor since freshman year. The dude's like fifty. It's fucking disgusting."

"Gross," Amanda said from next to me.

Cam laughed. "So Jess—"

"WHORE!" Lucy yelped.

Cam turned to her. "Baby, he gets it. She's a whore." Then he said to me, "So Jess—" He quickly moved to cover Lucy's mouth. "—is at this club, and she purposely spilled her drink all over Lucy. Of course, Lucy got pissed. Wait; she didn't just get pissed or mad. She like, *erupted.*"

Jake cut in, clicking his fingers in the air, and putting on a girl voice. "Twinkle twinkle little whore, close your legs they're not a door."

We all cracked up, including Lucy.

"She actually sang that one." Cam laughed again. He looked over at me. "She had her pinned against the wall, with her hands on her shoulders. Jess—"

"WHORE!"

Cam shook his head. "*Whore's* eyes were huge. She didn't think Lucy had it in her. Then Luce made some comment about *Whore's* breath smelling like wrinkly old-man ball sacs."

Amanda spat out her water and then started choking on her laughter. I patted her back, but I couldn't hold it together, either.

Classic drunk Lucy was always the best.

"Wait," Micky shouted. "There was one more." She wiped at her eyes as she tried to level her breathing. "Oh, yeah! Did it hurt when you fell from the top of the slut tree and banged every gray-pubed geriatric dick on the way down?"

The roar of our laughter filled the yard.

Lucy just sat quietly with a smile on her face as she drank her beer. She saw me watching her and winked. Fuck, I'd missed her.

———

"LOGAN," HEIDI CALLED out from across the fire pit. She didn't wait for conversation to die down. She just cut right in. Everyone turned to her. She hadn't said much during the night. I figured maybe she was embarrassed in front of Amanda for the way she'd treated her the last time we'd seen her, but looking at her now, she was beyond the buzzed state the rest of us were in. She was drunk, which was evident when she mumbled, "You ever think about what would've happened if you and I never broke up? We could've been good—you and me."

Her eyes were bloodshot, half-hooded. She struggled to hold her head up. I struggled to answer. "Um, I think maybe—"

"I mean, I know we just fucked ... a lot ..."

Amanda tried to wriggle her hand out of my hold, but I tightened my grip. I felt her body move away, but I couldn't take my eyes off Heidi.

"And when I told you that I wanted to date another guy—Dylan." She rolled her eyes. "I thought you'd at least try to stop me, you know. I thought we had something good. Not just the sex."

Amanda tried again to remove her hand. I held onto it tighter still.

We all sat in silence, but Heidi kept going. "We could have worked. You and I could've been the hot power couple through high school, maybe even college. Then I wouldn't be some college junior whose boyfriend dumped her for the Marines." She laughed once. "Remember how we'd lay naked in bed all day and teach each other *everything*. Those were good times, Logan. We should do it again sometime."

My eyebrows pinched. What the hell had happened to her while I was gone? It had to be more than just Dylan leaving.

Jake cut in. I'm glad he did, because I couldn't have formed words if I'd tried. "I think you've had enough to drink, Heids. Maybe it's time to call it a night."

I turned to face him.

"Yeah. You're right," Heidi agreed. "I've texted my friend. She's on her way."

I was too busy looking at Micky, who was frowning.

I followed her gaze.

Amanda.

Shit.

AMANDA

I KEPT MY head down, not wanting them to notice the stupid tears in my stupid eyes. Then I heard her speak, "Well, Logan, it was really nice seeing you again. I'm really glad you're home." I saw her feet stop in front of his from the corner of my eye. I still refused to look up. But then he released my hand that I'd been trying to withdraw, and the movements made me glance up at them.

And I wish that I hadn't.

Her arms were out, an invitation for a hug.

He stood up.

She placed her hands around his shoulders.

He wrapped his around her waist.

Then her fingers curled into his hair, bringing his face closer to hers.

And then their mouths connected.

She moaned.

Thump. Thump.

And then nothing.

My eyes shut tight.

My stomach hit the floor.

My head dropped.

His voice broke through. "I'll walk you out," he said.

And then he was gone.

Seconds passed. It felt like hours.

"Amanda?" Micky crooned.

I lifted my eyes to her.

"She's not in a good way. She's been struggling with a lot of stuff lately. It doesn't mean anything. He didn't kiss her back."

I nodded once. It was all I could do.

Then I cleared my throat. "It doesn't matter." It really didn't. Because I was here, and he was with her.

32

LOGAN

I TRIED TO take her hand when I got back, but she crossed her arms over her chest and looked down. I sighed and moved so I could speak into her ear. "I didn't kiss her back, babe. I pulled away as soon as I knew what was happening."

"It doesn't matter," she said quietly but refused to look at me. It did matter. *Obviously*, it mattered.

"Amanda," I tried again.

She chewed her lip, her exhale of breath causing it to quiver. I leaned in close and softly kissed her cheek. "I'm sorry," I whispered.

She raised her hand and wiped at her eyes. "It's fine. We'll talk about it later, not here." Her voice broke.

So did my heart.

I pulled back, not knowing what else to do. I placed my hand on her leg and watched as it began to tremble. She glanced at it quickly before staring off into the distance.

She didn't cover it.

She didn't comfort me.

She didn't speak for the rest of our time there.

We said goodbye earlier than expected. It was awkward, not just for us, but for everyone.

I kept my hand on her leg on the drive home. It hadn't stopped trembling. She kept quiet, eyes fixed on the road in front of her.

I spoke first. "You obviously didn't see it, but I pushed her away as soon as—"

"I don't care about that," she cut in. She sounded sad, and tired. Maybe she was tired of me fucking up.

"Then what's wrong? Will you please talk to me?"

"If you don't know—"

"No. I'm sorry, but don't pull that, *if you don't know then I shouldn't have to tell you* shit. Obviously I don't know. You *need* to tell me."

She sighed, glancing at me quickly. "I don't know, Logan. It's not just about her kissing you. It's that you just let her sit there and talk about you guys like that. You didn't interrupt her; you didn't ask her to stop. Do you know how that made me feel? She was disrespecting me, and you didn't even care."

Shit.

"Why didn't you say anything?" she asked.

I got defensive. I don't know why. Maybe because I knew she was right, and I felt like an asshole. "Why didn't *you* say anything?"

She got louder. "Because she's your friend, Logan. Not mine."

"It's just stupid that we're arguing about this right now."

"You think my feelings are stupid?" she cried.

"That's not what I said."

"How the hell would you like it if Tyson sat in front of you and all of my friends and started talking about us and how we used to *fuck.*" She spat out the last word, wanting to hurt me.

It did.

I stayed silent.

"You think it would be okay if he told you about how he took my virginity? And that I had no idea what I was doing, so he taught me everything, just the way he liked it? Maybe the things you like, that I do to you, are things he showed me." I felt the bile rise in my throat. I wanted to tell her to stop, but she kept talking. "You'd want to sit there and listen to how he used to sneak into my room at night so we could have sex? Or the times out in his car, when we had nowhere else to go? Or how about the first time we made each other co—"

"Stop!" It came out more forcefully than I'd intended, but I felt sick. Legit, sick to my stomach. I wanted to puke. "I get it, okay? Enough."

"You get it?" She laughed once, that bitter fucking laugh I hated so much. But it was different this time—quieter—as if she were still lost in her own thoughts. "That's not the point, Logan. The point is that I would never let him talk about that stuff. Not in front of our friends and definitely not in front of you. And you know why?" It wasn't a question. "Because I respect you, and I respect us. And you—you didn't. You just let it happen. And then you left me sitting there, feeling disrespected and pathetic, while you walked her out of the house to make sure *she* was okay." She took a few calming breaths. "I hope she was okay, because *I* wasn't."

Finally, I found my voice. "What did you want me to do? I wanted to make sure she got in the car safe."

She shook her head. "She had four other friends there. If they didn't know to look out for her, you should have asked one of them to. You should've known how that would make me feel."

The worst part is—is that she wasn't angry. She just stared straight ahead, letting the tears fall silently. She didn't raise her voice. Maybe if she was angry, it wouldn't hurt so much. She was sad, upset, disappointed.

I'd fucking disappointed her.

I caught her eyes lower to my hand on her leg. It wasn't trembling anymore; now it was all-out uncontrollably shaking. My heart beat so hard against my chest, it made my ribs ache. I waited for her to cover it or to hold it, maybe lift it and kiss my palm like she used to. But she didn't. Instead, I removed it from her leg, shook it out twice, and sat on it, hoping it might help.

"I'm sorry," I said quietly, staring straight ahead. I vowed to spend the rest of the night telling her, and showing her, how sorry I really was.

She parked next to her car when we got to the apartment's parking garage. I stepped out of my truck, but she didn't. Walking to her side, I opened the door and held out my hand to help her. She didn't take it, just jumped down on her own. She leaned against the car, rifling through her bag. "I think I'm just going to go home," she said quietly, refusing to look at me.

"What?" My chest ached, not from the thumping of my heart, but from the breaking of it. "Please, don't do this." I was begging. I didn't care. "I mean, I know I fucked up. And I'm sorry. It just seems so insignificant, so petty—" She finally looked up at me with her eyes wide, filled with tears. *Shit.* "That's not—" I sighed, trying to calm myself. "That's not what I meant. I just mean in comparison to everything we've been through—"

"Maybe," she interrupted. "But it doesn't stop it from hurting. Pain is pain regardless. And I need to feel that pain, deal with it, and I can't do that with you around. I just can't."

I sucked in a shaky breath.

She pulled out her keys and unlocked her car. I opened her door and watched as she took a seat and started it. She tried to smile up at me, but she couldn't.

Then she was gone.

I watched her taillights fade away while I hoped, prayed, begged for her to turn around and come back.

But she never did.

My hand shook against my leg. Lifting it, I inspected it closer. And then I snapped. "Fuck you," I growled. I turned around and smashed it against the side of my truck. It made the shaking worse.

JAKE CALLED AN hour later. I was wide awake in bed, staring up at the ceiling. I hit answer but didn't speak. He sighed. "Should I come over?"

"No," I answered quickly. I didn't want to see anyone.

Lie.

There was one person, but she didn't want to see me.

"Tonight was messy," he uttered.

"Understatement."

"Is she there?"

"No."

"Shit. Is she pissed?"

"Truthfully, I don't think she's pissed. She's upset. She said she was disappointed, thought that I let Heidi disrespect her."

He laughed. "That's pretty much the exact words Kayla used."

"Yeah?"

"Yup."

"Must be a girl thing."

He laughed again. "No, dude, it's kind of what happened."

"Fuck." I knew he was right, but hearing him confirm it was like a kick in the gut.

"Yeah."

"I just wanted to make sure Heidi was okay, you know?"

"Yeah," he agreed. "I totally get it. But Heidi—she's kind of been a mess since Dylan left. The girls have tried talking to her, but she won't talk to anyone. Honestly, if I had to watch Kayla's ex try to kiss Kayla, I'd more than likely beat the shit out of him. We all saw when Amanda slapped that girl for Lucy. I'm surprised she didn't do the same to Heidi."

"Valid."

He let out another sigh. "What are you going to do?"

"I don't know."

Truth.

I KNOW WHAT I didn't do, and that was sleep. Not a wink, the entire night. I lay in bed with the curtains open and watched the darkness turn to dawn. I wanted to call her. I wanted to beg her to come back. But she wanted to get through this, and she wanted to do it alone.

I looked at the time on my phone; it'd been in my hand the entire night, waiting for her to call.

5:15.

"Dammit." I pushed the covers off, stood up. At the exact same time, there was a light knocking on the door. I opened my nightstand drawer to retrieve the gun. I stared at it for a second before the knocking sounded again. It was soft, almost as if they knew how I'd react if it were any louder. I left the gun and shrugged on a shirt as I made my way to the door.

I looked through the peephole.

She stood, with her hair a mess piled on top her head and a nervous look on her face. She appeared as bad as I felt.

Unlocking the four deadbolts seemed to take forever. Maybe it was because I was so anxious to get to her that both my hands were shaking.

When I finally got the door open, her eyes snapped up and roamed my face. Surely she'd be able to see what a mess I was. She didn't speak as she stepped inside and walked into the bedroom. I locked all the locks on the door, checking them over three times before following her in there.

She stood in the middle of the room with her hands at her sides and tears in her eyes. I took the few steps until I was right in front of her. I wanted to speak, but I mentally couldn't. She looked up at me with a pained expression on her face. A tear fell.

I hated myself.

I hated that I was the one to cause her tears. I tried to wipe it away, but my hand shook against her cheek. She held it against her face and inhaled deeply and then blew out slowly. And then she kissed my palm. Once. Twice. By the third time, it had steadied. Then she dropped it.

Slowly, she slipped out of her dress and lifted my shirt over my head and onto her. I watched her every move in dead silence, wanting to remember it. Savor it.

She climbed into her side of the bed but faced the wall. I climbed in, lifted the sheets to our shoulders and snuck in close behind her. I didn't know if she wanted to be touched or talked to, so I tentatively placed my hand on her waist. She flinched slightly but didn't remove it. I moved in even closer, my chest plastered to her back. I wrapped my arms around her stomach and brought her in as close as possible.

Then she spoke. "Your heart's going a million miles. Did you take your Xanax?"

I sighed, relieved she was speaking. "I forgot," I told her truthfully.

"You can't do that, Logan. I felt your hand on my leg last night. You can't stop taking it."

I swallowed loudly. This wasn't the conversation I wanted to have. "Will you please turn around? I hate talking to you like this. Please?"

She shifted in the bed until we were face to face. Placing her palm against my chest, she looked up at me. "Did you sleep at all?"

I shook my head. "No. You?"

She leaned closer and placed her lips over my heart. "No."

"Amanda," I choked out. Clearing my throat, I moved her hair away from her eyes and lifted her chin to face me. "I'm so sorry. For all of it. For not thinking about you and the way you'd react to what happened. I'm sorry I made you feel the way you did. The last thing I ever, *ever* want to do is make you feel—"

"Sshh," she cut in. "I'm sorry, too. I think I overreacted—"

"No, you didn't. Not at all. You had every right to be upset with me. You were right, and I just didn't think. That's all. I didn't think. I'm stupid—"

"Stop. Don't call yourself that." She paused, waiting for her words to come together. "Maybe it's just another burst in our bubble, you know? Maybe something like this just needed to happen. But I don't like it, Logan. I hate being upset, and I hate that we hurt each other. I don't want us to do that. We can't be destructive, and you're right, after everything we've been through, it is petty. I let it form into something bigger than it should've been—"

"No, you didn't. It is a big deal. I should have spoken up *for* you. I won't ever see her again."

"Quit it." She kissed me once, slowly, letting her lips linger on mine. "That's not what I want."

"What do you want then?" I kissed her back, just as softly. I let my tongue slide along her lips, asking for entrance. She opened her mouth slightly, darting her tongue out to brush against mine.

"I just want you."

"You already have me."

"And I want sleep." She struggled to keep her eyes open. "And I want to wake up and be in your arms and forget this shitty night ever existed."

"That sounds perfect."

33

LOGAN

"AMANDA." I SHOOK her shoulders. "Babe, wake up."

She nudged my hands off of her. "No," she whined.

"You gotta get up."

She slowly turned over, her hair smeared all over the place. I chuckled as I moved it out of her face. She opened one eye tentatively. Then a slow smile formed. "How are you this hot in the morning?" She reached up and pulled my head down to her neck, tilting it for better access.

I ran my tongue up her neck to her jaw. "I could ask you the same thing."

"Mm," she moaned. "Morning sexy times." She curled her fingers into my hair and pushed my head down her body, lifting her shirt at the same time.

"Holy shit." I covered her nipple with my mouth, feeling my dick get harder and harder. "Babe, we gotta be quick, and you gotta be quiet."

"I can do that," she said, still half-asleep. She pulled on my hair to shift my mouth to her other breast. "I'm already wet."

"Shit." I started kissing her lower, licking down her stomach. She writhed beneath me, spreading her legs wider. I moved her panties to the side so I could feel her. I could already smell how turned on she was before I felt it. I looked up at her, chewing her lip, her eyes still closed. I questioned for a second if she was actually aware of what was happening. "Babe?"

"Shut up, Logan. Just get inside me."

She didn't have to tell me twice.

"OH MY GOD ..." She breathed out, her fingernails finally relaxing against my skin. "Why were you covering my mouth telling me to shut up?"

Why did I?

Waiting for the post-come buzz to fade, I kissed along her collarbone while one of her hands combed through my hair. And then it hit me. I pulled back suddenly, startling her. And then I laughed. I couldn't help it. "You gotta clean up and get in the shower. Heidi's here to see you."

AMANDA

"HEY," SHE greeted me. She looked about as good as I had at five this morning, when I'd finally decided my pride didn't matter as much as my relationship with Logan did. Hence why I'd shown up here fifteen minutes later.

"Hi." I raised my hand in a small wave.

"Um. I went to your house, but your brother told me you were here. I was hoping to talk to you, if that's okay with you—and Logan—of course."

He walked out of the bedroom with his hair still wet from the shower and his laptop in his hand. "I'll be up on the rooftop, just call me when you're done." Then he kissed my cheek quickly, over and over again.

"Stop." I giggled out, pushing him away. "Go!"

He laughed. "Lock the door behind me." And then he was gone. I did what he said, then turned to Heidi.

Awkward.

"So." I shifted on my feet. "What's up?"

"Can we sit?"

I led her to the sofa and took a seat.

She smiled, but it was well-practiced and clearly fake. Then she sighed, letting her shoulders drop and her features even out. "Obviously I'm here to apologize." She paused, waiting for my reaction. If she expected me to tell her that it was fine and that she didn't need to, she was wrong. "I was horrible to you—not just last night—but that first night at Lucy's bonfire..." She trailed off, away in her own thoughts.

"Look, I know that you may not understand—" She cut herself off and blew out a breath. "Can I just be honest with you?"

I nodded.

And waited.

"I'm just bitter. And jealous. And drunk. A lot."

My eyebrows bunched together. "You're jealous? Of me? Why? Because I have Logan?"

"No," she said quickly. "Well, I mean yes, and no. I don't know how to explain it."

"Just try."

"Okay." She nodded once, sucked in a breath, and let her words out all at once. "I was pregnant."

I gasped.

She nodded in confirmation, her eyes instantly welling with tears. "When Dylan told me that he'd enlisted, I was seven weeks pregnant. I didn't know. He came over to the house and I wanted to tell him, but he said he had some news, so I let him go first. He told me he was leaving. He'd enlisted, and he didn't think it was a good idea for us to keep seeing each other. Not when his future was unclear."

"Heidi," I consoled. "Did you tell him?"

She laughed sadly. "What was I supposed to do?" Her voice was strained as she wiped her eyes. "It's not like he was going and wanted us to work out. He told me he wanted to leave me. I mean—yeah—I could've told him. He could've stayed—but it wouldn't have been for me. It would have been for our baby." She cried now, her body folding over itself. "Our baby," she repeated.

I sniffed, trying to hold it together. "So you..."

"I had to, Amanda. I had no choice. I couldn't do it alone—and it wouldn't have been fair to ask him to stay."

I rubbed my own eyes. It made sense now—why she was the way she was and how she chose to cope with it. "I'm so sorry, Heidi. I had no idea."

She shook her head, frantically wiping at her cheeks. "No one knows. You can't tell anyone."

"I won't. Swear it."

She inhaled deeply and let it out in a whoosh. "I know it doesn't make sense to you, but that's why...I just wanted someone to blame. And you—you were there. I mean, he told you when he was thinking about joining... he never even mentioned it to me. I get that we had issues but nothing worth breaking up over. But he told *you*. And I don't know. It just felt like you could've been the one to talk him out of it. I know it's stupid, and there's no way you could have known..."

"I get it, though. I understand what you're saying."

"I guess I just got mad at you, and angry, because Logan came back, and you guys are together—and I'm happy for you, I really am. But I'm jealous as all hell because I want that. I want Dylan to come back and declare his love for me, you know?"

I'd started crying, too. I couldn't even imagine what she'd gone through. And she was right; Logan was back, he was here, and we were together.

She sniffed once. "I just needed someone to blame because there had to be a reason for it all, and I'm so sorry that I made you that reason. It's not fair."

"It's okay," I said truthfully. "Honestly, I get it. You're not bad people."

She nodded. We both tried to sniff back our emotions.

"Are you going to tell him, Heidi?"

She shrugged. "What good will it do?"

"I don't know. I just think he has the right to know."

She turned to face me. Our eyes locked for the longest time. "When did you get your tattoos?"

I gazed down at my wrists. "His birthday—the night it happened."

She gave me sympathetic look. "Did he know you had them?"

I shook my head.

"Why didn't you tell him?"

"Because it wouldn't bring him back."

"Exactly."

34

AMANDA

"DID HE TELL you a bunch of embarrassing stuff about me as a kid? Is that what you guys did all the time?"

"Yes," I deadpanned. "In fact, that's all we did. He even told me about how you can rap Vanilla Ice, word for word."

He glanced at me quickly, his eyes huge. "He did not."

I let out a laugh. "He didn't. But your reaction just told me you totally can."

"Shut up." He tried to push me away from him.

We were in his truck on the way to his dad's house. I'd been sitting under his arm with my hand under his shirt, playing with his abs the entire drive. The stuff that had happened last night—and today with Heidi—was emotionally draining. I was so glad we got through it quickly, and that things were back to normal.

I picked up his iPod from its holder on the dash and went through his playlist.

"What are you doing?" he asked.

Finding the track I wanted, I hit cue. I watched him with a smart-ass smirk on my face, and waited for the current track to finish. When it did and "Ice Ice Baby" started, he narrowed his eyes at me. "I don't know the words," he declared.

And right on cue, he started, "All right, stop..."

My laugh was as loud as the stereo. He bit his lip, trying to contain his own guffaw. "Fuck it," he announced. He turned the stereo up and made a show of knowing all the words and throwing Vanilla Ice-style fingers in the air. He was so damn beautiful in his happy, carefree state. My chest tightened as I watched him. This boy could've turned out either way, but he chose his life. He made his own decisions. He let the past stay in the past, and he made his own future—one that I hoped to be a part of forever.

He turned to me now, his dimples deepening. "What's up?"

I shook my head. "Nothing."

Placing a kiss on my cheek, he asked, "Sure?" He rested his hand on my leg.

"Yeah, I just love you a lot. That's all."

He curled his arm around my shoulders, bringing me closer to him and kissing my temple. "That's not *all*," he said quietly. "That's *everything*."

HE TOLD ME to wait while he got out and opened my car door for me.

"You don't have to open doors for me," I said, taking his hand as he helped me step out.

He shrugged. "You're my girl." Keeping my hand in his, he led me to the front of his truck and quickly turned to me. "And just so you know, I love you, too."

I beamed up at him and curled my arm around his neck, bringing his lips down to meet mine. He flattened his hand on the small of my back, deepening the kiss and pushing me until my back hit his truck. My hands fisted in his shirt, trying to hold on to something. His kisses made me weak. Not just at the knees, but in my head and in my heart. He pushed me further until my back was on his hood and he was above me. His hand went under my shirt, gripping my waist lightly.

"Ahem."

We pulled apart instantly and looked up at his dad. His arms were crossed over his chest; they lifted slightly with his chuckle. "Well, this is déjà vu," he stated.

We smiled at each other.

It really was.

"Baby, you don't need a YouTube video to show you how to cut peppers. I'll show you."

He moved his hand, holding his phone away from me. "No," he warned. "I'm gonna watch this video. You wait, I'm gonna be the best damn pepper cutter-upperer you've ever met."

I rolled my eyes. "I could've done it by now." I tried to remove the peppers from the board in front of him, but he slapped my hands away. "No, that's not the point. I need to learn to do this stuff."

Giggling, I crossed my arms and lifted my chin. "Why? Why is learning to cut peppers so damn important?"

"I don't know." His shoulders lifted. "You shouldn't always be cooking. It's time I learn this shit. What if you're pregnant and too tired to cook or whatever?"

I heard Alan's intake of breath. We both turned to him. His eyes bugged out of his head. "I'm not!" I assured him, at the same time as Logan said, "She's not."

He breathed out a sigh of relief before taking a swig of his beer. He pointed the bottle at me before placing it on the counter. "You should know by now that Logan needs to do things his way. He needs to learn the specific details of everything he does, over-analyze things. That's the way his brain works."

"See? Even Dad knows that about me." He looked down at his phone, frantically typing. "Geez, Amanda. What kind of future wife are you?"

Alan gasped again.

Logan laughed at him. "That one I said just to mess with you."

LOGAN

"You guys know I can cook other meals apart from taco casserole, right?"

Dad and I glanced at each other before glaring at her. "What is wrong with you?" I only half-teased, but the words were muffled by the mouthful of the greatest tasting food in the entire fucking word.

"I make a really mean pot roast," she declared.

I huffed out a sigh and turned my body to her. "Baby, quit it. You're ruining this moment."

Her eyes narrowed at me. "What moment?" I motioned with my eyes to the plate of food in front of me. "You're kidding, right?" She laughed out. "You're having a moment with food?"

Dad's chuckle caused us both to turn to him. "Sweetheart," he said to her. "I think he may love your food more than he loves you."

I mocked gasping loudly and covered her ears with my hands. Sticking my nose in the air, I joked, "Father, not in front of the child." She scrunched her nose and swatted my hands off of her. I lowered my voice and spoke in her ear, "Seriously, babe. I could never love anything more than you. Ever."

Her eyes lifted to glance quickly at my dad. She smiled a little, a blush creeping to her cheeks. I kissed her there, leaving a splatter of taco sauce. I chuckled as I wiped my mouth with a napkin and then wiped her cheek. "What am I going to do with you? Honestly, I can't take you anywhere."

She turned her head and lifted her chin to face me. Her smile caught me off guard. Our eyes locked.

Then: *Thump. Thump.*

But it was different this time. Not nerves or anxiety. It was like the world's way of telling me that I was alive and to pay attention, that the girl in front of me, the one who could make or break me, was here. But she did neither of those things. Instead, she healed me.

I love you, she mouthed. It made my thumping heart race but in all the good ways.

I opened my mouth to speak, but her ringing phone cut us off.

"Sorry." She grimaced. "It's Ethan. I should get that." She stood. "I'm sure I told him I wasn't going to be home," she mumbled to herself before exiting the room.

Dad cleared his throat. I gave him my attention. "You seem happy."

"Of course I am," I said, a sudden cockiness returning. I began to count on my fingers. "One. I have my girl." I paused. "Two..." I trailed off. There was no two. Nothing else really mattered. Shrugging, I stated, "I have my girl. That's all."

His smile got wider. "And she doesn't just make you happy. She makes you whole?"

I nodded.

"And Ethan? He's okay with it now?" He must've known Ethan was the one to do the damage on me, but he never brought it up, never accused him. That's the thing with Dad; he always took a step back and waited for me to make my own choices, but he never pushed; he only ever encouraged. Like in seventh grade when I told him I wanted to be doctor, he smiled, but all he said was, "If that's what you want, of course I'll support you, but you make sure you're doing it for you." I didn't get what he'd meant back then, but I get it now. He didn't want me doing it for him. Truth: in a way, I kind of was. I guess I wasn't doing it *for* him, but I did it because I wanted to be the kind of man he was. The kind of man who could give his life over to a complete stranger—a little boy who needed help—and not once expect a thank you for any of it. So I let the words flow out of me before I dared stop them. "Thank you, Dad." His eyes widened in surprise. "Thank you for never giving up on me and for always being there. And understanding me better than anyone else. You've done all this stuff for me, and I can't—" My voice cracked. I cleared the knot in my throat. "I can't thank you enough, for all of it. Taking me in—"

He raised his hand to interrupt. "That's enough of that." I didn't miss the moisture that welled in his eyes. "You never have to thank me for anything, Logan. You may think I saved you, but to me, it was the other way around. You gave me a family when I thought I'd never have one. I'm so damn proud of you."

"I'm sorry," her voice came from next to me. "I didn't mean to interrupt." She sat back down on her chair and placed her phone on the table and then settled her hand on my leg.

"Is everything okay?" I asked.

"Yeah ..." She seemed deep in thought.

I linked my fingers with hers and squeezed once. "What's going on?"

She turned to me now, with the same faraway expression as before. "That was Ethan," she said.

I already knew that. "Okay?"

"He, um, he found someone to take over my room." She chewed her lip, her eyes searching for a reaction.

It was instant—this stupid grin that completely took over my face.

Her own smile widened. "So, you still want me to move in?"

"What the hell kind of a question is that? You know I do." Letting go of her hand, I pulled out my phone and started typing notes. "You know what we should do? Split the spare room in half, and we can set up a desk on each side, so I'll have all my stuff on one side, and you can have all your girly Hello Kitty shit on the other. I should buy some more towels." I glanced up at her quickly. "You know, the fluffy ones you like. Oh, and gummy bears, we need to fill the house with those. I found this place online that sells them by the color—"

Her laugh cut me off. "Babe, there's no rush. I'm not moving in tomorrow."

My eyes narrowed. "What? Why not?"

"Oh." Her eyes widened. "I mean, I can if you want me to, but we need to discuss this properly. You kind of just said it in passing, and I wasn't sure if you were serious, but I told Ethan anyway—"

"Of course I was serious. What's there to discuss? It's not like we're not together all the time anyway."

She sighed. "It's different though. We need to talk about how much rent I'm going to pay and—"

"No," Dad cut in. I was so overwhelmed with her news that I'd forgotten he was even there. "I've covered his apartment for a year, and you will not be putting a cent toward it. Or anything else you need to move in. Logan will cover it all."

Amanda's voice was quiet. "I can't accept that. You need to let me pay—"

"No," he said with finality. "Besides, you need to save your money for my grandchildren." He stood up, his chair scratching against the floor as he did. Amanda and I gaped at each other, before turning to him. "That one ..." He pointed his finger between the both of us. "I said just to mess with you."

35

LOGAN

A Month Later

SHE SAID SHE'D wanted to talk about something important and to meet her on the rooftop when I got done at the cages with the boys. She spun around from looking out over the edge when she must have heard the door open.

"So, what's up?" I asked after greeting her with a kiss, or eleventy-three of them.

"I think this is a sit-down kind of conversation."

I led us to the outdoor sofa and sat down. Whatever it was, it had to be serious. "What's going on? You're kind of making me anxious here."

Her eyes darted quickly to my hands. They weren't shaking, yet.

I sighed and pulled on her shirt until she was sitting next to me. "Whatever it is, just tell me. Is it about moving in? Did you not want to?" My chest ached. "If you think it was too soon, then that's fine; we can work out something else. I just want to be with you, Amanda. If—"

"Stop. That's not what this is." She blew out a breath and closed her eyes, as if building the courage to speak. I was beyond anxious now, but I tried my hardest not to let it show. "I just don't want you to be mad at me, and all of this started before you came back—"

"Why would I be mad?"

She looked away from me before speaking. "Because I want to go see your birth dad."

And there it was—the trembling in my hand.

I cursed under my breath.

She kneeled down in front of me and took my hand in hers but didn't kiss my palm. She'd stopped doing that weeks ago. "It's okay, baby," she assured me. She made sure I was looking at her when she said the words, "Just focus." It's this thing she'd been trying to get me to do since Dad lowered the dosage on the Xanax. She was trying to get me to control it without the help of meds. "Just focus," she said again. So I closed my eyes and did what she said. She told me to keep a memory—a moment—in my mind, for this purpose alone, where I could think about it and feel all the emotions from that single moment in my life.

I chose her; she didn't know it, though. It was the moment she'd told me she loved me for the first time—and not just in my dreams. Her face had been so close to mine, and she had that genuine, effortless smile I loved so much. "I love you so much, Logan," she said.

I thought it was in my head, but when I opened my eyes, she had a knowing look on her face. Maybe she did know it was her I was thinking of. Or maybe she just said it to say it. We did that a lot—reminded each other of how we felt, took things slow so we could remember them. They'd become *our* moments. Part of *our* life. I felt her palm flat against my chest. "See, you're all better."

I sucked in a breath and tried to remain composed. I pulled her up until she was sitting on my lap. "So, you've wanted to visit him for a while?"

"Yeah," she said quietly, facing the ground. I tilted her chin up so I could see her face.

And then I waited.

"I just think it would be good, for closure or something. I thought about it a lot while you were gone, and then you came back, and I thought that maybe I wouldn't need to anymore, but it's still there, in the back of mind. I still feel like it's something I need to do."

I sucked in a breath and let it out slowly. "Okay ..."

We sat in silence for a few minutes while I thought. She didn't press on, she didn't ask me to speak sooner than I was ready. She knew me well; she knew me better than I faked it.

I continued. "If you want to see him, I'll support you. But I don't. I don't want to see him or even really think about him. I'm done."

She nodded slowly. "I understand that."

I kissed her quickly. "Do you know where he is?"

She nodded again.

"When did you want to see him?"

She swallowed audibly. "Tomorrow."

My eyes drifted shut. "I'll drive."

AMANDA

I TRIED TO ignore the skeezy looks I was getting from the inmates. I did my best to dress as least flattering as I could; I knew that Logan was concerned about that, especially because he wasn't coming into the building with me. He'd called ahead and spoke to someone to make sure that I'd be watched the entire time. I knew I would be and that I'd be *safe,* but if him making that phone call meant that he'd breathe easier while I was in there—then who the hell was I to say anything?

The thumping against my chest made it hard to breathe. I admit it. I was scared. I wasn't afraid that he'd hurt me—not physically, anyway. What I was afraid of was looking into the same monster's eyes that Logan had spent years trying to hide from. And I didn't want that for me. I didn't want to have to hide from him or be afraid of the dark or being alone. I wanted to let go of the hatred in my heart that I carried around because of him. Not so much for what he did when he showed up that night, but for what he did to Logan all the nights before.

Before he was finally *safe.*

HIS EYES WERE cast downwards when I sat down in front of him. He didn't even bother to lift his head. I cleared my throat. Nothing. "Hey, asshole."

That got his attention. Slowly, he lifted his chin. Dried blood and bruises covered his face. Not a single part of me felt sorry. Maybe that made me a bad person, but I doubt it.

"Who are you?" he spat out. The asshole couldn't even remember me. Then he chuckled lightly to himself. "Don't tell me I'm your father."

"No." I assured him. "You don't need to worry about that. My dad—he's an asshole. You—you're a waste of fucking air."

His eyes widened. "Oh. You have a mouth on you."

"Fuck you."

He rolled his eyes and sighed.

Valid. I needed to calm down. I came here to speak to him, to get closure. Not to cuss him out.

"My name's Amanda—"

"Fuck," he growled and then trained his eyes on the table in front of him.

"So you remember me now?" My name must have triggered something.

"What are you doing here, little girl?"

I leaned forward and rested my elbows on the table. "Little girl?" I laughed. I wasn't going to bring up the fact that his daughter was the same age as me. The same one whose sex he traded for drugs.

His jaw tensed, but he still refused to look up at me.

"I came here because I thought you had the right to know. Not because you deserved to, but because you *don't*." I paused, trying to find a place to start. "Logan—he's an amazing person. The best, actually."

His eyes lifted slightly.

"You know he's really smart? He's studying to be a doctor, just like his *dad*."

He lifted his chin now, paying more attention.

"And he's so genuine. He cares about everyone and everything and *always* puts himself last." I sniffed back my emotions. "You know he feels everything, right here." I pointed to my chest. "In his heart. And he *loves*. He loves fiercely, with this passion and emotion that's *all* Logan. Every part of him. He gives you every single piece." I wiped away the tears as I struggled to speak. "And you take all those pieces, and you cherish them, because Logan—that's what he deserves." I laughed to myself. "And he's so funny. He's cocky and rude, but he's so damn funny. He always makes the effort to make me laugh. All the time. And he watches me, with this intensity that knocks me back a step. And he doesn't know that I notice, because he's so busy giving me everything." I let it out now—all the feelings I had brewing inside, and I cried. I cried for the person I loved. My person. "He's always thinking. His mind's always churning. You know, he thinks about things that people our age don't even worry about. He wants to cure hunger, fight for world peace, stop slavery—he wants to do it all. He wants to change the world. And you know what? One day, he will." I leaned closer and lowered my voice. "But it won't ever be because of you."

His hands balled into fists on the table, and a low grunt escaped him. His lips formed into a sneer, but he kept quiet.

"No matter what you did to him, you couldn't bring him down. You tried." I laughed bitterly. "Oh, you fucking tried. But you couldn't do it. Because Logan—he's better than you. He's always been better than you. And you missed out on all of it. You missed out on watching this bright, amazing little boy turn into the best man possible. And he did it all without you. He could've played the 'poor me, I was an abused kid' card. But he never did. Not once. He left you exactly where you belong, in the past—where people leave all their regrets and mistakes and fuck-ups. Because that's what you are. A fuck-up. And you deserve to know that. So that five, ten, fifteen years from now, when you hear that your own son, the one who you abused every day of his life when you had him, has done something amazing, you should know that he did it all without you. And everything he achieves, every success he has, I want you to take it as personal *fuck you* from him. And from me, too."

I stood up, ready to leave, but his hand caught my wrist. I looked down at it and panicked for second, before remembering where I was. The guards had already taken two steps forward—ready to pounce.

"Amanda," he croaked. I flinched. My name leaving his mouth made my insides freeze. I looked from my wrist to his eyes. I tried to cover my gasp, but I wasn't quick enough. The monster's eyes I'd been so afraid of matched the ones I loved so much. Only they weren't lively like Logan's. They seemed expired. Beyond their date. *Used.*

He flipped my wrist up so he could see Logan's initials on permanent display. "You love him, don't you?"

I nodded once. "He's my person."

He pulled out a ratty, old envelope from his front pocket. "Jones!" he called out to the guard behind him.

The guard took the steps to cover the space between us. Picking up the letter from his raised hand, he opened it and skimmed it quickly and then handed it to me.

It felt like a ball of fire between my fingers.

I waited until I was in the foyer before reading it.

Thirty-four weeks post-Amanda.

How bad is it that I don't know how to greet you. Dear Dad? Dear Asshole? Maybe Dear Child Abuser? What do I call you? Sperm Donor? Monster?

Dear Monster,

Remember that time when I was six and you told me you'd stop hitting me for a week if I didn't speak for two hours? I didn't speak for an entire day, but the next morning, I got woken up with a fist to my stomach. You probably don't remember. You were too wasted, high, fucked-up in all other ways.

I dreamed about that last night. I woke up in a sweat. No piss this time. I'd say you'd be proud of me. But honestly, I couldn't fucking care less what you thought of me.

Here's the thing. I woke up today with a new outlook on life. It's this: fuck you.

I'm not going to live another day waiting for the darkness to fade or the shadows to pass. You and my mother—you're monsters who hide out in those places. In the shadows and darkness of my life and my thoughts and my dreams. For so long, I'd been afraid to close my eyes. But not anymore.

I almost let you win. You came back, and you turned my dreams into a nightmare. I walked away from the one person in the entire world who I let love me back—and it's because of you. Because you embedded my brain to believe that I wasn't worthy and that I didn't deserve to have the kind of happiness Amanda gave me.

So, fuck you.

Because you're wrong. I've worked hard my entire life to leave you in the past, to not let you have any control over me. And in one night, you came back and you ruined that. You ruined me, and I lost her. And letting you control that, letting you own that part of me, was the biggest mistake of my fucking life.

Because I gave up on her—and I gave up on us.

But I'm going back, and when I do, I'm going to fight for her.

It could take me days, weeks, months, years. It doesn't fucking matter. Because I won't just be fighting for her. I'll be fighting you, too. And if I ever get her back, it'll be my life's biggest achievement.

And the biggest fuck you I could give you.

Because you won't win. I won't let you.

EPILOGUE

September 24Th

LOGAN

ETHAN'S EYES WERE huge as he took in my words. "How the hell did you manage to rent out the entire place?"

Unlocking the gate to the minigolf center, I turned to him. "Let's just say I had to have a lot of sex with a lot of different people, some I'd rather forget."

Amanda's backhand into my stomach knocked the wind out of me. "You're an ass," she stated.

I opened the gate and waited for them to enter. "Baby, don't be mad. I thought about you the entire time."

I walked us over to where all the switches were and started turning them on, just like the owner showed me. Truth is, I came in and asked if it was possible. He said if I covered double the general takings for a Tuesday night, it would be fine, as long as we had a professional clean-up crew come in before opening the next day. He was kind of eyeing me weird the whole time, and I knew the instant recognition hit him because he took a physical step back. "Actually," he'd said. "That's not going to cover it." I'd dropped my shoulders and waited for him to continue. "You're friends with Jake Andrews, right?" It wasn't really a question. "If we can get him here for a day, do some signings, get some pictures, maybe he can donate a signed jersey or baseball to hang up—then I'll let you have it for nothing." I'd smirked. "Sure, bud. Won't be a problem."

Not until I actually told Jake about it.

Ethan came up next to me and nudged my side. "Seriously, dude. This is the best birthday present ever. I can't believe you did all this."

I shrugged, watching Amanda talking to Lexie, Tristan and James, Micky's ex and their new housemate. Tristan was play-punching her arm, counting off each one. She laughed, trying to get him to stop. "I have a lot to make up for," I told him.

"I don't know," Ethan started. "I mean, look at her." I already was. "I think you're done. You came back. You're both healed. You're both moving forward. What else can you do?"

A slow smile spread on my face. "Give her the whole goddamn universe."

An hour later, the place was packed. Alcohol was in full supply, and a handful of guys were actually trying their hand at minigolf. Jake was pissed when I told him that I'd basically traded his time for the place. He hated doing anything that made him the center of attention. I played the pity card and told him I just wanted to give Amanda and Ethan a good time; they deserved it after the hell I'd put them through. It worked. He changed his tone and said he'd be more than happy to do it.

"Have you spoken to Megan since you've been back?" Micky asked over the music.

I leaned forward on the table so she could hear me properly. "Not yet, have you?"

She nodded. "She's doing well, Logan. That new facility she was moved to helped her lots." She smiled proudly. "She's clean, and she's started to sort her life out." Then her features flattened. "It would mean a lot to her if you called or something. Just let her know that you're *safe*, and that you don't blame her for what happened. She's carrying around a lot of that guilt—"

"What?" I interrupted.

"Yeah," she said timidly. "She thinks it's her fault, what happened that night, and you leaving. She even called Amanda to apologize."

I looked over to Amanda, who was laughing at Ethan missing the hole from only inches away. "I'll call her," I promised. "I don't want her thinking any of that shit. I just wanted the time to make things right, you know?" I faced her again. She was nodding, understanding what I meant.

I just wanted Amanda.

AMANDA

LOGAN AND I left the party right after Cameron and Lucy did. They had to be up early to head home. Tomorrow was the anniversary of Lucy's mom's death, and, like every year, they went to visit her with the rest of her family.

"YOU PROMISE YOU can't see anything?" he asked.

I gripped his arm tighter and took the final step onto the roof. "Do *you* promise this isn't going to be like the last time you blindfolded me?"

"Holy shit, babe, my dick just twitched in my pants."

"Really?"

"Yup."

"Let me touch it."

The warmth of his breath from his chuckle hit my cheek. "Okay," he announced. "You ready?"

"Yes." I blinked a few times, adjusting my eyes to the small amount of night light that filtered through once the blindfold was off. We were on the rooftop of the apartment, like I'd suspected, but there was nothing different about it. "Um, I don't—"

His laugh cut me off. "Just wait right here, okay?" He moved swiftly to an outlet next to the door. "Ready?" he shouted.

I nodded.

Then the entire place lit up from above. My eyes darted up to the hundreds of fairy lights that were strung up above us. In the center was a bunch of different sized and colored paper lanterns. But that's not what made me gasp; it was the dozens of tiny glass vials weaved through them.

"See?" He stood next to me and followed my gaze. "Now we just wait for it to rain, and we can start collecting more moments."

I slowly turned to him. His eyes were still focused above us. But he wasn't seeing what I was seeing. What I saw was my future, my life, my world. "Logan, this is amazing."

His smile was instant. That all-out, carefree, deep-dimple-displaying smile I loved so much. He took my hand. "Come on." He led me to a rug set out underneath the center of the lights. I followed. Once we were seated, he said, "Hi." He chewed the corner of his lip and played with a loose thread on the rug.

"Hi," I replied.

We sat cross-legged, facing each other. Our grins matched each other's. "Happy birthday."

"Thank you."

"I got you something."

"No. You've already done so much. You've spent way too much money."

He rolled his eyes. "This didn't cost me anything."

"You sure?"

"Yes, babe," he drawled. "I'm sure."

I perked up. "Okay, then. Gimme!" I threw my hand out, palm up.

He sighed. "It's not—" He took a deep breath and let it out with his words. "It's not what you think it is, and I don't want you to get excited or mad or disappointed because you will, and it's—"

"Logan. Stop!"

"Okay ..."

I moved my hand suggestively closer to him.

And then I waited.

And waited.

It felt like forever.

But the instant the metal hit my palm and the lights from above shined reflectively on the diamond—I flipped my hand and dropped it.

I glared at him, my eyes falling out of my head. His expression matched mine.

I glanced down at the ring, now sitting on the rug.

Thump. Thump.

I looked away.

"I told you it's not what you think it is."

"No," is all I could say. My mind was racing. My palms were sweating.

"Amanda." He tried to get my attention.

I started to stand up, but his heavy hands on my legs stopped me from moving any further.

"What is wrong with you?" He'd started chuckling. I didn't know what was so funny.

"You're giving me an engagement ring, Logan. That's not funny."

He quit laughing. His tone was serious when he said, "It is an engagement ring, but it's not for you. I mean it's not *your* engagement ring."

My face must've shown how confused he just made me because he dropped his head and let out the sigh of all sighs. When he finally lifted it, his eyes were focused, determined. Picking up the ring between us, he asked me to come closer. I did. "Closer," he said again. I moved. "Closer." I was sitting across his lap by the time he was satisfied. "I'm not asking you to marry me," he started. My shoulders relaxed. I wasn't ready for that yet. "I'm not saying that I won't. It's just not our time—*yet*." I smiled, so glad we were on the same page. He continued, "Remember how I told you about Dad's Tina?"

"His high school sweetheart? The one who..." I trailed off.

He glanced away for a second. "Yeah, this is hers."

My breath caught.

"My dad..." He held my hand upright and placed the ring on my palm. I picked it up and started to examine it. It was beautiful. Beyond beautiful. White gold with a single stone, but the stone was huge, triple the width of the band. His words broke into my thoughts, but I kept my eyes on the ring. "He gave this to me when I was sixteen. He said I'd become a man." He laughed lightly to himself. "He told me that moments, the ones I create, the ones I hold on to—they're only worth remembering if I have someone to share them with. He said that when I found someone—someone I wanted to share all of my future moments with—to give them this. And hope that every time that person looks at it, they'll know. They'll know that I wanted to share my life with them.

"And that's what I want. I want that person to be you, Amanda. And if for some reason, shit happens—again—and things don't work out for us, I need you to *know* that. I need you to be able to look at this, for the rest of your life, and know that you're it for me. Because I love you. I've always loved you. I'll always love you. And I hope that that's what you *feel* when you think about this *moment*. Loved."

The tear fell before I realized that I was crying. Lifting my head, I tried to level my breathing. I opened my mouth, but the words didn't exist. He reached around me and gently pulled the chain over my head. After unclasping it, he slid the ring on and secured it around my neck again. I lifted it to see both the ring and vial. I curled my fingers around them, grasping tightly. "This chain holds all my dreams," I told him.

"Yeah?" He smiled softly. "*You* hold all of mine."

WE SETTLED ONTO the rug, me lying down with my head on his

shoulder and his arm around me. We gazed up at the lights above us, listening to them chime as the wind blew and they clanked against the vials. Only then did I take in the masterpiece he'd created. The lanterns all set up in the middle, the twinkling lights forming a circle around them. "Logan, do you know what it looks like?"

"What do you mean?" he asked. But it wasn't really a question. He already knew my answer.

"It looks like the universe."

ABOUT THE AUTHOR

Jay McLean is an international best-selling author and full-time reader, writer of New Adult and Young Adult romance, and skilled procrastinator. When she's not doing any of those things, she can be found running after her three little boys, investing way too much time on True Crime Documentaries and binge-watching reality TV.

She writes what she loves to read, which are books that can make her laugh, make her hurt and make her feel.

Jay lives in the suburbs of Melbourne, Australia, in her dream home where music is loud and laughter is louder.

For publishing rights (Foreign & Domestic) Film or television, please contact her agent Erica Spellman-Silverman, at Trident Media Group.

Made in the USA
San Bernardino,
CA